DAMIAN WHITTLE was born in Perivale, West London, England and currently lives in Leeds. He has had a variety of jobs and has a variety of piercings and tattoos.

FALLEN WEAPON

FALLEN WEAPON

Damian Whittle

ATHENA PRESS
LONDON

FALLEN WEAPON
Copyright © Damian Whittle 2007

All Rights Reserved

No part of this book may be reproduced in any form
by photocopying or by any electronic or mechanical means,
including information storage or retrieval systems,
without permission in writing from both the copyright
owner and the publisher of this book.

ISBN 10-digit: 1 84748 053 5
ISBN 13-digit: 978 1 84748 053 8

First Published 2007 by
ATHENA PRESS
Queen's House, 2 Holly Road
Twickenham TW1 4EG
United Kingdom

This is a work of fiction. Names, characters, places and incidents
are either the product of the author's imagination or are used
fictitiously, and any resemblance to actual persons, living or dead,
events or locales is entirely coincidental.

Printed for Athena Press

Chapter One

The ground was cold and his body bruised. That much he knew. A vague memory of being attacked flickered in his mind and was gone. He tried to shift his weight slightly and immediately stopped as pain burst through every part of his battered torso. Not yet. Sooner or later he would make another attempt, eventually he would stand up, but for now he would stay down here, looking up at the stars that glinted indifferently in the sky. Perhaps that was all he had ever done? But that couldn't be right. There must have been something else, a place before this. That made sense, didn't it? But all he could remember for the moment was concrete beneath him and darkness above, and he had no understanding of how he was connected to either.

Fear. That had always been there, too. It squirmed in his stomach and soon enough it would turn to terror. He could feel each breath, fast and desperate, in his chest. He focused his attention on the brightest of the lights that looked down at him, and tried to banish everything but that distant, uncaring star. It didn't help. The world around him wasn't real. At any moment it would all come crashing down, revealing, perhaps, whatever it was he couldn't remember. Even the blackness, as he shut his eyes, whimpering like a child, was an illusion. Without realising it, he had curled into a foetal ball, ignoring the shouts of protest from every limb.

Time passed. A minute, an hour, he wasn't sure. Wrapped into the warmth of himself, he almost felt safe. The hollow roar of his own breath blotted out the other noises prowling about him. The sensation was curiously familiar, as though he had experienced it elsewhere.

This couldn't last. He was going to have to confront whatever was outside, however bad it proved to be. Slowly, he forced himself to emerge from the cocoon of his interlocking limbs. For a while, he remained on his back, eyes still shut against the world, enjoying what little safety he had for a little longer. Then, he looked.

Everything was still in place, just as before. Vehicles hummed in the distance. Cars, probably. Strange that he knew what a car was but didn't know his own name. Still, that meant there would be drivers. People. Already he was confronted with a choice. Would it be better or worse if he were not alone? Either way, it was time to make a start. He was going to have to get to his feet. Now.

It took a while. His legs were extremely weak and there was no support for him to cling to. First, he rolled over on to his front, wincing as his sore ribs pressed against concrete. Carefully, he pushed himself up on to all fours. I must look like a dog, he thought. Assuming he was right about what a dog was. An animal that was kept as a pet? He stared down at the floor. There were tiny cracks in the ground and a red stain where his head had lain. His blood or someone else's? Running his fingers through his scalp, he was relieved to find that his hair was dry.

Suddenly, a siren screeched in the distance. Quicker than he'd intended, he forced himself to his knees, hoping he could run if need be. The shrill echo faded into the night.

Silence.

Nothing to do with him, then.

He examined his surroundings. He was kneeling in a wide, stone-paved plaza, bordered on three sides by empty roads and on the fourth by the looming hulk of a large, anonymous building. The only living things were a few withered trees and a cluster of litter-strewn bushes. Beyond the roads, shops – he was fairly sure that was what they were – stood in silent ranks.

It was a relief to find he was alone. Taking a deep breath, he stood up. There was a brief sensation of nausea and he thought that he might collapse again. He retched but nothing came. Maybe he hadn't eaten recently. The sickness passed, leaving him empty but a little calmer.

So, here he was, standing and with a clearer idea of where he was, if not why. But what now? He was shivering. Thankfully, he was wearing clothes, but they were gossamer thin. His feet were bare and the ground felt sharp beneath them. A car appeared on one of the roads, moving slowly, as though hunting for prey. Perhaps he could flag it down, see if the driver could help. But that would involve face-to-face contact and he wasn't ready for that. He decided to make for the building instead.

Walking was difficult. Each step reminded him just how much his body was hurting. Fragments of stone and glass buried themselves in the bare soles of his feet. Nevertheless, he wasn't quite so afraid any more. Moving through the dark was somehow less terrifying than lying in it with his eyes shut. As he drew nearer, he saw that the building was enmeshed within a network of scaffolding. There were graffiti-patterned boards over most of the windows and a cloying stench of long-ago fires hung in the air. Cracked steps, encrusted with the dried remains of what looked like oil, led to a pair of heavy, wooden doors. A metal panel hung above them, covered with metal squiggles that he couldn't decipher.

He studied the entrance, wondering how to get in. What little strength he possessed wouldn't be equal to forcing these doors. He would have to look for a back entrance or, failing that, a crowbar to rip away the panelling from one of the windows. He gazed up at the building. There were three storeys. He considered the possibility of climbing the wall to look for a way in and quickly dismissed it as absurdly dangerous.

Then he caught a glimpse of something: a window on the third floor, the only one that wasn't boarded up. From it, a pale face was staring back at him. He was too far away to read the expression. The face must have realised it had been seen, because the next moment it was gone.

He had been watched. All this time, as he lay in the dark, as he had struggled to his feet, someone had been observing him.

The doors were open. He hadn't realised before, but they had been forced, not very far, just enough to allow someone to squeeze through. The shattered remains of a lock lay to one side, among a coil of chain. He started backing slowly away, trembling.

'Are you all right?'

He turned quickly. Behind him stood two men. They were dressed in light-blue suits. One of them had curly brown hair while the other sported a bushy ginger bouffant with freckles to match. Both of them were tall and muscular. They were smiling broadly.

The one who had spoken, the curly-haired man, stepped forward. He looked concerned.

'Do you need somewhere to sleep for the night? Wouldn't go in there, if I were you. Place is falling down.'

'Yeah,' added the other one. 'You'll not be safe in there. Anything might happen.'

He was frozen to the spot, unable to think of what to say. Shouldn't he be the one asking the questions? Why did it feel as though he were being interrogated?

Curly Hair was very close now. He could see the man's perfect teeth as the grin grew wider.

'Been taking something, sonny? Never mind. You'll be OK now.'

Curly Hair grabbed him by the throat with both hands. He gasped helplessly as the man began crushing the life out of him. The grinning mouth filled his vision, laughter booming in his ears. He struggled feebly against the relentless grip, but it was no good.

'Fucking dosser,' Curly Hair spat.

The pressure of the hands was harder, tighter now. He was going to die.

'Dirty, stinking!'

A scream, loud and high pitched. The hands were gone from his neck and he collapsed to the floor, gulping down air. Curly Hair was staggering, gurgling, blood foaming from his mouth, red against the white of his teeth. A boy stood behind him. There was a long shining object in his hand. Curly Hair toppled on to his back with a final, despairing gasp. With a furious yell, Ginger Bouffant charged at the boy, swinging both fists like a gorilla. The youth somehow ducked under the oncoming blows and thrust the blade upwards. A shriek. Ginger was dead before he hit the floor.

Knife still held tight, the boy stood over his victims, panting slightly, a sheen of sweat on his face. It was the same face that had looked down at him from the window.

There was no point in trying to run. There was nowhere to

go. So he just looked at the boy, watching as he slid the splattered blade into his jacket pocket. He was about sixteen, tall and painfully thin. His bony, pallid face was covered in spots. Dark roots showed through spiky hair dyed blond. He was dressed in a black tracksuit that seemed to hang on his emaciated frame. His hands were protected by white surgical gloves. The boy smiled, revealing grey teeth.

'I couldn't let them hurt you,' he said, almost hesitantly. 'My name's Lee.'

The sound of his own voice surprised him as, at last, he spoke.

'I don't know what my name is.'

Lee considered for a moment.

'You're Jason.'

Chapter Two

The house stood by itself on a long, concrete platform. A squat, flat-roofed, one-storey building, it was painted a sickly shade of green. It had once been a railway station waiting room. Jason vaguely knew what a train was – a form of transport that was now obsolete. There was a wide pit in front of the house, in which the battered remnants of metal tracks rusted slowly among heaps of gravel. The trains must have travelled on these rails. Now the tracks ran for only a few hundred metres before being cut off by the base of a gigantic tower block that soared into the night sky, a neon logo blazing at its summit. All around, equally massive structures glowered down at the flimsy shelter at their feet.

Opening the triple-locked door, Lee let them into a cluttered living room. A long sofa, strewn with faded cushions, rested against one wall. On the facing wall hung a flat television screen. Beneath this there was a rickety bookcase, taken up with shiny silver discs and a few well-worn paperbacks. In one corner of the room was a compact unit with a sink and microwave. A chipboard door opened on to a tiny bedroom.

Lee collapsed on to the sofa with grateful sigh. He peeled off his gloves, screwed them into a ball and threw them into a corner. Jason hesitated before sitting down next to him. The soft cushions were comforting against his aching back. For the first time, he realised just how exhausted he was. The journey had been a difficult one. His body still hurt badly, making walking an effort. His young saviour had a crippled foot, made worse by running down three flights of steps. They had been forced to lean on each other as they hobbled through the gloomy streets. The few passers-by had given them odd looks and muttered angrily about drugged youths.

They sat for a while in silence. Lee picked at one of his spots, a frown creasing his forehead.

'So,' he said at last, 'you don't remember anything?'

Jason coughed, for some reason embarrassed by the gaps in his mind.

'Er, no. I know what things are and what they're for. But not who I am. You think I'm called Jason?'

Lee giggled. It was a high-pitched, almost girlish sound.

'I thought it kinda suited you. I don't know what your real name is.'

Jason nodded, disappointed. He'd hoped the name might be his first clue, but apparently it was as random and meaningless as everything else.

'Why? Why call me Jason?'

The youth smiled.

'When I was a little kid I used to like old films. The ones before everything went animated, when the monsters were made of clay and stuff like that. Y'know?'

Jason looked blankly at him. Lee shrugged.

'Oh. Well, in one of these films, people got moved around by gods. They just appeared in places, like you did. That's why I called you Jason. That was the hero's name.'

Was Lee right? Was he some sort of hero? No, it didn't seem likely. He certainly didn't feel strong or powerful. Without this boy and his knife, he'd probably have died out in the cold.

'You saw me appear?' he asked.

'Yeah. I was looking out of the window, 'cos I'm teaching myself not to be scared of heights, and I saw a blue fire. You were in the middle of it. The flames went out and I thought you were dead. But you got up and started walking towards the library.'

'Library?'

'Yeah. Y'know, books and discs? I was... collecting some stuff from there. Anyway, then I saw those two execs. I knew what the bastards would do.'

'How?'

'Just did. I've met that sort before. It's like a game for them.'

'Did you ever see anyone else appear, like I did?'

Lee shook his head.

'No, course not. It was amazing.'

Jason leaned back further into the sofa, thinking over what the boy had told him. He winced at the discomfort of his stiffening back. Lee got up and limped towards the bedroom.

'I've got some stuff that'll help.'

He returned with a foil strip and two beakers.

'Codeine Beta Four,' he explained. 'It's way better than Beta Three. Not even on the market yet.'

He ran some water into the beakers and popped two pills from the strips into each. The water fizzed happily. He held one out to Jason.

'What does it do?'

'Makes you feel better, Jason. What else?'

He took the beaker and sipped cautiously. The solution was bitter. Lee downed his in one and looked expectantly at him.

'Go on, then.'

Jason took a long gulp of the bubbling fluid, shuddering at the sour aftertaste.

'It's horrible!'

'Finish it. You'll want the full hit.'

Reluctantly, he did as he was told and handed the empty beaker back to Lee. A warm feeling began to spread through his stomach and the aching of limbs was already slightly subdued.

'Better now?'

'Yes. Thank you, Lee.'

The boy looked pleased and took the beakers over to the sink. A few plates covered with rivulets of gravy lay in the plastic bowl. He ran some hot water into the bowl and then turned back to Jason.

'Are you hungry? I can make you some sandwiches or something.'

Jason tried to remember eating, but had no idea what kind of food he liked. Besides, the drugs were making him sleepy.

'No, thank you.'

Lee giggled again, flashing him a grin of discoloured teeth.

'You're so polite!'

'Is that bad?'

'No. Just unusual.'

He finished washing the crockery, then came and sat down next to Jason again.

'You look tired.'

Jason's mind was hazy. Not the frightening confusion of before, but a drowsiness, like he was floating.

'I think I need to rest for a while.'

'I'll get you a blanket and you can sleep in here.'

Lee got up and disappeared into the bedroom. Jason stretched out on the sofa, shifting a cushion beneath his head for a pillow. Lee returned with a heavy blanket and spread it over him. Jason tried to say something, but his eyes were sliding shut and he could only mutter. He heard the boy's voice as though from a distance.

'If you wake up needing a piss, you can get to the toilet through the bedroom. Night, Jason.'

Jason suddenly realised that he hadn't thanked Lee for saving his life. He wanted to call out to him, but the light had been turned out and the bedroom door was shut. Alone in the dark once more, Jason tried to piece together the few snippets of information he had gathered so far. A minute later, he was sleeping dreamlessly.

The sensation that woke him up was new and Jason couldn't immediately identify it. An urgent, nagging desire. He needed the toilet. For a while he lay still, trying to ignore his bladder, but it was no use. Gingerly, he threw back the blanket and got to his feet. Movement wasn't as painful as before. The drugs had done their work well.

He crept to the bedroom door and pushed it gently open. Lee was curled up under the thick covers of a small bed, his breathing slow and heavy. Jason watched him sleeping for a few minutes. He knew so little about this boy. He was as much a mystery as Jason was to himself.

His need to relieve himself was still clamouring for his attention. He edged past the bed to a door on the other side of the room. He entered the bathroom and flicked on the light. Aside from the toilet, there was a small bath and a chipped basin, above which hung a large, bronze-framed mirror. Jason unzipped his trousers and eased out his penis. It was, he realised, the first time he'd seen it. Grasped in his hand, it seemed a pitiful and useless thing. As a yellow stream gushed into the pan, Jason couldn't repress a groan of pleasure.

When he'd done, he turned to the basin. His reflection stared back at him. It had not even occurred to him before to wonder what he looked like. Now, examining the face in the mirror, he was both fascinated and disappointed. Green eyes returned his scrutinising gaze. The features were heavy. Dark hair hung in an untidy fringe. The body was stocky, with a small belly showing beneath a blue T-shirt. His thin black trousers were baggy, torn and much too short. Could this unassuming figure really be him? Jason felt diminished, ashamed of such a mundane body. Why didn't his reflection show... what? What had he been expecting? An unworldly wraith? An angel? He turned away from himself.

In the bedroom, Lee was whimpering in his sleep. Jason approached him, concerned. The boy was twisting in the sheets, as though trying to get away from something. Jason touched his trembling shoulder gently, but Lee didn't wake up. He must be having a nightmare. A bad one. He needed to dream of something else. A safe place, where nothing could hurt him. An image formed within Jason. A field on a summer's day, wide and golden, the vista stretching to each horizon. He slipped the scene into Lee. The boy stopped struggling and lay still, his expression now peaceful. Jason ran his hand through Lee's hair. The new dream was in place, the nightmare banished.

He returned to the living room and the sofa, feeling slightly better about himself. It was good to help the boy who had saved his life. To help his... friend.

Sitting on the edge of the sofa, Jason found he was shaking. What had he just done? And how? He was certain that other people couldn't do... whatever he had done. Suddenly, Jason felt more afraid of himself than the world around him. He crawled back under the blanket, more confused than ever. To help him sleep, he thought of Lee, safe in the golden field. It brought him some comfort.

Chapter Three

People did not like Edward Cornish. It was his smile. His round, fleshy face was always stretched into a beaming grin. Happiness like that was unnerving, especially in an overweight, balding man of forty-eight. All his acquaintances had long agreed among themselves that he was covering something up. Given the chance, he would turn to rape or murder. Whenever his name came up in conversation, it was always with talk of strange looks and sly, unwanted touches. Men claimed that, given half the chance, they'd punch some decency into him. Women devised all manner of punishments for his imagined deviances.

Mr Cornish was well aware of his reputation. It didn't trouble him in the least. Whatever his customers suspected, they knew that his bookshop was the best. There was no text so esoteric that he could not track it down, nor subject so arcane that he wouldn't have a reference work. The same clients that damned him as a pervert came in secret to ask for dominatrix instruction manuals and tourist guides to Hell.

The bookstore nestled among a crop of ruthlessly competing antiques shops in a street that was easily missed if you weren't looking. When Mr Cornish had purchased the property, it had already served five years as a chemist's. Very few changes had been necessary. The walls were still an antiseptic cream colour and the metal shelves that had once carried pills and sanitary towels were still in place but now filled with books. It was all spotlessly clean, thanks to the attentions of a spry, middle-aged woman who was also his occasional and only lover.

Mr Cornish liked his routines. He would arrive for work at 6 a.m. and open at 9 a.m. The intervening time was useful for getting things done that he wouldn't want his clients to be aware of. Like meeting business associates.

It was 6.35 a.m. Outside, the world was shrouded in icy darkness. The agent would arrive in exactly five minutes.

Mr Cornish waited behind the counter, drumming his fingers. A tumbler of whisky sat at his elbow, already half empty. The Fracture made him uneasy. Extensive and exhaustive searching through his books had revealed no mention of them. It was as though their presence was hidden from the entire world, which was odd considering some of the claims they made. Nonetheless, they could always be trusted to fulfil a bargain. In the end, that was all that mattered.

He took another sip of whisky, savouring its warmth. For years now, each day would begin with whisky and each night ended with it. Ironically for a man rumoured to enjoy an almost unimaginable number of vices, no one had ever suspected him of alcoholism. Sometimes the dependence made him feel old. All the bars were shutting down now. The children had found new addictions.

With a swish, the automated door slid open and a cruel breeze accosted his skin. Mr Cornish leapt to his feet with unaccustomed speed. Despite the cold, there was sweat on his forehead.

'Good morning, Cornish.'

The figure was tall and slender. He was clad in dark brown leather trousers and a matching jerkin. His head was sheathed in a blank, grey metal mask. The only opening was where the mouth should have been. But there were no lips, just a small, circular orifice in which something red shuddered.

'Good morning...?'

'You can call me Phillip.'

His voice was surprisingly soft. The agent came forward, the door sealing itself behind him. His movements were curious, neither masculine nor feminine. Mr Cornish got the impression that it wasn't just his face that was damaged.

Phillip rested his gloved hands on the counter, observing the bookseller impassively. Mr Cornish tried desperately not to recoil. There were many strange creatures in the Fracture, but this walking ruin of a man was frightening even by their standards.

'It would appear that I disgust you,' stated Phillip bluntly. There was a trace of amusement in the gentle tones.

Mr Cornish's reply was little more than a squeak. 'No, no, of course not. No!'

This was ridiculous! He had done deals with these people before and knew their ways. There was nothing to fear. The Fracture were indifferent to him – a tool, little more. They only hurt those that mattered to them. He forced himself to take a deep breath.

'That is, you look strange, but—'

'You have known stranger?'

'Yes. Not many, but yes.'

The red flesh within the aperture wobbled as Phillip chuckled.

'I'd be surprised if that were true. But never mind.'

Phillip reached into his jerkin and drew out a small, paper-bound package.

'I have brought the book, Cornish.'

He handed it to the bookseller. Mr Cornish held it reverently for a moment and then tore away the brown wrapping, unable to wait. In his hands lay an old hardback volume. He flipped the pages tenderly and then clasped it to his chest. The book reeked of age. It was all he could do to stop himself sniffing the pages.

'You are pleased?'

'Oh, yes!' breathed the bookseller. '*Christina Alberta's Father*, 1925, a first edition. I'm more pleased than you can imagine.'

'You admire Wells?'

'He was a genius. He foresaw so much.'

'Not us, though.'

The pride was unmistakable. For a moment the agent caressed his mask with a gloved hand. Phillip clearly took some satisfaction in his shattered face.

'I doubt anyone could have foreseen you,' said Cornish quietly.

Another chuckle.

'True.'

Phillip's greasy jerkin creaked as he leaned forward.

'The boy will come here tomorrow. In all likelihood, he will bring the subject with him.'

Mr Cornish nodded. He was calmer now. The ancient book was a talisman. While he held it, no harm could befall him.

'What do you want me to do?'

'Nothing. Your part is played out now. Give the boy his reward and let him go.'

Now that it was nearly over, he found he was curious.

'Why did you choose him? I don't think he's a very stable young man.'

'He isn't. That's why we chose him. Enjoy the book.'

Phillip turned to go. Mr Cornish started examining the volume more closely. This one wasn't for selling. It would be added to his private collection. Early twentieth-century literature was his greatest passion – echoes of a naivety long since lost to the world. He would shut the shop for the day and withdraw into the back room to savour his prize. None of his gossiping acquaintances could have guessed that the fat man with the sinister smile wanted only two things in life – to drink whisky and to read old books. Doubtless they would have been disappointed.

'Oh, one more thing, Cornish.'

He looked up. Phillip was standing in the open doorway.

'Yes?'

'The boy has given the subject a name. He calls him Jason.'

With that, the Fracture agent was gone. Mr Cornish emptied his tumbler and activated the door lock. As he retreated into the back room, his bizarre visitor was already half forgotten. The book awaited him and that was far more important. Still, he reflected, perhaps he should have asked Phillip who was winning the war.

Chapter Four

The building across the street was being forced into a metamorphosis. Heavy men in lithe machines swarmed all over it, remorselessly altering its structures and redefining its functions. It was caught between two entirely different forms at the moment. One half was reserved and clinical, the other gaudy and elaborate: a hospital reborn as a casino. Or perhaps the other way round. Metal beds lay on the rutted ground outside, either torn out or waiting to be installed. In huge skips sagged the empty husks of machines designed either to spin roulette wheels or replace kidneys.

Although there was no such work being done on the side of the street where Jason was waiting, it seemed if anything even busier. A constant stream of people bustled past him, some sparing him a brief glance, but mostly with their eyes fixed resolutely forward. Clearly this was not a city where you should look at strangers for very long. Everyone wore similar clothes. Pastel jackets and striped black trousers for both sexes. The men were all clean shaven with thickly gelled hair. Few of the women were wearing jewellery, but their hair was piled high into elaborate styles and many of them had extraordinarily long fingernails. They all gave every indication of being totally oblivious to his existence. Still, Jason was scared of them. He expected one of the anonymous figures to suddenly turn on him. Someone that knew him, knew his secrets.

Over on the building site, two workmen had been arguing for the last five minutes. Even with the road and the stream of traffic between them, he could hear the conversation; the loud confident voices of men used to talking over the rumble of machinery.

'They're supposed to be put over there,' one was saying. 'How else are we gonna get the fuckin' things in on time?'

'They're in the way!' retorted the second voice, just as aggressive.

'No, they aren't! They're on the plan; the drivers expect them to be there. They don't expect them to damn well turn up in front of the gate for no bloody good reason!'

'Yeah, but this way it'll be quicker!'

'Quicker but still wrong.'

'But we're behind. You know we're behind.'

'And we'll be even more behind if everyone's tripping over stuff that's not where they damn well expect it to be.'

There was a pattern to the confrontation, thought Jason, a structure more solid than the heavy stones around them. One had power. The other wanted it and so pretended to have power. The second man knew he was wrong but he was putting on this display to save face. He would not surrender without a fight, even though the debate was so trivial. And yet, from the start, he had known that he must lose. Strange. Jason wondered if they could sense all this as clearly he did.

He turned to look up at the tower block that rose behind him. It was a rather uninspiring sight. Pale cream brickwork and beige detailing, broken up by ranks of black glass windows. According to Lee, several hundred people lived and worked here. The lower storeys were offices, the upper were apartments. He couldn't imagine what life must be like in such a place. It was almost as broad as it was high, but still, how could there be room for all those people?

Lee had been gone for almost half an hour now. What if something had happened to him? What if friends of the people he had killed last night had caught him? How could Jason survive, alone in this world where he knew nothing, not even himself? What if...

'Sorry. It took longer than I thought.'

Jason was so relieved to see Lee that he wanted to hug him, like a lost child found by its parent. Instead he smiled, hoping not to betray how scared he had been.

'Did you sell them like you wanted?' he asked, trying, not very successfully he thought, to sound relaxed.

Lee had told him that he had a 'client' in this building who kept a private collection of insignia from expensive cars. Apparently, this man was prepared to pay highly for the small metal symbols. Jason hadn't even tried to understand why. All he knew was that Lee had acquired some of these insignia and expected to sell them to his client at a good profit.

'Yeah. The dopey fucker wanted to argue about the price, but he wanted the stuff too bad. He...'

Lee broke off.

'You don't look too good, Jason. You want to go home?'

Home. He had only slept in the little house for one night, but it already felt like home, at least of a kind. The thought of it made him feel better. Somewhere to hide from this throng of nameless strangers. But he didn't want to let his friend down.

'I'll be OK. I just felt... weird for a moment.'

'You still can't remember anything?'

'No. Nothing.'

Lee nodded and scratched at his acned cheek with long fingers for a few moments.

'Well, I guess we should get you some clothes. You can't wear those for ever.'

Jason looked down at his top and trousers. He had been wearing them since the night before. He had even slept in them. The only addition was a pair of white trainers and black socks that Lee had given him.

'What sort of stuff do you ' began Lee. 'You can't remember, right?'

They both laughed and Jason had a sudden feeling of security. The shared joke was like a shield between them and the rest of the world.

'Well,' said Lee. 'I don't know much about fashion.'

'Fashion?'

'I'm sure we can find something.'

The shop was underground. There was no sign, just a flight of concrete steps leading downwards. There was only one long floor, stuffed to bursting with racks of clothes. The walls were painted black and decorated with tribal masks, their wooden faces surrounded by feathers. Jason wondered if they were for sale, too. He liked them. They gave nothing away and asked no questions.

Most of the clothes on the racks were like those he had seen on the street. Lee walked past them without a glance, heading towards the back of the store. A fat man in a salmon-coloured jacket gave them a hostile look as they passed and muttered something to the diminutive woman in cerise standing next to him. She laughed, her thickly piled hair wobbling as her head moved.

There were fewer clothes at the back of the store and they seemed to have been set out with little care. There weren't any masks on the wall here, just a sign covered with odd little black symbols.

'What do you think?'

Lee was trying on a silver chain. The chunky links emphasised the scrawniness of his neck. Jason thought for a moment. Did he like it? It made his friend's body look vulnerable, but was that his intention?

'It looks good.'

Lee smiled.

'Good. Now, what do you want?'

'I've been thinking. I'm pretty sure I like green.'

'That's a start.'

In the end, the clothes he chose were much like the ones he already had. A few pairs of black jeans and several green T-shirts. He chose a red top as well, just to have something different. He didn't know if he'd ever wear it, but having the option seemed to make sense. Lee found himself a warm-looking jacket of some shiny blue material. It was at least two sizes too big.

While they were waiting to be served by an impressively bored girl, Jason thanked Lee.

'No problem. I did well out of the insignia. And I've got a book to sell tomorrow.'

'A book?'

'Yeah. That's...' Lee looked round before continuing. 'That's why I was in the old library when I saw you arrive. I know a guy who'll pay a lot for old books.'

'So,' Jason asked hesitantly, 'is that what you do? Is that how you make money?'

'Pretty much. There's a lot of people who want to get hold of old stuff before it gets lost or turned into something else. They pay me to get it for them.'

He paused and there was an odd look in his eyes as he asked, 'Does that bother you?'

Jason considered.

'No.'

He was surprised by the relief in Lee's face.

'Good.'

The bored girl finally decided they were worthy of her attention. While she was contemptuously packing their purchases, Lee worked out how much money he had left.

'After we take this stuff back, do you fancy a drink?' he asked.

The Colossus Pharmaceutical Bar was a very popular place to be and most of the couches were already taken by the time they arrived. Small groups and couples lay talking quietly or sleeping side by side. Although a few of the customers were dressed like Lee, it seemed to Jason that many of them were a good deal richer. They had the sort of impractical outfits that, for reasons he wasn't sure of, he automatically associated with wealth. With their intricate accessories and tastefully matching colours, they looked like conservative butterflies. None of them spared the two boys so much as a glance.

The room was circular with the glinting chrome bar forming a ring at the centre. Behind the bar was a broad column supporting shelves full of brown and blue pill jars. The low couches radiated outwards from the centre, about thirty of them in all. Concave screens set around the walls played abstract, surreal images to an accompaniment Jason couldn't understand at first. When he asked, Lee told him it was called ambient music.

The woman behind the bar was short and dark, with a face that brooked no argument. Her smart, midnight blue outfit seemed like an afterthought, a half-hearted concession to the world. When she smiled, though, it made him feel that he was very welcome here.

'Hello, Lee,' she said, her voice gruff but with a strong trace of humour. 'You've found us a new customer, then?'

Lee grinned back at the barwoman. He was wearing a black tracksuit. Jason had changed into one of the new pairs of jeans and a dark green top.

'He's called Jason. It's his first time. Far as he can remember, anyway.'

She nodded as if that explained everything. She smiled at Jason again, though this time he couldn't read her expression.

'Well, Jason, we'll start you off with a Prozac and codeine Beta, I think. That's what young Lee started on, as I remember.'

She reached under the bar and brought out two glasses, followed by two large bottles of pills. Taking three tablets from each jar, she dropped them into one of the glasses. She produced a small water pump from beneath the counter and filled the glass.

'There you go, Jason,' she said, pushing the drink over to him.

'Er, thank you.'

Jason sipped at the fizzing fluid. It wasn't as bitter as the solution Lee had given him the night before and he felt the warmth spreading through him almost immediately.

'And what about you, Lee?'

'Codeine Beta and D-hydrochloride please, Kerri.'

The woman – Kerri – gave Lee his drink. He paid her and they went to look for a free couch. Eventually they found one on the outskirts of the room. They settled down on the soft cushions. Lee lay back and sighed contentedly. His medication was already half gone.

'You'll probably fall asleep pretty quick if you've not had it before. But Kerri lets her regulars sleep over, so don't worry about it.'

Jason nodded. He was happy. The drugs were easing the tension that had gripped him all day. Suddenly he realised there was something he needed to say.

'Thank you, Lee. For everything. For saving my life. For—'

The boy cut him off.

'It's OK; you don't have to keep thanking me. I had to help you. Knew that when I saw you. I think it's—'

There was a sudden commotion of loud voices. Three men had entered the bar. They were young; not much older than Lee. All of them sported bright yellow coats and one of them was wearing a matching wide-brimmed hat. They ambled towards the bar, shouting at each other and everyone around them.

'Fucking beer boys,' muttered Lee.

'Beer boys?'

'Some people still like that shit. Stupid rich guys who think it's "traditional". God knows why; it just makes you puke.'

The trio had been served by a reluctant Kerri and were now looking for somewhere to sit. They tried to join a pair of girls who quickly told them what they could do with their suggestions. The one in the hat approached Lee and Jason's couch. Bleary eyes stared out of his finely featured face.

'Room for three more then, lads?' he asked, obviously trying to make his voice deeper than it was. He removed his hat to reveal immaculately coiffured hair.

'No,' replied Lee bluntly.

'No need to be rude, mate.'

'Find somewhere else to sit.'

The other two had joined their companion. Nervous sweat trickled down Jason's back.

'These two being rude?' asked one.

'Yeah. Well, the spotty one is. His friend doesn't speak.'

'Maybe he's a thinker?' chortled the third man.

'Yeah,' said the first, leaning over Jason. He reeked of expensive musk. 'A bit of a chess player, maybe. All brain and no talk.'

There was a slight rustling. The man looked round. Lee was slowly and deliberately drawing the knife from his jacket pocket. His eyes told the man that he was quite capable of killing him. The drunk took a step backwards. When he spoke, it was little more than a whimper.

'Well, look, my friend, only—'

A woman's voice interrupted him.

'You'll be leaving now.'

The trio turned to be confronted by the short figure of Kerri. She held their gaze for a few seconds. Whatever they saw in her face scared them even more than Lee's blade. They scurried for the exit.

'Sorry about that, boys,' said Kerri. 'I don't normally let beer boys in, but I thought I'd give them the benefit of the doubt.'

She saw Lee slipping the knife back into his jacket.

'You know I don't like people waving knives round! Next time, call me, right?'

'Sorry.'

She ruffled his hair, a fond smile easing her hard features.

'Forget about it. You two sleeping over?'

'Yeah.'

'Well, I'll be waking you at six in the morning, no later. Coffee is the usual price.'

She strode away. Lee giggled.

'She's not so scary when you get to know her.'

'Would you have killed those guys?' asked Jason.

'Course not. I just wanted to scare them a bit. I've met their sort before.'

'I just thought because... last night.'

Lee frowned.

'That was different. They were a real danger.'

He looked angry. Jason realised he'd upset him. After all that the boy had done for him, he didn't want to hurt his feelings. He touched Lee's arm.

'I'm sorry. There's still so much I don't know.'

Lee nodded and seemed to relax. He downed the last of his medication.

'I know. But I don't want you to think—'

'I don't.'

'Good. You still look tired. Go to sleep.'

Jason lay back into the cushions. He was beginning to feel drowsy. Lee curled up on the couch, his face close to Jason's. The pale youth's eyes closed and his breathing was slow.

'Good dreams,' he murmured.

Dreams. Jason knew how he could thank Lee. He imagined the field again, a golden space of absolute freedom. Almost without thinking, he eased the image into his friend's consciousness. The boy smiled.

'Thanks,' he whispered as he fell asleep.

Jason's eyelids flickered shut and a second later he too was sleeping. All around them, the drugged customers chatted and slumbered, unaware of the strange creature in their midst.

Chapter Five

It was fortunate that Phillip was a patient man. He had an excellent view of Cornish's establishment from here but it was far from comfortable. The floor of the cramped store room was cluttered with piles of ageing furniture, and porcelain figurines lined the walls in solemn ranks. To get to the grimy window, he had been forced to jam himself between a black lacquered wardrobe and a glass cabinet housing the stuffed remnants of long extinct birds. His brown leather clothing was smeared with dust. Even his mask felt dirty. Still, at least he could be sure he would not be discovered here. As far as anyone knew, the owner of the antiques shop below had been away for a long time, hunting new stock in distant cities. It was unlikely that he would ever return.

He had been watching the bookstore for three hours before he saw them. Two figures approaching. Being careful to stay out of view, Phillip studied them. His eyes had been erased with the rest of his face, but the mask gave him all the information he could ever need. Its vision never tired and was unfailingly precise. It was better than sight.

The subject was as expected – nervous and confused, but beginning to adapt. He was wearing new clothes and looked surprisingly healthy. Phillip repressed the surge of loathing he felt at the sight of an enemy. This was not the time to indulge himself. There was too much to be done. Instead, he examined Lee. The boy did not look well. His greasy face was covered in pimples and he walked with a noticeable limp. Despite this, he carried himself with confidence. On the whole, Phillip thought, the youth would have fitted in well in the Fracture. A shame there could be no question of that.

The two boys entered the bookstore. Satisfied, Phillip turned from the window. He could leave this room of rotting relics. All was going as planned. Only a few more days and everything would be in place.

'An excellent find. Yes, excellent,' said Mr Cornish as he flipped through the book.

'It wasn't easy. It was with a lot of public records stuff.'

Cornish looked up, an eager glint in his watery eyes.

'Really? What sort of records? Public census?'

'I think so.'

'I may be interested in seeing some of those, Mr Stanning.'

Jason could not decide whether or not he liked the bookseller. He was cheerful enough and clearly pleased with what Lee had brought him. Yet he was sure that the bloated man was hiding something. His tone was too welcoming, his smile too broad.

All the same, Jason was feeling good this morning. They had both slept well at the Colossus bar, despite the strangers around them. Kerri had even cooked them a filling breakfast of bacon and eggs with their morning coffee. It was clearly a rare occurrence and the invitation hadn't been extended to her other customers. He got the impression that the fierce barwoman had a soft spot for Lee and looked kindly upon Jason simply because he was his friend.

'*The Mystery of Edwin Drood*. An incomplete classic,' Cornish was saying. 'The text itself is well known. But this edition is unusual. Edition and condition. That's the key in my line of work.'

Jason wandered away from the conversation and examined the shelves. The books came in all shapes and sizes, from thin, little pamphlets to huge volumes that had to be laid on their sides to fit on the shelf. All of them were covered in indecipherable black symbols.

He picked up a large, red book and scanned through it. There were no symbols on the pages, only photos. They were all of women clad in fur and feathers. From the state of the binding and the damp smell of the yellowing pages, it was very old; the women, whoever they were, must be long dead. Only their images had survived. He returned the book to its place on the shelf and picked up another, smaller one. He could make nothing of it; there were no pictures and the black marks on the pages were completely meaningless. He tried another, but again it was incomprehensible. He tried a third and then stopped.

Mr Cornish was waddling over to the old metal till on the counter.

'I'll get you your payment, Mr Stanning. Two hundred, I think?'

'Yeah, that's what we said.'

The bookseller handed Lee his payment and beamed at them.

'We'll make it two fifty for a job well done. Thank you Lee and… Jason, wasn't it?'

'Yes, that's right,' said Jason distantly.

As they left, Mr Cornish was thumbing through his book and mumbling happily to himself. Outside, the afternoon air was rapidly turning cold. Jason took a deep breath, pleased to be away from the shop. His friend was counting through a sheaf of red banknotes. Satisfied, he put them into a tan wallet, which he slipped, carefully, back into his jacket.

As they walked down the quiet street, Jason thought about the symbols on all the books. About what they must mean.

'Lee,' he said.

'Yeah?'

'I can't read.'

Lee stopped.

'What, not at all?'

Jason shook his head.

'No. I was looking through some of the books and I couldn't understand any of them. I never even realised before. I don't know how to read.'

Lee scratched his neck thoughtfully.

'Well, maybe it's something to do with you losing your memory?'

'I suppose that makes sense,' said Jason doubtfully.

'Well, don't worry about it. Either you'll remember how to read or—'

'Or?'

'Or you won't. Don't worry about it, all right? If it comes to it, I can try and teach you.'

'Thanks,' said Jason.

'What did you think of Cornish?' asked Lee, suddenly changing the subject.

'He's kind of strange.'

Lee nodded.

'A lot of collectors are a bit weird. Maybe the dust gets in their brains or something.'

'Maybe, Mr Stanning.'

The boy giggled.

'He's even more polite than you are. You wouldn't believe the rumours about him.'

'Rumours? What sort of rumours?'

'Pretty much everything you could imagine. I think he's all right though. Always pays up.'

Lee broke off, staring up at the window of a building across the road. An antiques shop. His hand was at the pocket with the knife.

'What's the matter?'

'I thought I saw someone watching us. A guy in a mask.'

He relaxed, taking his hand away from his pocket.

'Must have been my imagination.'

Jason shivered, drawing closer to the boy.

'You're making me nervous.'

Lee grinned.

'Sorry. Must be going crazy. It was nothing.'

'I hope so.'

'Don't worry about it. I have to set up something for tomorrow and then there's a film I want to show you.'

'A film?'

'Yeah. You'll see how you got your name!'

They carried on down the street. A blank mask watched them go.

Chapter Six

Straight lines. These were what needed to be considered. The lines that led from one point to the other with the least possible distance between. They had to be examined with a clear eye. Even the shortest line could be an illusion, leading not to clarity but to chaos and confusion. His decision must not be rushed. This place was primitive and half formed, but even here the choices were not clear cut. There were several options. All would lead, inevitably, to the desired destination. But which would take him there the quickest?

He was used to making these difficult decisions. After so long, it often felt as though he had done little else. He did not regret any of them. Each sacrifice had been justified. Every attack or retreat had been dictated by necessity. Sometimes you killed the enemy in their millions. Sometimes you killed only a dozen and waited patiently for the advantage their deaths would give you. It was all a matter of narrowing down the alternatives until only one remained.

He pondered the structure of the city. He could start at the bottom. Turn the disadvantaged into his tools with promises of power. But that would mean a delay. Those without power never knew what to do with it when you gave it to them. Either they were afraid of it or it drove them mad. They always required time to build the necessary experience. No, it was better to find those who had tasted a little power already. They were always the easiest to control.

He examined the records they had given him of this domain. There were many armed factions. Some were motivated by politics, religion or ethnicity. The majority paraded under the banner of law enforcement. Over a hundred rival organisations competed to be the heroes of the city. Without fail, they claimed to be providing a service that the State would not. Of course, the irony was that the State was quite happy to have these private armies enforcing their laws. It left them free to concentrate on other things.

Most of these vigilante organisations were small. That was good. A large army would be more difficult to get rid of when they were no longer required. He swiftly reduced the list down to the six least well-known. He wasn't going to risk using a group that had too high a profile. Then came the lengthy process of comparing their respective advantages. Each group had weaknesses that could be usefully exploited. Two were utterly corrupt, one almost bankrupt and the other three simply incompetent. Of those last three, one increasingly stood out. The greatest weakness there was the leader.

Excellent, he thought. Time to begin.

Professor Hayden had chosen his line.

Jason lay back on the sofa, paracetamol and codeine caressing his veins. In the flickering illumination from the screen, he could see Lee sprawled next to him. They had turned off the lights and drawn the heavy curtains, shutting out everything in the world but the film.

'It's really old, but it's good,' said Lee.

Stylised images of fabulous beasts scrolled across the screen as dramatic music swelled from the speakers. Thick lettering spelt out words that Jason couldn't read but that he assumed were the names of the actors.

'And this is where you got my name from?'

'Yeah, I thought maybe you'd been dropped to Earth by a… god or something.'

Jason considered. Could that be it? Was he the victim of some higher power? The idea didn't stir anything in his mind, but that didn't mean it couldn't be true. Perhaps this story might give him some clue as to where he came from. If nothing else, he liked being in the dark with his friend, watching these strange imaginings from a bygone age.

'I found a big book of the stories this was based on,' remarked Lee. 'They're kind of hard to read 'cos they're so old. Still interesting, though. Exciting. If they'd taught stuff like that at school, it might have been worth going.'

Jason understood exactly what a school was but he couldn't picture himself ever having been at one. Nor Lee for that matter.

'You didn't like school?' he asked.

'It was crap,' Lee retorted, suddenly angry. 'I didn't give a fuck about any of it, so I stopped going. Anyway…'

He broke off, as though there was something he didn't want to reveal.

'Yes?' prompted Jason.

'They were gonna kick me out anyway. I threatened one of the other kids. He was giving me shit all the time, thought he was funny. So I… it's pretty stupid really. I threatened him with a chisel. Nicked it from the woodwork room. I wouldn't even have done anything; I just wanted to scare him. Like I said, stupid. But they decided I was a problem case. Teachers didn't want me in their classes any more. Not that I wanted to be there. So I left.'

'Did you ever see the other kid again? The one that was giving you shit?' asked Jason.

'No. He left me alone after that.'

'Good.'

The boy managed a smile, the bitterness vanishing as abruptly as it had appeared.

'Anyway, we're missing the film.'

The tale that unfolded was a peculiar one. Jason's namesake was a young man sent on a mission by gods from a place called Olympus. He had to find a Golden Fleece that was kept at the end of the world. During his journey, he encountered flying devils, a bronze giant and a many-headed monster called a Hydra. It was all pleasantly hypnotic. The world was reduced to the screen in front of him and the boy beside him.

One scene caused him an unexpected reaction. An army of skeletons was summoned from the ground to fight on behalf of the forces of evil. The heroes were horrified by the sight of the walking bones of the dead yet Jason thought they were beautiful. The stark white figures possessed a secret poetry far more profound than the strength and prowess of their enemies. For a moment, he caught a shadow of his past, a flicker in the dark. A word drifted through his mind: Fracture.

He wondered if he should tell Lee. The boy's pale face was

intent upon the film. The light from the screen picked out his jutting cheekbones. He was reminded of the skeletons. Like them, Lee held a weird fascination. Jason didn't want to interrupt his pleasure so he stayed silent. But he was happy. At last, he had a fragile hint as to what he was.

From the shadows of the monumental tower blocks, Phillip watched the small house where the subject was staying with the boy. The curtains had been drawn and it was impossible to tell what they were doing now. It hardly mattered. All was going as planned. There was nothing to prevent him from returning to the Fracture until the next stage was due to begin. But if he did, the Committee would be waiting for him. He knew them well enough to know that they would demand an immediate and exhaustive report. This was, after all, the first time such a strategy had been attempted. There would be endless questions and counter-questions. He preferred to be alone for a while and indulge in nostalgia. It had been a long time since he had set foot in the city of his birth.

Once, when he was young and knew nothing of the Fracture, he had been considered handsome. More than that, he had been admired by everyone. It was not just that he was from a family with the kind of wealth that guaranteed a prestigious education and an excellent career. It was that anything he wanted he could take. No compromise had ever been necessary. If he desired a girl, he had her and then threw her away when he was bored with her. Any subject that he chose to study he quickly mastered. He could afford the best clothes and the newest cars. Phillip Pace was universally desired and envied. He was the essence of success.

No one, least of all Phillip, could have guessed how it would all end on what should have been the night of his greatest triumph. Mydia Hycron, even then the biggest corporation on the planet, had announced the beginning of auditions for the annual Face contest. One man and one woman would be selected from thousands of hopefuls to be at the forefront of every major advertising campaign for the next nine months. Their image would be on screens throughout the city and beyond. They would set the looks and styles that the ambitious would religiously follow. If they wore a certain cut of jacket, then the next day anyone that mattered would be wearing the same. If they endorsed a product, it would be in every good home within the week. Even after their nine months were up, their stories and scandals would be retold and reinterpreted in web shows and musicals for weeks afterwards. Perhaps even for years, if they made a big enough impression on the public consciousness. And Phillip Pace had decided that he would win. He would be the Face of this city and all others.

He had devoted a whole year to preparing for the auditions. At twenty-three, Phillip had developed an impressively – though not excessively – toned physique, but this was far from being enough. He had had his legs reshaped to more classical lines and his eyes were now tinted to a lighter blue with the pupils slightly enhanced for maximum impact. It had always troubled him that he was a shade too pale, so his skin had been permanently tanned. This was still a comparatively dangerous procedure and cancer in later life was a virtual certainty, but the results were worth it.

When the night of the audition came – it was a tradition that they were always held at night and with barely a day's notice – there had been no trace of doubt in his mind. He hadn't even been nervous. Phillip Pace would win. He always did. He had bought a new car for the occasion, long and sleek, the carapace a shining orange. It glided along the dark roads, lesser models seeming to part before it. The speakers were pumping out new ragtime and the screen was showing an advert for the five-thousand yendollar jeans that he was already wearing.

The car that wrecked him was a much older make. Its fenders were hanging off and he found out later that it didn't even have a screen installed. Phillip caught only a brief glimpse of it before it smashed into the side of his own car and then he was wrapped in a cocoon of contracting metal. Shards sliced through every part of him. His groin was impaled on the clutch. As his face bust over the dashboard, there was light and darkness and unbearable pain. After that, he had drifted, numb and sightless. Occasionally, he heard voices, doctors and nurses, discussing what should be done to keep his wreckage alive.

He never heard his parents or friends. Their absence didn't

trouble or even surprise him. Now that he was distorted and damaged, it was only natural that they would no longer care. He had lost and there was no place for a loser in their world.

From time to time, he felt painful little jabs as he was fed through tubes. The pressure on his face changed every day, as bandages were applied and removed. Cold hands explored the fragments of his genitals. He heard the word 'eunuch' whispered like a curse. He understood its meaning, but the drugs kept him from screaming out in horror. Sometimes they left a radio playing. New ragtime wasn't popular any more and someone called Liam was the new Face of Mydia Hycron. The web shows were in an uproar because, allegedly, he had never had plastic surgery.

After a while there was no more pain, except for the occasional pang of withdrawal when they were late with his medication. Other than that, his new world was a sightless, scentless void in which he could only hear. In a curiously detached way, he wondered what was to become of him. In all the hubbub of voices around him, he could find no one who would tell him.

One voice always seemed to be there, in the background. Its tones were calm and measured; the dignified speech of a well-paid consultant used to dealing with the wealthy and their wounded offspring. Each syllable carried with it a hint of restrained exasperation at the madness of his patients' lives. The nurses called him Doctor Channing. They used the name with admiration, fear and lust.

Phillip wasn't sure when the conversation took place. Most likely it was at night, but without eyes there was no way to be sure.

'What will you do with him?' asked Channing.

The other voice was unfamiliar, constantly switching from soft to hard and back again.

'He'll have no life here, Channing. You know that. Even if he survives, there is nothing left for him.'

'Yes, I know. But why do you need him?'

'The war. It's getting worse. We need new recruits.'

'You'll turn him into a warrior?' The doctor sounded shocked.

'Of sorts. It's a better offer than anyone else can make him.'

'But you aren't offering it to him. You are asking *me*.'
'That is so. You must make the choice for him.'
'That isn't fair.'
'No. It isn't. But there it is.'

For a while there was silence again. Phillip slept and dreamt of agony. Then Channing's voice had woken him. He sounded sad.

'I've given you to them. They can help you. I don't know what you'll become. But the Fracture protect their own.'

Pain at his arm again. More dreams. And then he had awoken in the Fracture. They had given him a new face and a new life. Later, they had given him a mission. He had all but forgotten the days of being handsome and adored. Now, alone in the darkness, Phillip tried to imagine what might have been and compared it with what was. The Fracture agent pondered on who Phillip Pace might have become.

He was pleased to find that he was without regret.

Chapter Seven

'Do you want to go back down?'

Jason could see the Adam's apple in Lee's scrawny neck moving up and down as he swallowed, desperately trying not to gag again. He was still trembling. Jason had never seen Lee afraid before and it was an unsettling experience. Surely it would be better to walk away from this place, back to where his friend and protector could be fearless once more?

'I can't, Jason. This is the only place he'll meet me.'

'Does he know?'

Lee managed a humourless smile.

'Probably. He says he likes to have the advantage over people.'

It was all Lee could do to look up from the concrete floor at his feet. He had had to stop several times during the long climb up the foul-smelling, filthy stairs. His whole body had started to shake in anticipation and dread. When they had finally walked out on to the top storey of the deserted car park, he had almost vomited on the spot. The only barrier against the sheer drop on each side was a low metal railing that ran round the perimeter. The chilling wind whistled against them, threatening to snatch them up and throw them into the abyss. The only other sound came from the gold and silver planes that rumbled overhead.

Jason could not help taking another look out over the city. For the first time he had a sense of the wider geography of the world in which he had found himself. The buildings were impassive monoliths of smooth grey and cold black, aligned in perfect ranks. In whichever direction he turned, they stood in formation against the skyline, the tallest somehow always at the centre, waiting for the day when they might reach even higher. Their makers' absolute certainty that they would never fall was inscribed into every line and angle. The smaller, brightly coloured blocks that clustered about them were transitory things that would inevitably be consumed by the greater mass. Yet for all its solidity, the city seemed to be undergoing a gradual transformation. Scaffolding wound its way up walls and different textures of brick mingled and clashed. New hues of green and orange stained the bases of the buildings, steadily consuming the grey. It was as though an infection had started on the ground and was slowly but inexorably spreading upwards. Even the straight, congested roads were not immune. Curving diversions had begun to branch out from the main routes. In places, they had already swarmed over and replaced the originals.

Jason found the sight fascinating, but he was more concerned for his friend.

'I'm… I'm trying to get used to… to heights. But it's not so easy,' stuttered Lee.

Jason remembered his face at the high library window, that first night. It was odd to think that they must both have been feeling frightened, albeit for different reasons.

'Do you want me to do this for you?' he asked gently.

'No. Peters won't deal with someone he doesn't know.'

There had to be something he could do to help. He wondered if he could put an image into Lee's mind to calm him. But when he had done it before, the youth had been sleeping or close to sleep. Would it work in the cold light of morning, when he was fully conscious? And shouldn't he ask his permission first?

'Lee,' he began. 'I can…'

'He's here.'

Peters was obviously a rich man. He wore tailored black trousers, a long red velvet coat and a white silk shirt. Gold clung to his neck and fingers. His grey hair was moulded into an enormous, rigid bouffant. It was difficult to place his age – it could have been anything between thirty and sixty. He strutted towards them, his thin lips parted in a beaming smile.

'Salutations, gentleman,' he purred in a tone that was friendly and patronising in equal measures.

Jason heard an intake of air beside him as Lee took a deep breath. He was shaking again and his face was slimy with sweat.

'I've… I've brought the money. Have you got the card?'

Peters looked offended.

'But of course! I am a man of honour; you should know that. I always keep my word.'

'Good,' was the murmured reply.

Peters' face grew even cheerier at the obvious weakness in his associate. There was a hard gleam in his clear, blue eyes.

'I just hope you spend the money well. You really should do something about those spots, you know. Dermatological treatment is quite affordable these days.'

Lee mumbled an incoherent response. He was so vulnerable in this high place that he couldn't even retaliate to the insults of this vain and ridiculous man. Jason decided that he couldn't stand by and let his friend be belittled by this bastard. Whatever his ability was, he would use it. The consequences could wait. He summoned a new image. Into Lee's mind he projected a ring of ancient, heroic warriors, standing in a tight circle all around him. Their swords were drawn, their faces determined. While they stood, no harm would befall their charge.

Lee's back straightened. For a moment he looked at Jason, gratitude in his pale face. Then he turned back to Peters.

'Just give me the Slavecard. I've got better things to use it for than a beautician.'

Peters looked surprised.

'Well, it's your loss. You could at least do something about your teeth. They don't look as though they've got any calcium left in them.'

Lee held out his hand. It was steady.

'Card.'

The older man frowned.

'Money.'

'Card.'

A long moment of silence passed. Peters produced a small, silver card from his immaculate coat and reluctantly handed it over. Lee examined it for a few seconds, running a finger over the narrow strip on the back. He grinned and drew out his wallet.

'It'll do.'

He counted out the money Cornish had given him for the book and then held the notes out to Peters. With a grunt of irritation he took them, not even deigning to check that it was the right amount before he shoved them into his pocket.

'Well, Lee, I think that concludes our business.'

'Yes.'

Peters looked at Jason for the first time. It was a critical, condescending gaze, intended to make him feel inadequate.

'Anything I can do for you, young man?'

'No, I don't think so,' he replied, trying to imitate Lee's firm tone.

The man nodded, barely concealing his anger. He had wanted to dominate the meeting and had failed. With a curt farewell, he swaggered away.

'I think we should get away from here,' suggested Jason.

Lee didn't answer straight away. His mind seemed to be elsewhere. Then he nodded.

'Yeah. It's cold up here.'

He limped back towards the stairs. Jason followed. He felt proud. It had been good to see that overdressed peacock defeated. But did Lee understand what had happened? Should he tell him? Would he be disgusted to know that his mind had been penetrated?

The journey down was quicker than it had been up. They still had to avoid the piles of rubbish and pools of bodily fluids, but Lee was no longer afraid of every step.

Halfway down, Jason stopped.

'What is a Slavecard? You never told me.'

'It knocks out a cash machine's security systems so you can get most of the money out of it.'

Lee paused, checking the graffiti-covered wall for unpleasant stains before he leant against it.

'You can only use it once, so you've got to choose the right machine. Peters knows a lot of people who are into... subversion of technology, I think they call it.'

Another crime. Jason was aware at some level that the society he was in would regard what his friend planned as morally wrong. It didn't worry him. If anything, he found the concept strangely appealing. Subversion of technology.

'Have you used one before?'

'No. But I've never had anyone else to support before.'

Jason found himself both grateful and slightly embarrassed at the risks Lee was prepared to take on his behalf. The sense of unworthiness he had felt when he first saw his own reflection returned.

'Is there anything I can do to help? I don't want to take your money and give nothing back.'

Lee looked down at the litter-strewn floor. That... thing you did.'

A cold shiver passed through Jason. How could he explain what he didn't understand himself?

'I don't know how I do it,' he said slowly. 'It felt natural, but I don't know what it is. You were scared and I wanted to help. Are you angry?'

To his surprise, the youth laughed.

'Of course not! You did it the night I found you, when I was having a bad dream. And when we slept over at the Colossus, right?'

Jason nodded.

Silence.

Lee looked him in the eyes.

'I'd like you to do it again.'

Chapter Eight

The office was so hot that he could barely breathe. Sweat drenched his hair and sealed the thin material of his pale blue shirt to his back. His throat was dry with a thirst no amount of coffee could quench. The new heating unit still wasn't working properly. It would be a matter of minutes to go downstairs and turn it off. But Johnnie Varney preferred to swelter. A little discomfort was a price worth paying for the prestige of owning a company that could afford a Mydia Hycron heater. Clients would no longer walk into cold, draughty premises but into a place where the manager could buy as much warmth as he wanted.

The weekly reports lay on his spartan desk, awaiting his attention. This was one of his favourite parts of the job: finding out what fresh victories his troops had scored. True, some of them were badly written, vague and full of gaps. But there was no disguising the nobility and bravery of his underlings or the evil nature of the forces they strove to conquer. When he had read each report, Johnnie would write his own comments with the old stylus pen that his grandfather had given him and then file it in one of the grey metal cabinets that half filled the office. It was an old-fashioned, almost archaic way of working, but he found it satisfying. Like the bound volumes of the works of Shakespeare prominent on the shelf behind him, it was a nod to tradition, to things that must be preserved.

He picked up the first one. It was a single A4 sheet describing a shoplifting incident. Clarke had given chase and caught the little bastard. Johnnie closed his eyes and pictured the stony-faced man cracking the scruffy child's fingers. Rough justice. An honourable solution to the problems of the age. He returned to the report. It seemed the shopkeeper, a comparatively recent client, had been so grateful that he had given the hero several free bottles of wine. Johnnie frowned. All tributes were supposed to be handed in and yet Clarke seemed to have kept the reward for himself. Obviously he would need to be reminded of the rules. A forgetful man sometimes, but fiercely loyal.

The next report concerned a group found taking the new Valium and decon combinations outside these very premises. They had been quickly dealt with. Johnnie had not been in the offices at the time, but he could well imagine his enraged troops sending the street scum scurrying for the gutters. Loyalty again. They would take the use of drugs near the Stauncher headquarters as an insult to their leader. Of course they would.

Loyalty was very important to him. The company that had owned this building before him had had no comprehension of such a quality, no understanding of honour in business. It had been in this very office that his manager had told him that, after ten years of service, he was being thrown away. Rejected. He had been a different man then, quiet and subservient, his spirit broken by a failed marriage and children who didn't even acknowledge him. Now he could have crushed the traitors with the power of his words. But then, he had simply pleaded and trembled and run away.

The memory of the meeting still lurked at the back of his mind. Pretending to have authority; no chance of promotion; mountains out of molehills; customer dissatisfaction; lies to excuse their petty abuse of power. So many liars in the world, crushing the honest man.

Five years and many further betrayals later, he had returned to the site of his humiliation. His employers had long since moved on, but taking this building was the first of many victories. The upholstered chair he sat in had been his manager's. Those that came to see him had to sit on the same plastic chair on which he had once squirmed. A symbolic reversal.

It was only the beginning. His army, the Staunchers, would bring Truth back to the world. They were admired and feared throughout the city. Those frightened and powerless against the scum that lurked in every corner were happy to pay for the protection that only they could offer. Inevitably, as the tales about them spread, so their numbers would grow. Johnnie could foresee a future in which he stood at the head of a huge force, waging war on all that was dishonest and unworthy. And when that war was won, there would be rewards and glory. A presentation from the old King, perhaps, or a maybe even a street named after him. History would remember him not as a small, sweaty, middle-aged man with curly brown hair going grey, but as a mighty warrior chieftain armed with a gleaming gun with which he never missed.

The next report detailed an investigation into suspected prostitution at a nearby tower block. The old couple who had reported it were rightly disgusted by what they suspected. They had even paid a little extra to ensure that there would be photographic evidence. Wilkins and Levine had visited the flats in question and attempted to persuade the women to leave. The report was surprisingly lacking in detail. He would have to speak to them about that. Correct intelligence was essential to the crusade.

He scanned the next sheet. A few days ago, two bodies had been found outside the old library. Both had been stabbed. The precision of the blows suggested a skilled killer. Johnnie suspected that the two men had disturbed a crime and been brutally attacked. He was determined that they would be avenged. Crowper was looking into the matter, but as yet had uncovered nothing. He was going away on holiday in a week's time, so he would have to get a move on.

The door opened. Johnnie looked up in amazement. No one entered the office without knocking. It was one of his most important rules. This was a place of power and must be treated at all times with respect and deference.

The intruder appeared to be somewhere in his fifties. He was small and tubby with a mass of grey hair. Large eyes were magnified by a pair of metal-rimmed glasses. He wore a dusty green suit and battered brown shoes. A stench of old tobacco hung about him. Even from behind his desk, Johnnie felt the smell catch at the back of his throat, making him want to cough and splutter.

He got to his feet, preparing to cut the old man down to size. The words froze before they could begin.

'Good evening, Varney,' said the intruder. His voice was husky and dry. For some reason, it made Johnnie think of insect wings.

'That's *Mister* Varney. Who are you? What do you mean by just walking in here without an appointment?'

In his office, people acknowledged his authority.

The newcomer chuckled, a deep, confident sound.

'There didn't seem to be anyone to stop me.'

'My employees are all engaged on important assignments elsewhere in the city.'

Johnnie waited for the humble apology that such an announcement ought to command. Instead, there was only more mocking laughter.

'What, all nine of them?'

For a moment, Johnnie was back in the past, being degraded and humiliated by a man more powerful than himself. The memory made him determined. This old fool would be brought to heel.

'Nine of the bravest, most honourable men you will ever meet.'

He could hear the tremble in his voice and hated himself for it. Uninvited, the stranger helped himself to the seat in front of the desk. Without thinking, Johnnie sat in his own chair. His head was starting to swim from the smell of cigars.

'Why Staunchers?' asked the old man.

'What?'

'Why did you call your army of nine "Staunchers"?'

He straightened in his chair. The response was a well-rehearsed one.

'Because we will staunch the flow of dishonour and corruption in the city. We will draw the line and make a stand.'

'Not a very big line, I should imagine. And from what I hear, honour is the least of their interests. It ranks far behind beating children and visiting whores.'

'I know my men! I am their commanding officer!' Johnnie blustered, repelled by the desperation so clear in his own words. He was a confident man! Uncertainty belonged to his past.

'I doubt they would agree. I have come to help you, Varney.'

'I don't need your help!'

'Oh, but you do. What can you do without help? Hide behind your desk while a few women's faces are broken in your name?

Fill in your reports while you wait for your pitiful organisation to fall apart? Attempt to delude yourself just a little longer that anything you do matters when you know in your heart that it is all without meaning? You need me, more than you have ever needed anyone in your unremarkable life. My name is Professor Hayden.'

Johnnie barely registered the name. He had lost control. In a matter of minutes, a fat old man reeking of cigars had taken from him every scrap of authority. Johnnie Varney was once again helpless. Shoulders slumped, he stared down at the floor. Some part of him was crying like a child. He hoped the tears didn't show.

'Help?' he murmured.

'Oh, yes. You are right in one thing. There is a war to be fought. Enemies to be defeated. A Fracture that must be found and punished.'

The vehemence in Hayden's voice surprised Johnnie. It was the sort of hatred that was both terrifying and inspiring. A hatred that could lead men. He forced himself to look the old man in the face.

'What do you want me to do, Professor Hayden?'

'When do you next hold a meeting for your... mighty army?'

He let the insult pass without comment. Johnnie knew that any defiance was unimaginable in the face of such a man.

'Five days' time.'

'Here? Oh, of course here. This is the only place you have. This small building. Still, it will serve, it will serve.'

'You want to talk to my men? They are a good bunch. You can always depend on them.'

Johnnie knew that he sounded like a little boy insisting that his gang was the best. Hayden was clearly amused, a slight smile twitching at the corner of his mouth.

'Oh yes, Varney. They are very dependable. That is why we chose you.'

'We?'

The old man ignored the question. He stood up.

'Hold the meeting as planned. Then I shall give you your orders.'

He turned to go, but stopped in the doorway.

'Soon you shall have war and all the honour you have ever dreamt of. If you have the strength to serve.'

Then he was gone.

Johnnie sat trembling and crying in his chair. Just as he had done before, in this very office, when told that he was no longer needed. He grasped the stylus pen tightly. The pen that had belonged to his grandfather, the hero. The upholstery of the chair was slippery with his sweat.

Unsteadily, he got to his feet. He had no right to sit in this office. He was no manager, no commander. Johnnie picked up the plastic chair from the front of the desk, took it downstairs and used it to smash the Mydia Hycron heater into fragments.

Chapter Nine

The machine could not have been better placed. It nestled discreetly in the wall of a small but exclusive bank that was surrounded on all sides by intertwining office blocks. As with all of its kind, it had been designed for a particular clientele: well-paid corporate workers needing funds for a night's entertainment. Naturally, it took only the very best cards. This cash machine was not for the convenience of those with average wages and inexpensive habits.

Having chosen the place, Lee decided to wait a week before using the Slavecard. They would need a time when the machine was as full as possible and there were no people around. They could only do this once and then the card would be useless. It would be stupid to waste the opportunity for a small profit. Each night, he walked past the bank three or four times, observing the flow of customers, studying the staff, weighing up the dangers. He left Jason at home. Two boys, he said, would attract far more suspicion than one.

Jason understood why he couldn't accompany Lee on these vigils, but he hated being alone. It felt unnatural, as though the experience was somehow alien to his very being. The time dragged as he waited for his friend to return. Even when he tried to distract himself by watching a film, it was just as bad. The fear would always come, stirring in his stomach, tightening round his chest, rushing in his ears. Sometimes he was sick, retching up half-digested food. It left him raw and empty and just as scared. Other times, he curled up on the sofa on which he slept each night, the blanket pulled over his head, reducing his world to a dark, warm cocoon.

It was not just being alone that frightened him. Jason was afraid for Lee. The city was a huge and incomprehensible place. Surely no one could ever be safe walking it alone at night? For all his skill with a knife, the boy was not physically strong and his crippled foot was a clear disadvantage. Any number of terrible things might happen to him.

When Lee returned, Jason would pretend that he had been patiently waiting, not counting every second. If his friend suspected the truth, he never remarked on it. They would take Beta Four and talk for a while. That was Jason's favourite time, when he knew that Lee was safe and could feel the drugs warming him inside.

It was then that they would experiment with Jason's strange ability. He was becoming more skilled each day, experimenting with shades of light and hues of colour. Each night, he created a new image for Lee. Mostly, they were landscapes – savannahs, mountain tops, forests and lakes. Places of freedom, ripe for exploration. Occasionally he added characters from the films they watched in the day. But although they were a rich source of heroes and villains, Jason found it hard to create a realistic, fluid representation of a living thing and he was never pleased with the results. They always seemed less substantial than the dream worlds he gave them to inhabit. His gift remained a mystery to him, but at least he was gradually beginning to learn its uses and limits.

They quickly realised that once Jason had transmitted an image, he did not have to do anything to sustain it. As long as Lee wanted it, the picture would stay in his mind. When it was no longer needed, it simply vanished. Free to study the boy's reaction to each vision, Jason began to take pride in pleasing him, in seeing his contented smile and hearing his faint murmurs of pleasure.

The week passed slowly. Most of the time was spent watching films. Occasionally they went to Kerri's for a few hours. They took pills in the day as well as at night. He often found himself thinking about the sensation they gave him hours before the next dose was due. He dimly recognised that it was probably some form of addiction. But Lee didn't seem worried by their dependence, so why should he be?

When he was not alone and terrified, Jason was almost happy. The unanswered questions about himself seemed more distant and less important. It was easy to let himself imagine that things might stay this way for ever. There was a guilty comfort in the idea that was hard to resist. But as the time of the robbery drew nearer, he knew it would, somehow, mean change. He was fascinated to see the Slavecard in action, yet... something might go wrong.

Still, at least Lee had agreed that Jason could come with him. That was better than waiting alone for him to return. Whatever the night held, they would discover it together.

All too soon, the time came. They did not leave the house until one o'clock in the morning. All the executives would be in their clubs by now, snatching a few desperate hours of freedom from their suited and appropriate existence. The two boys walked slowly towards their destination, just another couple of young men out for the night. Lee was wearing a black tracksuit, the jacket zipped up against the gnawing cold. Jason was in black jeans and a beige jumper. In their dark clothes, the shadows swallowed them up. The rich and the beautiful, their eyes hazy with painkillers and antidepressants, did not spare them a second glance as they migrated from club to club. Only one person stopped to speak to them: a pink-haired boy in a shiny, metallic jerkin with pointed shoulders. He tried to sell them capsules of a new, 'semi-legal' drug called cy. Lee looked tempted but refused. With as much of a shrug as the restraining outfit permitted, the pink-haired boy moved on in search of other potential buyers.

At last they reached the bank. There was no one about at this hour. The only sound was the droning of the wind as it scraped across the plaza and around the jutting office blocks. A few plump pigeons, tired after a day's relentless scavenging, rested against the black glass windows. Even here, there were signs of the city's metamorphosis. A fragile scaffold exoskeleton clung to the largest building. Heavy boards shielded one of the doorways.

Lee limped towards the machine. Following close behind, Jason stood at his shoulder as he studied the small rectangular screen. There were two keypads beneath and a narrow slot above. Instinctively, Lee looked around, though he knew they were alone. He took the Slavecard from his jacket. The youth was calm, his hand steady. Jason could feel the warmth of his body through the chill of the night.

Lee sighed softly to himself. 'OK. Let's do this.'

The card slid into the slot. After a few seconds, a green cobweb pattern began to creep slowly across the screen. Lee started tapping at both keypads, the flood of numbers helping the Slavecard to erode the machine's defences.

'Keep an eye out, Jason. If you see or hear anything, let me know right away, OK?'

'OK.'

Reluctantly, Jason moved away, turning to watch the deserted streets. The sound of his footsteps echoed back from the concrete and glass all around them. In the distance, he could hear music. A repetitive, slow drumbeat. For a while, he tried listening to it, but the rhythm was beyond his understanding.

'Fuck!'

The anger in Lee's voice made him turn round.

'What's the matter?'

'The fucking thing's been upgraded.'

'Does that mean it won't work?'

'No. But it'll take longer.'

Lee returned to the keypads, long fingers jabbing aggressively. His movements were faster now and his breathing quick and shallow.

Jason hesitated before he spoke again. 'Do you... do you want me to entertain you?'

The boy turned to face him. Nervously tugging at his lip, he considered the idea. 'Yeah. That would be good. Something relaxing.'

'How about a desert?'

'Yeah. Try that.'

Lee turned back to the machine. Jason envisioned a golden landscape of sand stretching in all directions. A perfect blue sky. The lightest of breezes stirring the air, carrying the promise of rain. He drew wind patterns in the sand, gentle ridges and swirls. When it was perfect, he eased it into the boy's mind. Lee's whole body relaxed. For a moment he stood still, each breath deep and calm. Then he started work again. His vigil forgotten, Jason watched him, fascinated by his friend's criminal skills. He was pleased to have contributed to the robbery, to have proved that he could help.

'Yes!' hissed the boy triumphantly.

The machine emitted a desperate chocking sound. The whole of the screen turned a nauseous green. Notes spewed out of the slot. Lee began stuffing the money into his jacket pocket. Relief washed through Jason. It was going to be OK.

'What have we here?'

Jason and Lee turned in unison. The man behind them was squat and muscular, with no discernable neck. Tiny eyes stared out of his tanned face and his wide mouth broke into a smile. He was clad in a pristine grey uniform. Black lettering on the breast pocket gave the name 'Clarke'.

'Two little boys out after their bedtime, eh, lads?'

Jason cursed himself. He should have been watching the streets, but he had wanted to see the cash machine defeated. This was his fault. Out of the corner of his eye, he saw Lee reaching for his blade. So did Clarke.

With terrifying speed, Clarke had the youth by the throat, slamming a huge fist into his stomach. He dropped Lee, whimpering with pain, to the floor. The boy curled up, arms wrapped round himself, uncontrollable tears trickling down his pale face.

'Not a good idea, sonny!' bellowed Clarke.

Anger burnt through Jason's mind. A rage so massive, no words could ever hope to encompass it. Without realising what he was doing, he focused his fury and slammed it into the smug, gloating man's mind. Clarke screamed and staggered back. Jason struck again and again, relentlessly driving his hatred into the enemy. He didn't think about how he was doing it. That didn't matter. This man had hurt the one person Jason cared for and he was going to suffer for it. The once arrogant figure collapsed into a heap, sobbing in uncomprehending fear and agony.

In the midst of the attack, Jason felt himself somehow beginning to detach and suddenly his consciousness was slipping from his body. The scene around him flickered, broke up and was gone. He was elsewhere. A cold, echoing, black void. There was no up or down and yet snowflakes floated through the dark, picked out by flickering, dancing lights. His senses were changing. Sharpening. Stretching out into realms he could not have dreamt existed. Close by, he could feel life. Not visible, but near. Life that struggled against itself. A billion parts of it flaring and vanishing, only to be instantly replaced. Each one unique to itself. Then he understood. It was not one life, but many. All fighting. He was in the middle of a battlefield. And every changing instinct told him that he belonged here.

Attack parameters flooded his mind. This was his war, even though he did not know why it was being fought. Pain seared through him as one side took massive casualties; a thousand minds like his own, snuffed out in a microsecond. Retaliation was swift and deadly. Another thousand warriors howled and died. The satisfaction of victory was in Jason's heart. The enemy was being taught a lesson.

He could feel his fellow troops flocking towards him. Still he could not see them, but they were there, drawing ever nearer. He was, of course, irrelevant in himself but he would help to swell their numbers. Perhaps his presence might give them the essential advantage that would tip the balance towards a final and absolute triumph. He did not fear what was to come. There were no doubts, no weaknesses, no indecision.

An image flickered through him. An ill-looking, scrawny boy lying on a concrete floor. A short, heavy man staggering to his feet and snatching up the youth's knife. Lurching forward, murder in his tiny eyes. Memories followed in quick succession. A terrifying world where he was exposed and vulnerable. Fear in the night. And this crippled, ugly boy protecting him, keeping him, Jason, safe.

In that moment, he knew he couldn't stay here. He was indebted to the boy. Joined to him. A million, million voices roared in anger as he turned his back on the battle. Traitor! But this fight wasn't important to him. Not now. He focused on where he had been: in another realm, in a vast city with his friend who was in terrible danger.

He fell through the void, back into his flesh. The fragile frame of skin and bone wrapped round him once more, binding him to the world he had chosen. He stood at the centre of an inferno of raging blue fire that had followed in his wake. He drew the flames into himself and then, with deadly accuracy, he flung them in one searing bolt at Clarke, burning the man out of existence.

Jason's legs gave way and the hard ground slammed into him. For a moment he lay still, waiting for his surroundings to stop heaving about him. Getting used to the notions of up and down again. Just as before, his whole body ached with the shock of this environment.

Concern for his friend soon overrode exhaustion. He crawled towards Lee. The boy was still curled up, whimpering. Jason took him in his arms, wrapping him in soothing, protective dreams. He felt him relax, his breathing gradually steadying.

'It's all right, Lee. He's gone. I... killed him. I'm... I was somewhere else. I was some sort of... weapon. But I came back.'

Lee awkwardly got to his feet. His stomach would be bruised, but otherwise he was unhurt.

'A weapon?'

Jason got up too, ignoring the pain.

'I don't know where I was. They were all fighting. All weapons. But... I chose not to stay.'

Lee nodded slowly. Jason wondered what he was thinking. Would he walk away in revulsion from such a strange creature? Abandon him to the city? Had Jason come back only to find himself alone?

'Lee—' he began.

The boy interrupted.

'So what do we do?'

'I don't know. I don't understand why I was fighting or where I was. But... I'm sure I don't want to go back.'

They stood for a few moments in silence. Lee reached down and carefully picked up his knife. Clarke had been holding it when he died and the blade was slightly melted. He studied it briefly and then slid it into his jacket pocket.

'Then I guess,' said Lee, 'we should...'

'Yes?'

'Go to Colossus for the night and see what new stuff Kerri has. Is that OK with you?'

Jason nodded earnestly. Lee smiled weakly. 'And we'll worry about everything else later.'

'Sounds good to me,' agreed Jason.

They walked away from the bank, leaving an empty cash

machine and a burn mark on the pavement. They were close, shoulders rubbing together, both boys needing the proximity of the other. Jason felt the sense of invulnerability he had known on the battlefield slipping away. He let it go without hesitation.

And in the Fracture, Phillip was awoken and told that the plan was nearing completion. Success was assured.

Chapter Ten

No one wanted to sit next to Johnnie Varney. While the rest of the Staunchers sat in a tight huddle of chairs in the middle of the room, he sat alone at the back. It was to be expected. He was a defeated man, an overthrown and irrelevant relic of their pitiful past. His presence was tolerated, nothing more. Johnnie understood this and accepted it. He deserved no better. Once, long ago, he had sat in this same room during company meetings and desperately tried to please his superiors with indifferent suggestions and meaningless figures. Later, he had stood at the front and tried to rally his army of nine to victory. Now he sat here once more, isolated, despised and ignored.

The meeting room hadn't changed much over the years. It had never seemed big enough, despite taking up a large section of the building. The walls were a discouraging off-white and the floor was covered by a well-worn carpet, the pattern an eye-straining mess of browns and yellows. The plastic chairs seemed to have escaped from a school classroom.

Professor Hayden would arrive at exactly six o'clock. He was always punctual. The entire group bar Clarke was here, eager to give their reports. They were a very different army to the one Johnnie had led, smart, alert and disciplined. In the three days since Hayden had first addressed them, everything had changed. The night-time patrols had been regulated so that there were always two men on duty at any one time. The once optional grey uniforms were now compulsory and in the pocket of each was a freshly printed rule book. They had even been promised weapons. It was the dawn of a new era for the Staunchers.

Johnnie looked up at the old digital clock above the door: 5.56 p.m. Only four minutes to go. The Professor gave a speech every night. The men looked forward to it. Johnnie remembered giving speeches. How they used to snigger and mutter to each other. How he had tried to strike a commanding figure but had always been intimidated by his men's expensive watches and tailored clothes. He had tried to pretend they were listening but knew they never did. Why should they have?

Now he had seen the true power that words could wield. With Hayden, they sat electrified, their eyes fixed and adoring. Even Johnnie was swept along by his talk of triumph and glory. For those fifteen minutes or so, all his shame would disappear. Afterwards, he could never remember exactly what Hayden had said, only that it had been inspiring and profound. That was all that mattered.

5.59 p.m. The pungent odour of cigars was wafting towards the room. You could always smell him before you saw him. Johnnie wondered if the other men had noticed the stench, too. But that was a disrespectful thought and who but an embarrassment and a failure like him would think it?

Johnnie suddenly realised that Clarke still wasn't here. That would go badly for him. It was certainly out of character. Of all the men, Clarke had embraced the new regime most wholeheartedly. Only the previous night, he had been talking loudly with Billington of what they could achieve once they were armed. If the others were aware of his absence, they said nothing. He could tell that all their thoughts were of the speech to come.

6.00 p.m. The flimsy door swung open. Professor Hayden strode in. Johnnie tried to stop himself from coughing as the smell caught at the back of his throat. He glanced over at the other Staunchers to see if it had affected them too. There was no sign that it had. Their faces were full of love for their leader.

'Good evening, gentleman,' purred the Professor. He stood at the front of the room. He never sat during the meetings.

'Good evening, sir,' they chorused back.

For a few moments, there was an expectant silence. Hayden stood, eyes closed, one hand tapping his nose. As one, his audience leaned forward, keen to hear what he would say. The old man's eyes opened. He cleared his throat with a gargling cough.

'Clarke is not here,' he observed.

Crowper, a mass of muscle with a thick new hair implant, got hesitantly to his feet.

'No one's seen him since he went on patrol last night. We thought you must have sent him on other duties, sir.'

Hayden smiled but his eyes were heavy.

'Clarke will have no more duties. He is dead. Murdered. There is nothing left of him.'

Some of the men gasped, others got to their feet. All of them began to speak at once, their voices merging into a furious babble. Only Johnnie Varney remained seated and silent, alone in this as in everything else. He did not even have the right to anger. Hayden motioned with his hands for them to sit down and be silent. Without hesitation they obeyed.

'I know who was responsible. I know their names and their faces. They are the scum of the streets. Foul children of this despicable age.'

'Children?' repeated Levine, his double chins wobbling in disbelief.

'Children,' affirmed the Professor. 'Yet old enough to kill. Convinced they can strike down honest, honourable warriors and not pay the price. But they will pay. You and I, my friends, shall see to that.'

Levine got to his feet, fists bunched and eyes bulging. He had always had a quick temper. Before he became a Stauncher, he had been a security guard but he had found the regulations too restricting.

'Where are they, sir? Tell us and we'll sort the little bastards out for you. Tonight.'

With the barest hint of regret, Hayden shook his head.

'I understand your feelings, Levine. I sympathise. They are natural. But we must be patient. The time for vengeance is not yet upon us. For now, we must watch and wait. There are other, darker forces involved in this crime. Our enemies have used these evil boys to strike down one of our number. They are too cowardly to deal plainly and in the open. But, when the time comes, we shall take the fight to them. For now, we observe. We watch these boys and wait for the moment when the enemy makes himself known. Then we will have them.'

Hayden seemed to have reached a crescendo. Sweat was running down his face. Johnnie was sure that the stench of cigars had grown headier. Without realising it, he had started to clap. All the men were applauding their commander.

Someone stood up. Hayden looked at him in surprise. It was Billington, the youngest of the group. His long hair had just been re-dyed blond. The Stauncher uniform emphasised his toned physique. He and Clarke had been good friends. The older man had been trying to get him into his exclusive golf club and had even let him use his family yacht. The applause died away.

'Well, Billington?'

'Sir,' he said nervously. 'I don't mean to be disrespectful. I am sure that you know best. But—'

'Well?'

'Why don't we just capture these boys and force them to tell us what we need to know? Wouldn't that be quicker?'

'We can't be sure how much they know. It is better to wait.'

Billington looked unconvinced by the answer.

'But what about Clarke, sir? He's dead! We can't just forget him. We've got to make them pay! How are we going to do that if we wait?'

There was a horrified pause. No one had defied Hayden before. With surprising speed, the Professor moved towards Billington until they were face to face. He looked deep into the young man's suddenly frightened eyes.

'You are here to obey orders. Triumph can only come through discipline. You know that!'

In the pause that followed, it was as though Billington had seen everything he most dreaded written in the old man's face.

'Yes, sir,' he whimpered, visibly trembling.

'In time you shall have all the revenge you want. That I promise you. Now sit down.'

Billington sat, staring at the floor like a naughty child caught out lying. Hayden returned to the front of the room.

'I shall give you a rota for surveillance. The boys will be watched at all times. For the moment, this takes precedence over everything.'

He smiled.

'Gentleman, we are on the verge of our first, great victory.'

The Staunchers were applauding again. Johnnie joined in,

palm smacking against palm until his hands felt raw. They were going to win. Professor Hayden's army would triumph. Looking round, he noticed that the men had all drawn their chairs away from Billington. There was a circle of space all around him now. Although the young man was applauding, he was still staring at the floor. His eyes were moist. For a moment, Johnnie felt sorry for him. Then he realised that he was no longer the most hated man in the room. It was a good feeling.

Chapter Eleven

Phillip had only met Dean Elliott once before. He hadn't made much of an impression in the agent's memory. His bland face with its covering of stubble was instantly forgettable. His voice was quiet and utterly toneless. Even his brown hair lacked life. His slender frame looked as though he might have enjoyed sports before he opted for this subterranean existence but it seemed unlikely he had seen daylight since.

Still, thought Phillip, who better to work in surveillance than a man so easily ignored? Slumped in a high-backed chair, Dean scrutinised the flickering, changing images on the six screens before him with the detached nonchalance of a seasoned professional. Even though he was only in his twenties, his body language was that of a tired old man. In one hand he held a remote control pad. In the other was a pack of mints. He popped one in his mouth, crunching the sweet noisily between his teeth and returned the pack to the pocket of the tan jacket that appeared to be moulded to his back.

Standing behind him, Phillip tried to control his impatience. 'Anything?'

'Not yet,' replied Dean. 'But not all the cameras are working. Even in the high-security sections, things get missed. Your two boys might have been lucky.'

'I can't take the chance. I have to be sure no one links them to the robbery or that man's disappearance.'

'Far as I know, it's not been reported yet.'

'It will be. No one must know they killed him.'

There was no need for caution. They could speak quite plainly here. This small, bare room, buried far beneath the enormous police tower, was a well-kept secret. It was the centre of a mesh of CCTV cameras that entwined most of the city. Even the rest of the police force were kept largely ignorant of its existence. After all, how could they have gone about their day-to-day activities if they knew they were being watched? Occasionally – very occasionally – it was deemed necessary to release recordings of the more violent interrogations. Just to keep the public happy. The repeat fees always came in useful.

Dean swallowed the remains of his mint.

'This them?'

Phillip leaned forward.

'Show me.'

He fiddled with the pad and all six screens showed the same view. The picture was sharp and clear. They were looking down at two boys by the wall of a bank. One stood watch while the other worked intently at a cash machine. A heavy-set man in a grey uniform appeared behind them.

'That's them,' said Phillip quickly. 'Delete the record for the entire night. I want no trace left.'

Dean pressed a button and all the screens turned white.

'It's done.'

'You're sure?'

'Yes. Anyone looking will think the camera broke down.'

'Good.'

The security man shifted in his chair. For the first time, something approaching an expression appeared on his face. He looked hungry.

'And my reward?'

'Of course.'

Phillip hesitated before he handed over the slip of paper. It was a strange thing to send someone to their death, no matter how willingly they went. Still, it was the payment he had chosen for three years of loyal service. Dean took the paper eagerly and scanned the single line of writing. An address and a number.

'The Slaughterhouse,' he breathed.

'We have arranged a booking for you. Tonight. The door will be marked. The chefs are aware of your wishes.'

'And I will be...' Dean broke off, too excited to continue.

'Cooked. Yes. The procedure will be painless, I'm told. Your body will be divided, roasted and served to a party of... gourmets.'

'Thank you.'

Phillip turned to go. This was no longer his business. Dean's voice stopped him.

'I don't know who they'll get to replace me. I can't guarantee that they'll help you like I have.'

'I'm sure we will find ways of persuading them if the need arises.'

'Yes. Probably. Goodbye.'

Phillip looked around the surveillance room. Tomorrow it would be empty, as though Dean had never existed. With technology like this, the security man could have lived like a spider at the heart of its web, watching and waiting for his victims to become entangled in their own lies and corruption. But he preferred to be a fly. To be consumed. And during his dying moments, he would be blissfully happy.

'Goodbye.'

The burger had the texture of rubber but the milkshake was delicious. Jason sucked greedily at the straw, drawing up the thick, pink fluid from a large cardboard cup. Cold tingled at the back of his throat and behind his eyes. Lee smiled at him.

'You really like those, huh?'

Jason nodded enthusiastically.

'Yeah. It almost makes up for the food.'

Lee pushed his cup across the small, chipped table.

'You can have mine if you want. I'm not really thirsty.'

'Thanks.'

Gratefully, Jason took the drink. As he did so, he noticed that Lee had barely touched his burger. He didn't blame him. Parts of it seemed to be raw. Then again, he never seemed to eat much anyway. Jason wondered if he just didn't like food.

'Anyone?' muttered Lee.

Jason glanced around the restaurant. The walls were painted in varying shades of green. All the chairs and tables had been designed to look hand-crafted despite clearly being made from mass produced plastic. Artificial plants stained with coffee were crammed into every corner. Pan pipes playing soothing melodies in the background were drowned out by the noise from a huge screen behind the counter showing an endless stream of music promos. Even at this early hour of the morning, the place was almost full. Suited men and women forced down speedy breakfasts while harassed parents looked despairingly at their squabbling offspring.

Jason shook his head. As far as he could tell, they weren't being watched. Not this time.

'Not that I can see. Maybe they just couldn't stand the idea of eating here.' The boy giggled.

'Yeah, well, I could understand that. You know they designed these places to look natural? After most of the big fast-food places went out of business, they reckoned people wanted to think they were eating somewhere, er, ecologically conscious. Still serve the same food, though.'

A new video had started on the screen. Four young men, three muscular and dark, one slim and blond, danced slowly on a beach. The image of their writhing, supple bodies was tinged with a sepia glow. Lovingly, the camera panned up and down their denim-clad torsos, occasionally pausing in a close up on their soulful eyes. At a nearby table, two hyperactive girls started a heated debate on who was their favourite member of the band.

'Alpha,' observed Lee. 'Some people reckon the blond one's a eunuch.'

Jason looked up from his milkshake in surprise. 'A eunuch?'

'Yeah. I mean he – I think his name's Jordan – he's never said anything about it one way or the other in interviews and stuff. But if you look at the way he moves, I can see how he might be. Though it's probably just a rumour they put about to get good sales.'

Jason tried to make sense of the sound accompanying the images, but he couldn't. Even the rhythm was incomprehensible, as though designed to create a response that he was incapable of. How did people tell which songs they liked and which they didn't? How were you supposed to judge?

'I don't think I understand music,' he said.

'Neither do they, probably.'

For a few moments, they sat in silence.

'Still,' began Lee. 'I can see... how it must be nice. Knowing that people are looking at you and like what they see.'

Jason remembered the crushing sense of worthlessness when he had seen his own reflection for the first time. It hadn't occurred to him that Lee might feel the same way about himself. Perhaps because he found the boy so intriguing. The way he moved, the way he spoke. His physical afflictions – the acne, grey teeth and crippled foot – held a compulsive fascination for him. Maybe he should tell him? He was about to speak when his friend cut him off.

'Sooner or later, we'll have to decide what we're going to do.'

It had been four days since they had robbed the cash machine. Four days since Jason had killed a man. The experience had drawn the two of them even closer together. They were both murderers now. Each had killed to protect the other. The secret was always there, unspoken between them. It separated them from the people eating, talking and arguing around them.

'Who do you think they are?' he asked. Lee scratched at his scrawny neck.

'I don't know. At first I thought they must be vigilantes. There are a lot of groups now; some of them are pretty big. Most people go to them instead of the police. Fuck knows why; they're just as bad. But I reckon they would have done something by now. They just seem to be watching us.'

For the last two days, they had had known they were being observed. Always by hulking figures lurking in crowds. Some they saw several times, others only once. But always it was the intensity of their stare that gave them away. Their eyes wide and unblinking, indifferent to everything except their prey. Whoever they were, they weren't very good at concealing themselves. However, as soon as they realised they had been seen, the watchers would vanish.

An attack of some sort seemed inevitable. Lee's hand was never far from his new, shiny blade. Jason forced himself to prepare to use his ability to hurt again. The assault had not come. Not yet anyway. The men waited and watched, hatred etched into their faces. In its way, that was more frightening. The two boys were never apart now. Even at night, Jason slept in a sleeping bag at the foot of Lee's bed. The youth was having bad dreams and needed his friend's calming mental images to banish them.

'Could it be anything do with that battlefield where you came from?' asked Lee.

Jason considered the idea.

'Maybe. But I don't think they come from there. The things that were fighting there were totally different.'

He had tried to describe his experiences in the void. It was difficult when he had barely understood it himself. All he was really sure of was that he had been fighting in a war that he no longer wanted any part of. Lee had accepted this with surprising ease. Maybe it made some sort of sense to him.

'Whoever they are, we can't just wait for them to get us.'

Jason gulped down more milkshake, uncertain how to reply. He had no idea what they should do. Even with their combined skills, confronting the enemy might be suicide. Besides, he wasn't sure he felt ready to kill again. The ease with which he had done it the first time disturbed him.

'Maybe we should leave,' said Lee suddenly.

'Leave?'

'The city, I mean.'

The idea was an obvious one and yet it had not even crossed his mind. Somehow he had assumed that their world was limited to this city. He hadn't thought about what lay beyond it.

'Where could we go?'

'On the outskirts of the city there are communes. I think that's the word for them. People go there who want to live by their own rules. You have to pay to get in, but that's not exactly gonna be a problem.'

Jason thought about the stash of stolen money under the sofa. It was a good thing they hadn't spent it all in the first few days.

'Won't they want to know who we are?' he asked.

'I don't think so. Once you're in, they pretty much leave you alone. As long as you don't hurt any of the other members, you can do what you want.'

'How do we get there?'

'To the outskirts? It's a full day's drive. But hiring a car would be way too expensive and we'll need the money to buy our way in. I reckon we should use the buses. It'll take longer, but if anyone follows us, it'll be easier to lose them. Most of the stations have cheap motels nearby where you can sleep over. What do you think?'

Jason nodded. It sounded a good plan. At any rate, it gave them a chance. 'OK. When do we go?'

'Now. We'll go home, get the money, pack some stuff and just go. There's a station about twenty minutes' walk away. We'll get on the first bus that comes along.'

Jason drained the last dregs of his milkshake with a loud slurp. None of the people in the burger bar looked round as they got to their feet. None of them knew that the two young men just leaving were killers and now fugitives. The girls at the nearby table were still discussing Alpha. They had finally agreed on who was the best-looking member of the band and were now trying to choose their favourite song. A middle-aged mother with four children looked at the girls with envy and shouted at her youngest to shut up and eat his forest fries.

Chapter Twelve

The plan could not have gone better. The subject's responses had been exactly as predicted. Trapped in an unknown realm with his powers massively diminished and memory erased, his nature had altered almost beyond recognition. He had found a name and a friend. He had learnt about fear. Most importantly, he had turned from the battlefield. Never again would the Block be able to use him. Of course, the loss was unlikely to trouble them unduly. They had billions more. Their military intelligence would most likely assume that it was an isolated breeding malfunction and disregard it. Even the best technology occasionally went wrong. Of course, a second such incident would make them suspicious. That was why the plan had been so meticulously prepared. It could only be tried once.

Phillip slipped silently through the shadows of the city. It was dusk, the sky rusty with a melancholy haze. Sometimes he caught the eye of a passer-by, but they would always hurriedly avert their gaze from the masked figure. He was too much at odds with the world as they knew and understood it. Moments later they would forget, the strange sight buried in the depths of their subconscious. Only their dreams would remember. A pretty girl in a tight red skirt brushed past him with the smallest of shudders. He felt a sharp pang of lust. Many such girls had come willingly to him when he was young. He had lost count of the virgins he had taken. It would be good to experience such pleasures again. Still, he reflected, there were many ways for a gelding to make love to a woman. One day he would try them.

Phillip was within sight of Lee's house. This would be the most difficult stage of the plan. His appearance would doubtless be a shock to them, but that was only the beginning of the problem. It was going to be far from easy to explain what was happening. They would have to understand the war and the reasons behind it. They would have to understand the

Committee's intentions. And hardest of all, they would have to understand that their friendship was required to end. Phillip regretted that Lee would have to be abandoned. The boy possessed many of the qualities most admired in the Fracture. Quick, imaginative and damaged, he might even have made an effective agent on future missions. Instead he would be left behind, alone. But such things happened. The war had made loneliness universal.

If they resisted the reality of their situation, then further, more aggressive demonstrations would be necessary. He hoped it wouldn't come to that. Even if one of them had once been an enemy and one deserved better.

Johnnie Varney took a deep breath before knocking on the office door. His legs were shaking. Once more he had to report failure to a superior. Once more his inadequacies were to be exposed and ridiculed. Had people felt like this when he had been the one to summon them? It seemed unlikely.

The Professor's voice was a musty growl. 'Enter.'

Timidly, Johnnie opened the door and scurried across the short distance to the waiting chair, not daring to meet Hayden's gaze. The new seat was metal and smaller than its wrecked predecessor. He felt as though its hard surface resented the touch of his body. It wasn't the only change. Most of his old filing cabinets were gone, rendered obsolete by the compact screen that perched proudly on the desk. The men had burnt all his paperwork two days ago. He himself had struck the match. Even the Shakespeare plays were gone. Still, he had never got round to reading them.

'Well, Varney?'

'I... I'm sorry, Professor.'

Scenes from the past ran through his mind. Please... don't sack me... just one more chance... please, I'm begging.

'Sorry? What has gone wrong?' asked Hayden evenly.

He forced himself to look up. The old man's face was unreadable. The smell of tobacco was as strong as ever but Johnnie hardly seemed to notice. It was drowned by the stench of his own fear.

'We lost them. They aren't at the house or the pill bar. We can't find them. They must have gone... somewhere.'

'Of course they've fucking gone somewhere,' spat the Professor.

Like a frightened child, Johnnie slid his chair back a little. The old man looked ready to explode. Saliva trickled from the corner of his wizened mouth and veins pulsed at his temples.

'Who saw them last? Who failed?'

He didn't know. He'd only scanned the reports, more worried about the consequences for himself than the precise details.

'I... it... I...' he stammered.

'Was it you, Varney?'

'Billington. It was Billington, sir.'

'Bring him here. Now.'

Johnnie Varney didn't think. Not about the lie. Not about his cowardice. Not about the danger in which he'd placed his comrade. All that mattered was that the blame would not be his. He went down to the meeting room and told the younger man that he was wanted. He responded with a wide grin. There was pride in his face as he ascended the stairs. No one had spoken to Billington since he had disgraced himself at the last meeting. They never even referred to him in conversation. Perhaps he thought he had been forgiven and selected for a special mission. Maybe he saw a chance to redeem himself.

Johnnie waited outside the office door. He could hear the rasp of Hayden's angry voice and the occasional protesting whimper from the Stauncher. He ignored the sounds. Instead, he thought of his grandfather. The hero. The man who had saved a child from drowning. The memory gave him some comfort. There were at least a few drops of courage in his blood.

'In here, Varney.'

Reluctantly, Johnnie entered the office. He had come to hate this room with every fibre of his being. All the terrible events in his life had happened here. And now, here was something far worse. Billington lay sprawled across the chair. His long hair had turned silver. Dribble laced his chin. His eyes stared vacantly up at the ceiling as he murmured a series of incoherent words: 'Not... no... my... problem... there... no... not...'

Johnnie retched at a smell worse than that of cigars; Billington had soiled himself.

Professor Hayden smiled bitterly.

'We will leave it here. It will feed on its own waste and after that starve to death.'

He could only nod. What was there to say? The old man had to be obeyed or Johnnie Varney would share the fate of the excrement-stained husk on the metal chair.

'What do we do, sir?'

'We go hunting.'

As Phillip looked round the empty house, he cursed his bad luck. If only he had come sooner! The signs of a hurried departure were all too clear. The cupboards open and bare; tins of food that had been snatched up and then thrown down littered the floor. Rejected clothes lay in tangled heaps everywhere. The bedroom was as much a mess as the living room. The bed was a nest of knotted sheets. A sleeping bag was bunched into a corner, one corner flapping out like a broken wing. Here, too, drawers were open and the contents thrown about. He sat on the bed, trying to ignore the scattering of underwear.

Something had gone wrong. Something neither he nor the Committee could have anticipated. But what? Incriminating evidence had been removed. Cornish had no cause to betray the Fracture to the authorities and, besides, he was a coward. So what had scared the boys into flight? And more importantly, what was to be done?

There were two choices. He could return and report the failure of the operation. The Committee would then be able to devise a counter-plan. But that would take time. Their decision-making process was always a drawn out and exhaustive affair. And while they deliberated, Jason and Lee were unobserved and unprotected. Phillip knew that the people of this city could only be predicted so far. While the Committee plotted, the subject might die at the hands of a random assailant. It would all have been for nothing. Which left the second choice: he could search for them. There were other contacts in the city; men like Cornish, willing to trade information and help in exchange for rarities. With luck, he could find the boys before the Committee even realised there was a problem.

Brown leathers creaking softly, he got his feet. It was an easy choice. This was his mission and he would see that it was a success. Whoever threatened Jason and Lee would be dealt with. And then he would make the boys understand that to run was pointless.

Before he left, he took a last look round the small house. It was a strange place, a hovel compared to the home of his childhood. Nevertheless, he could see why they might have been happy here. For a few minutes he stood motionless, the red flesh in the aperture of his mask trembling gently. Then he turned and went out into the twilight city.

Chapter Thirteen

After six months, Andrea had become used to the smell of exhaust fumes. For the first week, the heavy odour had made her head ache so badly she had thought she would die. It clung to her clothes and her hair, permeating every pore of her body. She had almost given up her patch, even though she had had to fight so hard to get it. Now the stench was just another part of her daily work. She had almost come to like it. After all, if there were fumes then there were buses and that meant customers, tired people at the end of an uncomfortable journey, who just might want to treat themselves to a necklace or a bracelet to brighten their weary day. Better still were the long-distance travellers. Hobbling from the buses, legs cramped with pins and needles, they would suddenly remember that they needed a present for the neglected relatives or friends that they were visiting. Handmade jewellery had just that right hint of the personal touch, even if it was bought in a panic and at the last minute.

Andrea's stall was a very basic affair, a square, fake wood table, covered by a ragged awning. The metal trinkets for sale were neatly laid out, some plain and simple, others glinting with tiny pieces of glass and engraved with intricate patterns. Stowed safely beneath one corner of the table was the battered red suitcase where her profits were stashed. She had used card to divide the interior into compartments for the different notes. It was as close as her life got to an ordered system.

Behind her squatted the disheartening shape of the station itself. Low and long, it was painted in harsh stripes of yellow and black. She had always thought it looked like a huge wasp, overwhelmed and brought to ground by the stink of diesel. People streamed in and out of the glass doors, looking at their watches nervously and trying to make some sense of the incomprehensible timetables in their hands. On the wide tarmac lanes in front of the station, the buses arrived and departed, their engines roaring and spluttering. Since the railways had been abandoned, they had become the new lifeblood of the city. There were accidents, of course; dozens of people were killed every day by careless drivers at the end of a long shift. Still, as yet, there was no better alternative for a public that always had somewhere else to be.

It was 4.30 p.m. The sky was rapidly darkening, the full moon already a distinct white sphere. Andrea pulled her fake fur coat tighter round her broad frame. Another twenty minutes or so and she would pack up and go back to the motel. A relaxing bath and then she would settle down in front of her screen for the evening. Today had been good; she might even be able to afford to take tomorrow off. The thought brought a smile to her fleshy face. A full day to herself. When was the last time that she had enjoyed one of those? She ran ringed fingers through her pink hair. Perhaps she should take the chance to do her roots. At the moment, she looked like a psychedelic skunk.

A bus wheezed to a stop in front of her. With a frown, she noted the Mydia Hycron emblem on the dirty, white chassis. Was there anything they didn't own?

The doors hissed open and the passengers began to troop off. Some looked briefly at her wares; others strode past without a glance. This was the hardest time to make a sale. Night was coming and everyone just wanted to be inside and warm. She had heard that the best traders knew how to take advantage of the hours of dusk and dawn, when the human nervous system was at its most vulnerable. It was not a skill she seemed to possess.

'Handmade necklaces!' she called. 'Special, unique, patterned bracelets! Sir? Madam? These are special, nothing like them anywhere else! What about you, sir?'

They weren't interested. Most of the passengers were old and clearly regarded a woman in her twenties with pink hair as a hazard best avoided. Maybe she should just give up now. It might be easier and less depressing to pack up early. Andrea was considering the idea when two boys got off the bus. One was pale and scrawny, dressed in a blue tracksuit. His friend was stockier and was wearing black jeans and a brown jumper. Both were carrying bulging holdalls. They looked tired. At a guess, they had travelled further than their fellow passengers. The pair stood near the bus for a few moments, talking quietly and occasionally glancing round. She had the distinct impression that they didn't want to be noticed. The one in black jeans looked at the stall for a few moments. He suggested something to his friend. The skinny boy smiled and nodded in agreement. He handed him a few notes and walked towards the station. As he passed the stall, she noticed that he had a limp.

The other youth approached her. He looked down at the metal jewellery, not making eye contact with her. There was an odd quality about him, but she couldn't put her finger on what it was. He seemed to be trying to shrink into himself. Without his friend, he seemed lost.

'Anything interest you?' she asked gently. She had been shy herself once. A very long time ago.

He looked up at her. His eyes were an attractive green. All the same, the boy's features were far too heavy to be considered handsome.

'I'm looking for two necklaces – matching ones, maybe?'

How sweet, she thought. Teens had a habit of buying things to mark their friendships. A few years from now, they'd probably be getting tattooed together. She pointed to a pair of pendants, each on a brown leather cord. Both were representations of a rearing snake, one facing right and the other left. Tiny red pieces of glass represented the reptilian eyes.

'What about those? Or if you don't like snakes, I've got a similar design with eagles.'

'Eagles?'

'An extinct bird. Like the dodo, only they were hunters.'

The boy picked up one of the snake pendants and looked in the direction of the station. He seemed to be trying to decide whether or not it would please his travelling companion.

'I think they would look good on both of you,' she ventured. Suddenly he smiled. It was an odd, lopsided grin.

'Yes. You're right. How much are they?'

'Twenty-five each. Forty for the pair.'

'I'll take the pair.'

He hesitantly gave her two crisp twenties, as though unsure

that they were the right notes. She handed him the other pendant. Awkwardly shifting the bag on his shoulder, the boy slipped them both into his jeans pocket.

'Anything else?' asked Andrea hopefully. A few more sales and maybe she would be able to afford to take two days off. Two whole days!

'Er, no, thanks all the same. Though…'

'Yes?'

'We need somewhere to stay for the night. Is there a motel nearby?'

Oh well, she thought, never mind. One day it would have to be.

'Yeah. If you go out through the station, out the main doors near the coffee place, there's a motel just over the road. I'm staying there myself. It's nothing special but it's OK.'

'Thanks.'

'No problem.'

The boy disappeared into the station. Andrea watched him go. Strange kid, she thought. Still, you met all sorts in her line of work. She started packing away the jewellery. Already she was planning a day's rest. A long lie in, takeaway meals and an afternoon with the screen. Soon, she'd forgotten the boy altogether.

The inside of the station was like a hive. It was the only word Jason could think of that came close to describing the madness before him. People swarmed everywhere. Heaving throngs passed back and forth, absorbing anyone that strayed into their path. Determined groups clustered tightly around stands showing charts that just seemed to confuse them more. Long, impatient queues stretched out of shops, from which heavy, greasy smells were emitting. The air was full of raised voices and stilted announcements. Middle-aged women with clipboards stalked the crowds, waiting to pounce on anyone who didn't get past them quickly enough.

Jason felt utterly lost. Lee had told him that he would be in the pharmacy, buying pills for the next few days. Jason looked desperately round but he could make nothing of the signs over the shops. Perhaps he should just wait here for Lee to come looking for him.

But it was impossible to stand still. He was swept along by two large families, all shouting simultaneously at each other.

'This way, this way! Come on!'

'But they said Pavement One!'

'No, no, we arrived at One but we leave at Three!'

'He's taken it, Daddy!'

'If you don't shut up, I'll smack your bloody face!'

The living tide deposited Jason near a magazine rack. Grateful to stand still, he pretended to scan the glossy covers as though undecided on which to choose. As he couldn't read the titles, he looked at the pictures instead. Most of them were photos of well dressed people kissing each other or holding babies, presumably their own. The short, bald newsagent sitting nearby scowled at him impatiently through gold-rimmed glasses.

A hand tapped Jason on the shoulder. He turned with relief.

'Excuse me, have you got a minute? I'd just like to ask you a few questions.'

The woman's cerise suit was almost as stiff as her lacquered hair. Her heavily made-up face formed a well-practiced smile as she tapped the clipboard with a pen. Jason was so disappointed he could have hit her.

'Are you considering upgrading your mobile? The Lusitanian is—'

'I'm sorry, I don't have a mobile,' said Jason as calmly as he could.

Neither the woman nor her smile were to be deterred. She scribbled a brief note on the top sheet and then flipped to another page without hesitation.

'Well, are you thinking of getting one? The Lusitanian is the best model on the market, a good investment for a young man like yourself.'

'No, I don't want one,' he snapped and pushed past her. The woman's voice behind him was terse.

'Thank you very much for your time!'

He found himself once more in the midst of the crowds. Should he ask someone where the pharmacy was? They all looked too busy, enclosed in their own angry, resentful worlds. The only people that looked as though they would speak to him were trying to sell things. Jason cursed his stupidity. He had wanted the necklaces as a mark of his friendship with Lee. What good would they be if he had lost him?

'Boy.'

The voice was quiet. Jason turned slowly. Standing behind him was a tall man in an orange suit. His thinning hair was plastered across his head in some sort of attempt at a fringe. His huge eyes made Jason momentarily think of a fish.

'What's your name, boy?'

'Jason,' he replied evenly. Somehow he knew it would be a mistake to show fear in the face of this stranger.

'You were talking to the jewellery woman outside. Do you know her?'

The question caught him by surprise. Was he being interrogated because of what he had bought? Perhaps the stall was illegal. Was some moral code against buying snake pendants?

'No, just wanted to buy some necklaces.'

'Are you sure?' he said, leaning closer. 'You looked very friendly to me.'

'I've never met her before in my life.'

Or had he? With the gaps in his mind, how much could he be sure of? For all he knew, the pink-haired woman could be a fellow refugee from the battlefield. The man was clearly not satisfied.

'Are you sure?'

'He's sure.'

Relief flooded through Jason as he felt Lee at his shoulder. His friend was returning the man's gaze steadily.

'And how would you know?' asked the man.

'I know.'

Lee moved closer to the man, deliberately invading his personal space.

'He's got nothing to do with her. Leave him alone.'

The man smiled suddenly.

'Never mind, then. I'm sorry to have troubled you.'

He turned and stalked away. Lee watched the retreating figure, a look of distaste on his face.

'He kept asking about the woman outside,' muttered Jason. 'I don't know why.'

'He's an assassin.'

'How do you know?'

The boy frowned.

'I've met them before. It's better to steer well clear. They'll kill someone just to prove they can do it. Even if it's the wrong person.'

Lee shuddered slightly, the ghost of a memory seeming to flicker before his eyes. 'I shouldn't have left you alone, Jason. I forgot what these places can be like.'

Jason wondered if he could have killed the assassin first. Slammed so much pain into his mind that he would have died in an instant. Perhaps he could have. But in front of all these people... they would have torn him apart.

He suddenly remembered the pendants.

'I bought these. I thought you'd like them.'

He took the necklaces out of his pocket and showed them to Lee. He took one, studied it and smiled. He put his holdall down and tied the leather cord round his emaciated neck.

'Good choice.'

'Guess I must have some fashion sense after all!' Jason replied, pleased.

He put on his own necklace, slipping the pendant under his jumper. He could feel the pendant through the thin material of the T-shirt beneath. It was unexpectedly comforting. Symbols, he thought, they have a strength.

'It'll be night soon, Jason. We'd better find somewhere to sleep.'

'The woman with the pink hair said there was a motel nearby. Near the entrance with a coffee place, she said.'

'Oh yeah. It's near where I got the pills. Come on, then.'

Lee led him through the milling crowds. It all seemed less bewildering now. If Jason concentrated, he could almost discern a pattern to the people's movements. Like all swarms, they were driven by common instincts. If you could understand the structure underlying it all, you could find your way. They were just approaching the exit when Jason stopped. A thought had occurred to him. A disturbing one.

'Lee?'

'Yeah?'

'You said that man was an assassin. He was asking about the woman with the pink hair. So that means—'

The youth sighed. He looked uncomfortable.

'Yeah, well, I think we've got enough problems, Jason. We can't get involved in other people's.'

'I guess you're right,' agreed Jason. 'But—' He felt Lee's hand squeeze his for a moment.

'We can't do anything, Jason,' he said softly. 'It's too dangerous. We're being hunted ourselves.'

Jason nodded. 'I know.'

This world seemed full of predators and prey. No wonder some animals became extinct.

As they walked out of the station and on to the busy street, he thought about his relief when Lee had found him in the crowd. And the feeling when the pallid boy had held his hand. Perhaps he would do it again. Perhaps.

Chapter Fourteen

'Do you think all the rooms look like this?'

Looking up from the bed where he was rooting through his holdall, Lee shrugged.

'I guess so. At least it's cheap.'

Jason couldn't decide whether their room was hideous or beautiful. The walls and carpet were decorated with a pattern of large, interlocking blue and orange triangles. Disconcertingly, the design continued across the sheets and pillows on the small, almost child-sized beds. Even the doors were covered with the hypnotic shapes. A large mirror on one wall reflected back the pattern. It was as though the room and everything in it was one solid block.

Lee pulled a white T-shirt out of his holdall. He peeled off the top he was wearing. After six long hours on the bus, it was creased and sweaty.

'I'm gonna go and wash. There should be enough hot water if you want a bath afterwards.'

Jason nodded, unable to stop himself staring at Lee's wiry, hairless torso. The boy's ribs stood out clearly beneath his pale skin. He wondered what it would be like to trace the shape of the bones with his fingers. The image of the skeletons from the first film they had watched together drifted through his mind. His friend smiled at him, apparently oblivious of the attention.

'Those buses are horrible, aren't they? You look really tired.'

Forcing himself to look away, Jason picked up a strip of pills that Lee had left on his bed.

'Do you want me to set these up?'

'Yeah, please. I think we could both do with 'em.'

As Lee turned away, Jason saw that his back was as acne ridden as his face, pimples spreading outwards from his spine. The boy pushed open the bathroom door and disappeared inside. A few seconds later, the sound of running water started.

Jason lay back on his bed, eyes closed. His hand stroked lazily at his crotch. Beneath the coarse material of the jeans, he could feel that he was hard. Even though it was the first time, he knew what it meant. Lee's body had always fascinated him. That fascination was turning into something new. It was a need now, stronger, more urgent and consuming than any other. He would willingly sacrifice anything to be intimate with him. Even though he wasn't sure what that intimacy would involve.

He was still hard, the sensation both pleasurable and painful. If only he could touch himself, could satisfy this urge... but what if Lee walked in? He forced himself to stand and move over to the small window. Jason looked out at the night, waiting for the feeling to pass. Their room was on the second floor of the three-storey motel. Traffic still flowed across the main road outside, but there weren't many pedestrians at this hour. An old man shuffled past, laden with carrier bags. A late-night shopper or a homeless derelict. It was hard to be sure. A young couple dashed down the street, hand in hand, rushing towards or away from something.

Jason pressed his hand and the side of his face gently against the glass, the cold cooling his skin. Trying to deal with these desires made him feel like a child. He didn't even understand what he wanted. He was still a mystery to himself. Now more than ever.

Something caught his eye. The narrow window frame was different to the rest of the room. Above, beneath and to his right, it continued the colour scheme of blue and orange. But the left-hand part of the frame was green. He ran his fingers slowly down it. Although made of the same material as the rest, the surface wasn't smooth, but engraved with a spiral pattern. Jason was pleased to find a break in the uniformity. It was obviously new, a replacement for a damaged piece. Perhaps its influence would spread and one day the whole room would be like this, organic swirls overwhelming their sterile surroundings. He hoped so.

'You OK, Jason?'

Lee's voice close to his ear made him start. He turned. The boy had washed and changed into his white T-shirt. He had taken off his tracksuit trousers, revealing the baggy white boxer shorts beneath. This close, Jason could feel his breath against his face.

'Er, yeah. I was just taking a look outside.'
'Did you set up the codeine?'
'No, not yet. Sorry.'
'It's OK, I'll do it.'

Lee sorted through his bag and took out two plastic beakers and a bottle of water. He set them on the cabinet between the beds, picked up the strip of pills and broke two into each beaker. As he filled them with water, he looked back at Jason.

'You look worried, Jason.'
'No. No, I'm not worried.'
'Good.'

Lee swigged down his fizzing beaker in one gulp. A shudder ran through his emaciated body.

'God, I needed that! Are you going to have a bath?'
'No, I'm too tired. I'll wash in the morning.'

Lee lay down across his bed, eyes closed, one hand resting on his flat stomach.

'Fair enough. The walls look exactly the same in there. Whoever built this place must have really liked triangles.'

Jason sat on his own bed, picked up the remaining beaker and sipped at it. The taste was slightly different to what he was used to, with an odd, sweet aftertaste.

'What time do you think we should leave tomorrow?' he asked.

'About ten, I think. We can catch an early bus. The further we can travel each day, the better.'

Jason gulped down the remaining fluid in the beaker. The familiar, comforting warmth was beginning to spread through him, taking the edge from his cravings. Tugging his shirt off, he gazed down at his podgy flesh. He didn't like being exposed in this cold room. It felt as though he was laid on a dissection table. He looked over at Lee, to see that he was sliding beneath the covers of his own bed.

'Turn the light off, will you?' he muttered.

It took Jason a while to find the light switch. Eventually, he located it at the intersection of two triangles. He flicked the switch and the room was plunged into darkness. Carefully, he felt his way over to his bed. Pulling off his shoes and slipping off his jeans, he climbed beneath the sheets. The material was soft against his bare skin.

For a while, they lay in silence. For all that he was exhausted, Jason wasn't sure that he would be able to sleep. His mind was turning over questions without answers. Lee broke the silence.

'Last time I was in a place like this was when I was a kid. We used to stop over at this big motel, much bigger than this one, when my mum and dad took me on holiday to the seaside. I used to get so excited. I think I was more excited by the motel than I was by the beach. Don't know why. 'Cos it meant living somewhere different for a night, I suppose.'

He had never mentioned his parents before and Jason hadn't thought to ask him about his family. Somehow, he had assumed that the boy had always lived alone. An eternal orphan, like himself.

'So, your parents—' began Jason, trying not to sound too curious.

'My mum died five years ago. Cancer. My dad married again a year later. His new wife, she's a fucking idiot. I was never gonna get on with her, so I moved out. He writes me sometimes. That's about it.'

His voice was steady, but Jason thought the memories must hurt. Not with a searing agony, but a dull ache that would probably never leave him. He wanted to hold and comfort him. But even the thought of that consolation had an erotic undercurrent.

'I'm sorry, Lee.'

'It's OK. I don't feel sorry for myself or anything.'

Jason spoke without thinking.

'If I ever had parents, and I'm not sure I did, I've forgotten them. You're my family now.'

Silence.

'I always used to wonder what it would be like to have a brother. I guess now I know.'

A brother. He wanted to be far more than that to him. But, perhaps it would do. For now at least. Jason wrapped his arms around his body, imagining what it would be like to share his bed. Normally, the drugs would be lulling him to sleep by now, but his limbs still twitched with a repressed energy.

'Jason, I know you're tired, but have you got any new pictures for me? I don't want to dream about those fucking triangles!'

In the darkness, Jason smiled to himself. He summoned up an image of a lush, green, delicate forest, alive with exotic birds. The trees were patterned like the mismatching part of the window frame. He transmitted it to Lee, hearing him sigh with satisfaction. The sound made him harden again. A few minutes later, the boy's gentle breathing told that he was asleep.

Jason couldn't sleep. Not with this tormenting need between his legs. Clumsily, he took hold of his penis, tugging at it, unsure of what he was doing. In his mind's eye, he pictured Lee's back, his scrawny chest, the warm feel of his pale body... It took seconds. Back arched, it burst out of him. He collapsed, exhausted and relieved. The bed was sweaty now. A new smell clung to the sheets. He drew his fingers through the small, sticky white pool on his belly, exploring the strange, slippery texture. Jason turned on to his side, aware that his fluids were trickling down on to the sheet beneath him. The agony was gone. He could sleep now.

A few hours later, every alarm in the motel roared into life.

Chapter Fifteen

Flopped across her bed, a bottle of decongestant medicine in one hand and a remote in the other, Andrea was waiting for her favourite web show to start. The screen was positioned on the bedside cabinet, angled so that she could watch in comfort. At the moment, an advert was playing for a neo-Christian concert. Clips showed strident girl groups extolling a variety of virtues. It was all very irritating, but she couldn't be bothered to flick to another site. There were only a few minutes to go before the icon for the new episode was due to appear.

After half a year spent living in this motel room, she was used to the decor. Like Jason and Lee's room, there was a stark, uniform design for both walls and furniture: vertical red and blue rectangles. Aside from a framed photo of a chubby young girl that hung over the bed, she had made no attempt to personalise her surroundings. There didn't seem to be much point as she might have to move on at any time.

A small green icon manifested itself in the corner of the screen. Eagerly, she pointed the remote at the PC and selected the new option. A sequence of industrial images in muted pastels began, accompanied by a synthesised guitar solo. Heavy, metallic letters announced the title: *Children of the Earth*. With a contented sigh, Andrea tossed the remote on to the bedcovers and took a swig of medicine, savouring the thick, sweet taste as it rolled down her throat. This was a weekly ritual. Even on the run, she had never missed an episode.

The story picked up where it had ended last week. Three middle-aged men were running across a high, concrete bridge between the twin towers of a manufacturing complex. Alarms blared all around them. The animation was smooth, without the jagged cuts that had become so popular of late. The picture changed to show a smartly dressed businesswoman. She was watching the fugitives on a monitor, her frighteningly glossy lips forming a tight smile. The picture switched back to the heroes. One of them had had an idea. An idea that was just crazy enough to work, probably.

It was all rubbish, of course. A formulaic echo of the old television shows from the mid twentieth century. The villains were inevitably outwitted at the last moment, though they usually found a way to come back and fight another day. There were even attempts at old-fashioned spiritualism, with a dandified ghost occasionally appearing to reveal useful plot points. Even though she knew full well that *Children of the Earth* was nonsense, Andrea loved it all the same. The show reminded her of the dreams that she had had when she was young and believed that one day she would make a difference.

Andrea had been fifteen when she had realised that she could paint. As an art form, painting had been in and out of fashion so many times over the years that no one seemed sure of whether it was a thing of the future or the past. All the same, she had enjoyed it and had begun to experiment with other media until eventually she discovered her true passion – sculpture.

It was an almost mystical process, taking a lump of lifeless stone and giving it shape, form, meaning. She had found that she could create both realistic representations of solid objects and abstract, nebulous shapes born of her dreams. Teachers that had ignored her for years suddenly realised that they had a protégé on their hands. While most of her friends were being forced to resign themselves to a corporate future, she was being groomed to be the next big thing in the art world. A name to watch.

It had all gone wrong on her very first exhibition. She had worked for over a year on it, preparing her pieces. Each one had to be perfect. Some were traditional, others wildly experimental. The main exhibit, the one she was sure would be the making of her, was a sculpture of a little boy holding a gun. The juxtaposition of images, the contrast of the innocent with the fatal, the soft with the hard, contained everything she wanted to say.

The day after her exhibition opened, a child from the prosperous Xavier district shot one of his friends. It was probably an accident. By all accounts the dead boy's parents had kept a gun on their premises for years and his friend, apparently very excitable, had found it quite by chance. But the incident caused an outcry. The web shows demanded that someone must be responsible for this outrage. Then they heard of Andrea's sculpture. There was no proof that the child had ever seen it and then decided he wanted to play with a gun too. But the web shows were sure there must be a connection and that was all that mattered.

The murdered boy's parents demanded that she closed her exhibition. And because she had worked for so long on it, because she believed in it, she refused. A few days later, she received another message from the family. There was a price on her head now. Andrea closed the exhibition and issued an apology for any offence that she might have inadvertently caused. She waited for a message to tell her that she was now safe but none come. Then came the first attempt on her life.

Andrea had been on the run ever since. There was always someone pursuing her, always a stranger who turned out to be more than they seemed. Isolation was a necessity. She had long ago lost contact with her family and could not risk forming friendships. Her only companion now was the screen. Making jewellery was a self-taught skill from childhood, one that enabled her to feed and clothe herself without depending on anyone else.

As she watched the show, part of Andrea's mind was turning over the question of whether she should move on. She had been here a long while now. The more familiar she became to people in this area, the greater the risk. Perhaps another week and then she would head towards the centre of the city. Losing herself there should be easy enough. For a while, at least.

The trio on the screen had made their escape. Not surprising, really. She wished the world was really like that: a place where you could have adventures and be sure of a happy ending. She remembered the two boys at the station. So keen to have a symbol of their friendship. So incomplete without each other. Were they staying at this motel? Maybe she should look for their room. Tell them to cling on to their dreams before they were snatched away.

A footstep outside the door. Measured. Determined. Andrea picked up the remote and turned off the PC. A shame. She would have liked to have seen the ending. She put the remote and the medicine on the cabinet. For a second, she gazed at the chubby girl in the picture. If only she had known, she thought. She sat, cross-legged, waiting for her visitor.

The door swung open. The assassin was a man with thinning hair and bulging eyes. He was wearing an unpleasant orange suit. The man was smiling. Always a giveaway.

'First time?' asked Andrea.

The assassin frowned as he pushed the door shut behind her.

'What?' he asked. There was the barest hint of a tremor in his voice. It was difficult to tell if it was fear or excitement. Both probably.

'First assignment? Will I be the first notch on your gun handle?'

Andrea was amazed at how calm she felt. She had always known this moment would come sooner or later and now it was here there seemed little point in acting surprised. Taunting her killer was almost enjoyable.

'I won't be using a gun,' said the man quietly.

'You going to strangle me, then? Is that it? Do you get off on doing it with your hands?'

The man voice's was high-pitched as he replied.

'You have to pay for what you did.'

'So you can get paid?' she snorted. 'Very noble.'

'I won't be paid. My family will. They get the money. I get the honour!' screeched the assassin.

The jacket of his suit was open. A small package was taped to the inside. A short cord hung from it. The man gripped the cord with a shaking hand.

'You deserve this.'

'No, I don't. You know I don't.'

Andrea spread her arms out in an extravagant gesture.

'Come on, then. Cut to the big climax!'

The assassin yanked on the string. The explosion blew the motel room apart. The man with the bulging eyes was dead in a second. Andrea had a few brief moments of life before the fireball engulfed her. Her dying thought was that she hoped those two boys would be all right.

As he watched the motel's death throes, Jason thought it was a shame that it would never get the chance to become something else now. The fire had consumed the whole building. It couldn't be much longer until it collapsed. Smoke was belching up into the night sky, filling the air with the noxious stench of burning timbers. Around them, people stood in shocked groups, muttering about an explosion in one of the rooms and a woman with pink hair.

When the alarms had gone off, they had barely had time to dress before the smell of burning and the sound of screams sent them running for the fire escape. Neither of them had thought about the money. Now they were watching it burn with everything else. All they had left were the clothes they were standing in. Jason hadn't even had time to put on his shoes. The pavement was rough beneath his bare feet. Lee was standing close, his shoulder pressed against Jason's. He was still wearing the black T-shirt he slept in, with a pair of blue tracksuit trousers and unlaced trainers with no socks. The boy was trembling and exhausted. It was hard for him to run with his bad foot. Jason had had to pull him along as they made for the exit. It must only have taken a few minutes for them to get outside, but it had seemed like hours.

'At least we're both safe,' Jason whispered to him. Lee nodded but said nothing.

With a dismal crunch, the motel toppled into itself. A collective sigh ran round the onlookers. A middle-aged woman started crying. A man started to shout at his wife and a child was screaming with rage. Jason felt Lee's arm in his.

'I think we should get out of here, Jason.'

They turned from the devastation, leaving the wailing, shouting, frightened throng behind them. For a while they walked silently, arm in arm. Lee's limp was worse than normal, slowing their pace. Jason winced as sharp stones stabbed into his feet. Away from the warmth of the blaze, the night air was freezing cold through his thin top.

'What do we do now?' he finally asked.

Lee stopped.

'I don't know.'

Chapter Sixteen

Under the soft light of dawn, the city seemed unusually fragile. The looming buildings looked as though they might dissolve into the pink clouds above them. As he studied the view from the office window, Phillip felt a little life creep back into his tired limbs. Though he existed in perpetual darkness, every detail, every nuance and texture of the scene before him was revealed through his mask. A sunrise had its own unique sadness. He surrendered to the emotion, allowing it to fill his exhausted mind.

He was beginning to miss the Fracture. This city, once his home, was a dull prison of rigid lines. How had he ever endured a childhood here? How did anyone?

Phillip found himself recalling the time he had first arrived in the Fracture. Still dazed by the journey, it had seemed to him overwhelming and incomprehensible. A fathomless spiral where even time was not linear and a journey of a thousand miles could be undertaken in seconds. Thankfully there had been teachers, cartographers who had taught him how a path could be traced. Soon enough, he could find his way with ease through the myriad complexities of his new home.

By comparison, searching this city was a simple matter. His contacts had given him details of every vigilante group. The man that Jason had killed had been wearing the sort of uniform that such organisations favoured. Although Dean Elliott had erased the security recordings of that night, the man's associates might have somehow learnt who was responsible. If so, then they would want revenge. Perhaps that was why the two boys had fled.

He had interrogated members of each group on his list. Some had been willing to answer the masked stranger's questions. Others had needed persuading. Everywhere it had been the same. No one had known anything about Lee and Jason. This place had been one of the last on his list. The Staunchers were considered a joke by their rivals. A potentially dangerous one, but a joke all the same. Their leader was an inept fool and most of them could be bought off with the smallest favours.

As soon as he had entered the building, Phillip knew that the Block had been here. The after-stench of one of their agents was unmistakable. The realisation had shaken him. The Committee had been certain that the enemy would not act on the loss of Jason. He was but one of a countless army. Could they have somehow learnt the details of the plan? It was hardly likely. The Committee were so wrapped up in secrecy, it was a wonder they knew what they were doing themselves. And if the Block had known all along, surely they would have acted sooner? The longer they left it, the less likely a successful retrieval became. By now, Jason would be far beyond repair. So what was their agent doing in the city?

Phillip had searched the building for answers. Renovations seemed to have been undertaken recently. The reception room was full of new chairs, waiting to be unpacked from their cocoons of bubble wrap and cellophane. Laminated timetables and schedules were pinned to newly painted walls. At the foot of the internal staircase, empty crates were scattered about. With mounting unease, Phillip realised that they had contained weapons.

In the manager's office, he found an expensive computer. Phillip broke through its security like a child unwrapping a present. He didn't even have to touch the keys. These laughably crude boxes that this century put so much faith in were defenceless against Fracture incursion. He ran through its memory and found his worst fears confirmed. A man calling himself Professor Hayden had put together a rota for the observation of two boys. From the descriptions, they were obviously Jason and Lee. Phillip cursed his arrogance. All the time he had thought that the plan was going well, the Block had been watching and waiting.

He found something else in the office. The shell of a man. His eyes were vacant, his clothes swimming with bodily fluids. Phillip's presence barely registered with him. His attention was entirely taken up by his own excretions. Occasionally he muttered to himself; a gurgling, miserable mantra.

'Not my fault. Not me. Not my fault. Not me. Not my fault. Not me.'

A typical Block assault, reflected Phillip. Magnified a thousand times, they used such powers to leave Fracture troops mindless and motionless on the battlefield. It was surprising that the victim was still alive. The agent seemed to have left him with just enough mind to appreciate his suffering. A predictably graceless act. Most likely a punishment. Maybe he had been the one who lost track of the targets and let them flee.

Phillip ran a gloved hand down the cheek of his mask. It was at times like this that he almost missed food and drink. A glass of wine might have helped him think. The presence of the Block changed everything. His next step should have been obvious: return and report to the Committee. But that still left the problem of the two boys. They were in terrible danger. He did not like to think of them reduced to the same state as the sodden ruin in the chair. Not when he had been entrusted with their protection. He wasn't prepared to wait for his superiors' orders to make sure they were safe.

Phillip knew that he was becoming reckless. He had started to see Jason and Lee as his project alone and was ignoring protocols. Such behaviour wasn't unknown, especially when acting in a non-combat domain. Separated from anything familiar, objectives could easily turn into obsessions. Was he succumbing to dislocation? Many agents were forced to retire as a result of such afflictions. He might return to the Fracture only to find himself assigned to archive duties. That thought only made him more determined. If this was to be his last mission, then he was going to make sure that it was a success.

A whimper. The young man in the chair had slid to the floor and was toying disconsolately with a turd. Phillip looked down at him. Murder would be an act of kindness. But he could be useful. He slid the brown glove from his right hand, revealing long fingers and dirty nails. A small thorn-like bone jutted out from his palm. The red flesh in the aperture of his mask quivered. It was a long time since he had done this.

With a leathery creak, he crouched down beside the gurgling man. Gently, he wrapped his fingers round his throat. The victim's gasp of fear was cut off as the grip tightened.

'No pain,' whispered Phillip. 'There'll be no pain. Not any more.'

The man's face was suddenly content. He smiled slightly, welcoming what was to come. With the barest pressure, Phillip pressed the bone into the soft flesh of the neck. Impressions begin to drift through his mind. Echoes that had survived the assault.

Graham Billington, that was his name. So proud of his new uniform... wasn't going to... a schoolyard... a gang of which he was... his favourite web show... there are robots taking over the patients... so many people... make an impression... laughter... happy to be laughing with them... a great song... sweaty bodies in the night... over too quick... the taste of ice cream in a child's mouth... didn't win that, should have done... not fair... never fair...

Phillip allowed Billington to experience the memories one last time. Permitted him that bitter pleasure. Then, with the delicacy of a surgeon's blade, he removed them. There was the smallest of despairing groans and then the young man was silent. Phillip cut deeper, deleting every frame of reference, hunting down and slicing away race memories and genetic imperatives. Sleeping visions from a time when there were no words to describe them flickered and were gone. He flung them into a dark space inside of himself and locked them away for ever. When he was done, Billington was a blank slate. Not just mindless, but utterly hollow. A husk waiting to be filled.

Phillip stood. Although the operation had taken only seconds, it had left him exhausted. He would need to rest before his next move.

'Stand,' he said quietly.

Obediently, the object that had been Billington rose. Its eyes were locked on to Phillip's mask, awaiting orders. The pool of faeces and urine at its feet was forgotten.

'Go and find somewhere to wash. And find some clothes. Clean ones. Then come back here.'

Billington nodded and left the office. The shattered young man was now simply an expression of Phillip's will. A slave and a tool. A Seeker.

Turning to the window, he eased the glove back on to his hand. The implant had hurt when it was first installed but he had learnt to be glad of it. Examining their battle wounded, the

Fracture had discovered something that the Block would never even have noticed. An empty mind could be used. Devoid of any sense of self, the victims were extremely sensitive to their surroundings. They were able to detect an object or a person over huge distances. Finding Billington was a fortuitous turn of events. All Phillip had to do was to describe Jason and Lee in sufficient detail and the Seeker would be able to find them. The whole city was open to it now.

Once his newly made tool returned, he would look for somewhere to sleep for a few hours. And then the search would begin in earnest. Speed was of the essence now. The vigilantes were no longer his main concern. There was a Block agent active in the city. A ruthless and cunning enemy. A creature that must be killed.

As he heard the returning footsteps of the Seeker, Phillip reflected that not all agents retired. Some died in the field.

Chapter Seventeen

The toast was slightly burned at one corner and heavily smeared with butter. It was the best thing Jason had ever eaten. He was already on to his third slice while Lee was still nibbling at his first. If they had had more money, he would have suggested that they order another plateful. As it was, they were lucky to be able to afford what they had. Lee had found a few notes stuffed into his pockets; not much, but enough for breakfast.

The bus station café was busy, even this early in the morning. At a table nearby, frighteningly orange businesswomen were discussing an impending merger. Two men in shiny golden suits sat near the counter, bellowing weak jokes at each other. Gangs of children whispered conspiratorially among themselves, trying not to catch the eyes of the patrolling staff. No one paid much attention to the two scruffy boys sitting quietly in the corner, not even speaking to each other.

Their table was shoved awkwardly into a corner, with no room to stretch out their legs. Jason suspected that wherever they had chosen to sit would have been equally uncomfortable. Even half full, the café seemed overcrowded. He swallowed down a mouthful of coffee. The taste was bitter and grainy, yet strangely addictive. He was starting to feel better for his meal. They were in trouble but at least they had food in their bellies. Of course, in a few hours' time it would be a different matter. Lee was clearly worried. He picked at his chin as he ate, sometimes glancing round as though scared they were being watched. Jason had never seen him look quite so vulnerable.

A waitress appeared at their table. Like the rest of the staff, she was dressed in an unflattering combination of yellow and green. The short skirt and top seemed to have been designed for an overweight schoolgirl. She tapped rhythmically at her notepad with a pencil, drumming to music playing only in her head.

'Would you like anything else?' she asked, managing to sound surprisingly interested.

Looking up at her, Jason was struck by how out of place the girl seemed here. She was in her early twenties, with strong, striking features and a wide mouth. Thick, long brunette hair was tied into a smart ponytail. She held herself with a natural poise as though she had been born with it.

'Er, I'm not sure. Lee?'

His friend looked at Jason's half-empty cup and smiled slightly.

'Two more coffees, please.'

'Are you sure?' asked Jason. He knew they couldn't waste what little money they had, but the idea was very tempting. Lee picked up another slice of toast.

'Yeah, why not? I don't think we can afford lunch with what we've got left, so we might as well enjoy it.'

With a spasm of guilt, Jason shifted his feet in his new trainers. They'd bought them from a market stall before they came to the café. Cheap, white pirated copies that made his bare soles itch; they at least kept his feet from being cut to ribbons. The waitress was studying her two customers closely.

'Down on your luck?' she asked.

Lee hesitated before replying. He scrutinised her and then seemed to decide that it wouldn't hurt to talk to the girl.

'We've got problems, yeah. We lost all our money in a fire.'

She nodded, a flicker of understanding in her face.

'You were staying at the motel that burnt down, right?'

'Right,' muttered Lee. 'Now we've no way of getting home.'

The girl's tone was suddenly suspicious, as though she had detected a hidden agenda in his words.

'We never do free food here. I'm sorry.'

Jason suddenly found himself angry at the waitress. Who did she think she was, this stranger prying into their business? If she couldn't help, why all the questions? Why didn't she just take their order?

'We aren't asking for free food,' he told her, aware of the anger in his voice.

For a moment the waitress looked offended. Jason wondered if they were about to be thrown out. Then she shrugged slightly, as though dismissing them.

'I'll get your coffees.'

'Wait!' said Lee suddenly, the gleam of an idea in his eye. 'Do you need any new staff? Just for a few days.'

'No. We've no vacancies. Sorry.'

She turned and walked away. Lee sighed.

'Well, it was worth a try. I probably wouldn't make a very good waiter, anyway.'

Jason smiled at the idea, imaging how his friend would deal with difficult customers. Lee seemed to know what he was thinking and grinned.

'And I reckon you'd just eat all their food before it even got to the table. The place'd probably shut down in a week.'

They both laughed. Nervous laughter that didn't make their situation any less desperate.

Rebecca was disappointed. The boys were a mystery, but one that she was unlikely to solve. It was a shame. Sometimes customers caught her interest, the ones that looked as if they had a story to tell. Of course they would always leave before she could strike up a conversation and vanish from her life. Perhaps it was her fault. She had never been very good at getting people to confide in her. Her questions tended to sound like interrogations. As she poured hot water into two cups, she wondered if she should have another try. Maybe if she didn't approach them as though they were an essay subject...

'Those two you were talking to – are they homeless or what?'

Mary was standing behind her, frowning at the two boys sitting in the corner. Younger and slighter than Rebecca, her face was continually locked into an expression of pained irritation. They did not like each other. Mary had previously worked for a company that had been absorbed by Mydia Hycron. The experience of redundancy had left her paranoid about the world in general. For some reason, she had soon taken it into her head that Rebecca looked down on her.

'I think so,' replied Rebecca, choosing her words carefully. 'They won't be any trouble.'

'Make sure they aren't,' said Mary tersely and picked up a tray of bacon sandwiches from the counter. Shifting her uniform into an even more unflattering position, she carried the tray to an enormously overweight young man sitting alone at a table. He gave an audible gasp of delight.

Rebecca spooned powder milk into the coffee, still lost in thought. When she had first seen the two boys, she had been intrigued. Not by the scrawny one with the spots and bad teeth, but by his friend. He was stocky and heavy featured, but there was an unearthly quality about him that was rather fascinating. Instinctively, she had wanted to get to know him. A secret part of her had wondered if he might be the mysterious stranger that she had occasionally let herself dream of; the one who would rescue her from the banality of this existence. And then she had seen the way he was looking at the other boy and knew that she had no chance.

The coffees were ready, but still she stood, stirring one cup and staring listlessly into the thick brown fluid. She often found her mind wandering like this. Dreaming of things that never were and never would be. It made the day more bearable. Waitressing was a dull, frustrating job for which she was eminently unsuited. But what else was there? To go and work for Mydia Hycron with all the other graduates? To sell insurance, gazebos, holidays or whatever else was doing well this year? Even if she tried a career in the arts, she would probably just end up writing for the web fashion shows, telling people which celebrities to like and which to despise. And so she stayed in this job simply because it was no more and no less dull than any of the alternatives. Until recently, the café had been an unfashionable sushi restaurant. There was still a mural of a fish eye on one of the walls. Quite why anyone had thought that sushi would sell well in a bus station she couldn't imagine. Still, if she waited round long enough, it might transform again.

Of course, frustration was expected after graduation. Higher education was the great adventure that you would look back on fondly all your life. The time when your mind was opened by great art and even greater parties. Except that, as far as Rebecca was concerned, it wasn't. She had spent five years learning to produce perfectly written accounts of her tutors' literary opinions without once venturing an idea of her own. At the end of it, she didn't feel she had any more insight than she had started with.

The social aspects had been no better. It didn't matter how many men she slept with or how many pharmaceutical drugs she took, it had all been done before. That was at the heart of her problem. She wanted to do or experience something totally new. It was a childish desire, but one she wasn't ready to surrender.

'That coffee's gonna be tar if you stir it much longer, Bex.'

Snapping out of her reverie, she smiled at Kelly. A friendly, pretty girl, not smart but bright. She wanted to be an actress and Rebecca hoped she would make it. The arts could do with someone who hadn't devoted an obscene amount of hours to breathing exercises and endless monologues.

'Sorry. Miles away.'

'No problem. That big guy is trying to chat up Mary.'

'Yuck! Hope he's had inoculations.'

They both giggled. Dislike of Mary was one of the things that united them. Rebecca picked up the coffees and walked over to the two boys sitting in the corner. She had already made up her mind to try and talk to them again. 'I could call my dad,' said Lee suddenly.

Jason looked at him in surprise. It was the first time he had mentioned getting outside help. For some reason, the idea made Jason uncomfortable. It would mean letting an intruder into their world.

'Would he help us?'

Lee took another bite of toast, chewing it thoroughly before replying.

'I'm not sure. We've never got on that well since he got married again. He might lend me some money, but... I think he'd want to know everything. Once he knew about you and the people we've killed... I don't know.'

Someone stood up, scraping their chair loudly across the floor. Lee twitched at the noise. He looked over at a coffee-stained and battered screen that stood on one table.

'I guess I could call him. Make up some sort of story. It'd have to be convincing.'

'What about Kerri?' suggested Jason. He'd liked the bar-woman. It might be easier to explain all this to someone he already knew.

'That'd mean going back home. We're being hunted, remember?'

'Your coffees.'

How long had the waitress been there? Jason tried to read her face but it was enigmatic. He could tell Lee was thinking the same thing as she set the cups on to the table. His hand had gone automatically to his pocket, reaching for a knife that wasn't there.

'Anything else?' she asked sweetly.

'No,' replied Lee, keeping his voice steady. Jason shook his head, not trusting himself to speak.

The waitress observed them for a few moments and then spoke quietly.

'You're in trouble, aren't you?'

Jason felt a knot form in his stomach. Would he have to kill her? Could they escape with all these people around them? The café suddenly seemed quiet. Even the men in shiny suits were subdued.

'I told you,' began Lee. 'The motel fire—'

'I heard what you said,' interrupted the waitress. 'You're being hunted.'

Jason and Lee stood up in unison.

'We're going,' said Lee, placing the banknotes to pay for the meal on the table.

'No,' said the girl, with a sudden urgency. 'You don't have to. Look, you can sleep over at my place; I've got a spare room. I just want to help.'

'Why?' asked Jason, suspicious. He remembered two men offering to help on the first night. Remembered hands about his throat.

'I just do,' said the girl. 'You obviously need help. You've no money. There are people after you. How long are you going to last without food or anywhere to sleep?'

'And what do you get out of it?' asked Lee.

'I want to know your story. That's all. Look, I can take this afternoon off. I'll take you back to my place. It's only ten minutes' drive away. You can get cleaned up and have something to eat. I'm a good cook, everyone says so. My name's Rebecca, by the way.'

Jason didn't understand why she wanted to help and he didn't trust her. They should just get away from here. He looked at Lee. His friend was clearly considering the idea. Rebecca picked up the notes and handed them back to him.

'Sit down, drink your coffee and think about it. Don't worry about paying; you can have it on me. It won't matter just this once.'

'Thanks,' muttered Lee, sitting down. Reluctantly, Jason followed suit.

'What are you called?' asked Rebecca.

'I'm Lee. This is Jason.'

'Lee and Jason. Well, like I said, think about it.'

The waitress returned to the counter. The orange businesswomen were leaving and a heavily wrapped quartet of old women was critically examining the selection of cakes. The shouting men were had returned to full volume and were debating their prowess at simulated sport.

'What do you think?' asked Lee.

'I don't see why we should trust her,' replied Jason. He wanted to leave as quickly as possible. They could worry about food and money later.

'We don't have to trust her, Jason. We'll just tell her that we're on the run from a gang. She doesn't have to know about you and... everything.'

'She might be working for the people that are following us.'

'I don't think so. They were really obvious. If they were gonna trick us, I don't think it'd so subtle. Anyway, she's right. We'll be an easy target sleeping rough.'

Jason nodded. He knew Lee was right. They had to take the help that was on offer. Even if it meant trusting a stranger. Even if meant an intruder coming into their world.

Rebecca watched Jason and Lee. She was sure that they would take up her offer. She felt a warm thrill inside her. At last she was going to have a proper adventure. Part of her mind was shouting that this was madness. But she had always envied the mad anyway.

'Three croissants, a cheesecake and tea for two,' rattled an old lady with false teeth at least two sizes two big for her.

She smiled at the ancient customer. 'Of course. I'll bring them over to you.'

Putting teabags into four cups, she could barely contain her excitement. She desperately wanted to know the boys' story. Who was pursuing them? The police? Other criminals? Someone else? As she filled the cups with hot water, she recalled what the ugly one, Lee, had said. The phrase that had most excited her. 'The people we've killed.' She remembered the way his hand has moved to his pocket, searching for a weapon. There were so many questions and Rebecca was determined to have all the answers.

Chapter Eighteen

Varney felt sorry for the driver. His home was that of a lonely man, full of history books and relics of times gone by. Inoffensive paintings hung on the walls, pastoral landscapes and bright-eyed dogs. Volumes of timetables and schedules were everywhere. It reminded him of his own house. In a different time and place, the two of them might have been friends. The driver was too old to be a Stauncher of course, but he might have made a confidante, someone to listen to Johnnie Varney when no one else would. Not that it made any difference now. The driver was going to die. Very soon.

He was a big man, as tall as any of the Staunchers that stood in a circle round him. Although he had grown fat over the years, the remains of a once-powerful physique could still be discerned beneath his blue and green checked shirt. His name was Sean and he was cringing in the faded, comfortable armchair like a frightened child. His body was bloody and bruised. Spittle tricked from his open mouth. None of the Staunchers had touched him. Professor Hayden had lost his temper and done something. Johnnie had seen it but couldn't remember what it had been like. He was grateful for that. When the time came for the driver to die, perhaps he would be able to forget that, too.

'You have seen the boys we are looking for,' said the Professor hoarsely. 'They got on to your bus. We know that. We have searched the records of your manager and we have visited your colleagues. You are the one. You saw them and you know where they got off. You have only to remember and this will be over.'

'Can't remember, sir,' whimpered Sean. 'Please, I can't remember!'

He was crying like a baby now. Embarrassed and ashamed, Johnnie turned away, looking at the faces of his former troops. They were impassive. Waiting. As the hunt progressed, the seven Staunchers had begun to change. They rarely spoke now. They obeyed but did not react. Sometimes they didn't even seem to breathe. He was beginning to have difficulty telling them apart.

Professor Hayden was unmoved by Sean's distress. His voice ground on relentlessly.

'Two boys. One dark-haired and stocky. The other blond and thin, with bad skin and a limp. Talking to no one but each other. Criminals that I must find and bring to justice.'

Johnnie found himself thinking of his grandfather. Like Sean, he had been a big man. Big and brave. A hero. Could he have stood up to Hayden or would he have been left a broken, whimpering mess? Maybe the Professor would have sensed and admired his qualities and chosen to spare him. But then, Professor Hayden didn't seem interested in getting to know those he interrogated. He just wanted information. They had been to many places today, before they found Sean. And all the people had… but Johnnie couldn't remember that.

'You will tell me, Sean. You want to tell me. All you must do is to recall, to reach into the back of your mind. It is a small place; it will not take much searching.'

There was a sudden gleam of desperate hope in the man's eyes as though he had seen a chance for mercy.

'I do remember. One of them, the kid with the dark hair. He looked like my son. Like Scotty. And I thought maybe I should call him, but it was time to go and I was running late, so it slipped my mind. But it's Scotty's birthday next month. I'll call him then. I will.'

Johnnie wanted to tell Sean that he was right. That he should call his kid before it was too late. Just tell the Professor what he wanted to know first. But the words couldn't make the leap from his mind to his mouth. So he remained silent.

'And where did the boys get off?' asked Hayden, his old body trembling with excitement.

'I will call him this time. I'll buy him that model bus he wanted when he was ten. When he wanted to be like his dad. He'll laugh but—'

'Where did they get off?'

Sean told him. Two minutes later he was dead. And forgotten.

Rebecca's flat was far too smart to be comfortable. Most of the furniture looked as though it had barely been used. The cream walls of the living room were lined with shelves on which ranks of carved wooden ornaments stood sentry. At one end of the room, a pristine sofa and plush armchairs faced a large screen. At the other end were a circular dining table and a cabinet full of plates and wine glasses. Everything was ordered. There was no clutter, nothing that was unplanned.

Sitting on the sofa, Jason felt awkward. He fidgeted with the cup of coffee in his hands and tried to avoid looking at Rebecca. She was rearranging the African masks on one of the shelves, humming to herself. He wished Lee would hurry up and finish his bath so that he wouldn't have to spend any more time alone with her. He didn't trust the girl. He had barely exchanged a word with her during the journey in her compact car or the long trip up six flights of stairs to her flat. Lee had seemed quite happy to talk to Rebecca about the fire at the motel, though he had carefully avoided telling her anything more about their situation. It puzzled and frightened Jason that Lee had accepted her offer so readily.

'Are you all right?'

Now finished with the masks, she had sat down next to him with an obviously forced smile on her face. Reluctantly, Jason made himself look up at her.

'Yeah. I'm fine.'

Rebecca took an audibly deep breath.

'Lee should be finished in the bathroom soon. Do you want to wash, too?'

'Maybe.'

He was being rude and he knew it, but he couldn't help himself. Her presence, this close, made him angry.

'You're very strange, you know that?'

A spasm of fear gripped him. Was she fishing for information? Or did she already know?

'I suppose I am. In some ways.'

Rebecca hesitated before replying, as though choosing her words with care.

'When I first saw you, I got the impression that you were different in some way. Unique. That can be dangerous, can't it? Being unique?'

'I suppose it can.'

'You're lucky to have someone like Lee to look after you.'

As he replied, Jason found he was smiling, not at the girl but at the thought of his friend.

'Lee's always helped me. For as long as I can remember. There are things I don't know and he makes sure I don't get hurt.'

'There's just the two of you, right? No other close friends or family?'

'No. There's just us.'

'I see.'

'We've never needed anyone else,' he added, unable to stop himself.

Rebecca opened her mouth to speak and then closed it again. She stood up. Her expression was unreadable to him. He thought maybe she was angry but it was impossible to tell.

'Do you like lamb casserole?'

'I've never had it. Or, at least, I don't think I have.'

'It's one of my specialities. Much better than the stuff I make at work. We can have a nice meal together tonight. The three of us.'

Jason couldn't think of a reply that wouldn't sound insincere. He was relieved when the door opened and Lee walked in. The grime of the day before had been washed away and his dyed blond hair was re-spiked. He was wearing a white T-shirt and black jeans that had belonged to one of Rebecca's old boyfriends. They were at least two sizes too big for him. He flopped down next to Jason.

'Better?' asked Rebecca.

'Yeah. Thanks.'

He turned to Jason.

'Are you gonna have a bath, Jason? It'll make you feel better.'

Just for a moment, Jason forgot Rebecca, the flat, everything else. There was just him and Lee. The boy he didn't want to share with anyone. Then she spoke and the moment was broken.

'I've probably got some clothes somewhere that'll fit you, Jason. You can both watch the screen afterwards if you want.'

'Cool,' said Lee with a smile. Jason noticed an unusual mint tang to his breath. He must have brushed his teeth. Was he trying to impress Rebecca?

She held out a hand and he automatically handed her the half-empty coffee cup. 'Go on,' she said. 'It'll help you to unwind.'

There was no good reason he could give to refuse. Jason forced himself to stand up and left the room. The walls of the immaculate hallway were hung with pictures that he didn't understand. As he walked slowly towards the bathroom, he heard Rebecca and Lee talking. Their voices were too quiet to make out what was being said.

Jason pushed open the bathroom door. The bath tub was huge. A dirty, black ring ran round the white ceramic surface and clumps of foam still clustered around the plug hole. In one corner, a damp towel lay where it had been carelessly thrown. Jason wondered if Rebecca would be angry if she knew what Lee had done to her bathroom. Part of him hoped so.

He twisted the taps and water began to gush from them. Jason began peeling off his clothes. They were sweaty and seemed half stuck to his skin. Lee was right: a wash would do him good.

As he sank into the tub, Jason closed his eyes and tried to shut everything out except the darkness behind his eyes. The hot water was good, soothing aches and pains that he hadn't even noticed. Without realising it, he had taken hold of his cock and was gently tugging at it. He wouldn't go all the way this time; he was too tired. Besides, this was Rebecca's bath; it would be wrong to release himself here.

Inevitably, he found himself thinking of Lee's body. The boy was beautiful. He saw the way that other people looked at his friend and knew that they thought he was ugly. But they were wrong. He was incredibly strong and incredibly fragile, all at the same time. There was something wondrous in the contradiction.

His hand was moving faster now, each motion firm and determined. He had told himself that he wouldn't do this, not here, but he couldn't stop…

A knock at the door.

Jason stopped at once. Was it Rebecca, demanding to know what he was doing in her nice, wholesome bathroom? With relief, he heard Lee's voice. Relief and embarrassment. How would he have reacted if he knew Jason thought of him as he touched himself?

'Do you want to watch a scary movie later, Jason?'

He looked at his erect penis. The skin drawn back from the tender flesh of the head beneath, a little clear fluid seeping from the eye.

'Probably,' he replied.

Chapter Nineteen

Phillip had always found this place rather absurd. Certainly it stood out from its surroundings. All around were half-demolished houses that clung desperately on to a life-support system of rusted scaffolding. Skips brimming with bricks sat at odd angles in the road. Despite all this, the proprietor had managed to give his venue a veneer of glamour. Golden columns stood at either side of the single red wooden door. On the garish sign above, multicoloured letters spelt out the words 'Waterfield Movie Theatre'. The walls of the narrow building were lined with posters behind thick glass. This week's film was a dour tale of mid-century governesses and God. Next week's was about prostitutes. It didn't really matter: no one went to the pictures any more.

Phillip pushed the door open. At his shoulder was the Seeker. There was no interest in its empty eyes. This was just another place for it to be.

The foyer was no more than a narrow passageway ending in two doors, one leading to the sole screening room, the other with a sign reading PRIVATE. The walls were panelled in cerise and pink. A frosted glass partition to the left opened on to a cramped ticket office. An unpleasant metallic tang of disinfectant pervaded the air.

The man in the ticket office didn't look up at Phillip. He was busily engaged at a screen, a frown on his brow.

'*Salome's Child* doesn't start for another hour,' he said dismissively. 'I can sell you a ticket, but you'll have to wait elsewhere.'

Pompous as ever, reflected Phillip wryly. But a useful contact.

'I don't want a ticket, Waterfield. And if I did, I'd expect a private screening.'

Waterfield looked up in surprise. For a moment, he was shocked by the masked figure at the partition. Then, recognition dawned and he managed a smile.

'Phillip. It has been a long time.'

'It has indeed. I need your assistance. Your local knowledge.'

Waterfield nodded. A tall, fat man wearing a deeply unflattering cream suit, he was in his mid-fifties but looked older. His haggard, tired face told of many past addictions and misadventures. Behind the thick-rimmed, ostentatious glasses, his eyes bulged with broken red veins. This was a man who had seen and done more things than he had the capacity to remember.

He manoeuvred himself out of the ticket office and led them to the door marked PRIVATE. It opened on to a surprisingly large living room. The antique furniture was fading and inviting, piled with well-worn cushions. Posters covered the walls, mostly originating from late-century Hollywood. There was even an old movie camera standing in one corner, looking like an alien invader that had opted for a quieter life. An oak bar sagged under the weight of decanters and pill bottles. A heavily carpeted staircase led up to the next floor.

'Angelique!' called Waterfield. 'We have a visitor. Phillip. From the Fracture. Oh, and a... friend.'

A warmly accented voice floated down the stairway. 'I'll be down in a moment, Eddie.'

'Sit down,' said Waterfield, pouring himself a generous measure of brandy from a decanter.

Phillip sat on a long sofa, leaning back into the comfortable upholstery. He liked this surreal, eccentric room. He felt almost at home here. The Seeker stood stiffly, eyes fixed on nothing.

'Sit,' ordered Phillip gently. His slave sat next to him. Waterfield scrutinised the vacant young man, obviously wanting to know more.

'Is your friend all right?'

'Better than it was. It was a victim of our enemies. It's better off this way, believe me.'

Waterfield gulped down half of his drink. 'I'm sure.'

He looked up with a smile as a woman appeared on the stairs. Like him she was old, but she still possessed the remnants of a former beauty. Her short, grey hair held the memory of lustrous, brown locks. The slight stomach was an indulgence for a previously perfect figure. Her elfin face had the happy look of someone who had had everything once and was now content to settle for less.

'Hello, Phillip,' she said as she almost skipped into the room. 'It's good to see you again. You always seem to bring excitement into our lives.'

When he was younger, Phillip had never appreciated the appeal of mature women. Now he understood it completely. He allowed himself to picture his injured body in Angelique's arms. She would not be revolted. She would explore him; a new world for old eyes. Perhaps, he thought, when Waterfield dies, she will choose to come into the Fracture, to experience fresh wonders.

'Phillip needs my assistance,' announced Waterfield, with more than a touch of pride.

'Oh,' said Angelique, helping herself to some tablets from the bar. 'Are you recruiting?'

'No,' Phillip replied. 'Searching. There are two young people that I need to find. Boys who are in danger from the enemy.'

Her clear eyes settled on the Seeker.

'I never really pictured you as the protective sort, Phillip.'

She was teasing him. Most people treated him with respect or fear, but this woman was quite happy to banter with him. To challenge him. He found it quite charming. Cunning, too. She knew that the more confident she was, the more answers she would get.

'It's a Seeker,' explained Phillip, his blank mask turning briefly in the direction of his slave. 'It can detect people or objects over great distances. It's sensed the two that I'm looking for, heading for the outskirts of this city. I need to know what's out there that two refugees would make for.'

'Well, let me see,' began Waterfield, tapping at his lips with a forefinger. 'There's quite a variety out there. None of them places to go to lightly.'

'Are they running from you? Or someone else?' asked Angelique. Her tone was cautious. Phillip knew that if she thought he was hunting someone to harm them, she would never help. And knowing her, she would stop Waterfield assisting him, too. He might as well be honest with them.

'They are part of an experiment that we are conducting on Block technology.'

Waterfield leaned forward, face alive with interest. His wife's expression was more reserved.

'Go on,' she said.

'The Block war effort is dependent on this technology. Without it, they will be unable to fight. They will leave us in peace.'

'What kind of technology?' asked Waterfield. 'A bomb or—'

'I imagine it's very different to anything like that,' said Angelique quietly.

Phillip nodded.

'Yes. Their technology is of flesh and blood.'

'Like yours?'

'Yes. Like the Fracture's. But the Block create theirs differently. They are mass produced in breeding farms so huge that they have their own moons. The Block's entire military campaign depends on their loyalty—'

'And these boys,' interrupted Waterfield. 'What have they to do with all this?'

'One of them was created by the Block. A product of their farms, like millions of others. But we have taken away his knowledge of what he is. We are attempting to change his nature.'

'That seems rather cruel,' observed Angelique.

'Not entirely. I arranged through one of my other contacts for him to be protected. On his first night here, he met a boy called Lee. Our intelligence had identified him as a suitable guardian. They have formed a close bond. Closer than anticipated.'

'And has this experiment of yours been a success?' she asked.

'Oh yes. His conditioning is all but gone. He is his own creature now. He even has a name. Jason.'

Angelique smiled gently at him. 'You must be proud.'

Could she read the thoughts behind his mask? Did she understand how obsessed he'd become with his task?

'I am,' he agreed.

'Something went wrong, though?' prompted Waterfield.

'Yes. Jason and his friend, Lee, are running from a vigilante group. I've no way of knowing how Jason is being affected. And there is a Block agent hunting for them, too. He is controlling the vigilantes. The Committee never anticipated this. If he finds them…'

He gestured at the Seeker. Was it imagination, or did the young man shudder slightly, as though still plagued by the ghost of a memory?

Waterfield and his wife sat in contemplative silence. Angelique went to the bar for a gin, chewing her lip in thought.

'Communes,' said Waterfield triumphantly.

Phillip's mask swung towards him, devastated flesh pulsing eagerly in the aperture.

'Communes?'

'There are breakaway communities at the edge of the city. They've rejected politics and a lot of the laws. They have food and resources. Even weapons. Everything they need to be self-sufficient. If I wanted to disappear, that's where I'd go.'

Angelique nodded as she sat down again.

'Yes. A friend of mine spent a few days in one. She got out very quickly, though. They're dangerous places. But I suppose if you were desperate...'

Excellent, thought Phillip. At last he had the clue he had been looking for. Thank you. That's what I needed to know. Here...

He reached into his jerkin and produced a small, dusty reel of film. The metal was rusted with age. A yellowing label on one side was inscribed with illegible writing in black marker pen.

'Footage from Charles Laughton's incomplete *I, Claudius*. Ten minutes that were filmed and then lost. Quite a find for you, Waterfield.'

Reverently, Waterfield took the reel. His face broke into a boyish grin. Just for a moment, the ravages of age were diminished.

'Thank you, Phillip. This is marvellous. We'll do a special screening, Angelique. Invite descendants of the stars. It'll be... I'd best go and put this in the safe.'

He lumbered up the stairs, muttering happily to himself. Angelique watched him go, an indulgent expression on her attractive face. They were very different, mused Phillip. Both had known a multitude of dangers and pleasures. But experience had made Waterfield pompous whereas it had granted Angelique insight and humour. Hers was the better bargain by far. It was fortunate for them that they loved each other.

She stepped closer to Phillip and touched his arm gently. The empty place within him stirred. His fingers burnt with life.

'Take care, Phillip.'

'I will.'

Chapter Twenty

The web movie was frightening, but Jason was enjoying it. For the first time in days, he was relaxed. Rebecca hadn't lied about her cooking skills. The meal had been delicious. The casserole was rich and full of flavour and had been followed by a sweet, smooth dessert. She had offered them wine, but they had both refused. She'd seemed disappointed at that, but had managed to find some Codeine Beta Four instead. Now the familiar numb feeling of the drug was spreading through him. None of them had spoken much during the meal. Rebecca had asked a few more questions to which Lee had given non-committal answers. Jason had concentrated on eating.

Now that the meal was over, the two boys were sprawled on the sofa. Rebecca, still looking smart and precise, was sitting in an armchair to their right. She had told him that the film they were watching had a large cult following and an equally large number of watchdog organisations trying to ban it. It was called *Shadows* and this was the first instalment of a new 'franchise'. Whatever that meant.

The hero, his angular limbs moving with a fluid grace, was confronting the evil clown who was the principal villain. The harlequin's white mask peeled away. Beneath was a ravaged mass of crisp, scalded flesh, every detail lovingly picked out by the animators. A choking, gurgling laugh rattled in his throat as the hero recoiled, revulsion in his tiny, purple eyes.

Jason heard Lee's voice in his mind. He was afraid of the monster disguised as a clown.

'God, that's horrible. Like the thing I thought was in the wardrobe when I was a kid.'

'Don't be scared, Lee.'

The two boys looked at each other in surprise. They had spoken without talking. Jason hadn't even been aware of what they were doing. It had simply happened. He opened his mouth to speak, but Lee motioned for silence with the smallest gesture. Jason gave a slight nod.

On the screen, the clown had been undone. The hero had turned his power against him and he was consumed in blazing light and crashing chords. The hero led his unfeasibly proportioned girlfriend to the safety of the world outside. Strange music began and the end titles flickered by, quicker than the eye could comprehend.

Rebecca got to her feet and stretched.

'I'm going to bed now. You two stay up as long as you like.'

'Night, Rebecca,' said Lee.

'Goodnight, Lee, Jason.'

'Night,' Jason muttered.

She looked at them for a moment and then left the room. Lee waited until they had heard her bedroom door open and shut in the hallway before he spoke.

'What just happened?'

'I don't know,' replied Jason slowly. 'I heard your voice in my head and I answered. I didn't think; I just did it.'

Lee scratched his neck, brow furrowed in concentration. When he spoke, he sounded nervous and bewildered.

'The clown was freaking me out. I wanted to tell you but I didn't want Rebecca to know. So I said it but... without talking.'

They had drawn closer on the sofa, leaning towards each other, heads almost touching. Lee's breathing was loud in Jason's ear. A new web show had begun but its noise belonged to a different world.

'I knew you could put pictures in my mind, Jason. I didn't know I could send stuff back to you.'

It had been a long time since they had talked about Jason's origins, about his unearthly gifts. The subject was always at the back of his mind, but he had chosen to ignore it.

'If only I knew what I was,' he mumbled.

'You said you were a weapon.'

'Yeah, but I still don't understand what that means. What I'm capable of.'

'Try to talk to me again,' said Lee. The fear was gone from his voice. In its place was curiosity.

'OK. I'll try.'

He closed his eyes, the darkness vast and terrifying. Just for a second, he thought he saw falling snowflakes behind his eyelids. He reached out to Lee as he had done so many times before, only this time with words instead of images. It was so easy. So natural.

'Can you hear me?'

'Yes. I can hear you Jason.'

He opened his eyes. Lee was smiling at him.

'Wow. You're full of surprises, aren't you, Jason?'

'But,' he began, 'you did it first. You spoke to me first.'

The pale boy leaned back on the sofa.

'Maybe it's 'cos we've spent so much time together. Your power is starting to rub off on me.'

'Yes. That could be right. It sounds right,' agreed Jason.

He liked the idea. It would mean that they were even closer than he had thought. Intimate. No one could come between them. But just because he liked the idea, it wasn't necessarily true.

'Do you think it would work with other people?' said Lee suddenly.

A shiver ran down Jason's back.

'I don't know. Probably not,' he replied, trying not to betray just how much the idea terrified him. He knew what was coming next.

'We could try it with Rebecca, if she'd let us.'

'No,' said Jason sharply. 'No, I don't want that.'

His friend looked at him in surprise.

'Why not? We wouldn't have to tell her everything. Just what she needed to know.'

'No, Lee. I don't want her involved in this.'

'I know she's stuck up, but I think she's all right.'

'We can't trust her,' he insisted.

'I think we can. Without her, we'd be out on the streets with nothing to eat.'

It hurt to hear him defend her. Were they such friends so quickly?

'We should get away from here. Now,' he insisted, trying to make it sound rational, trying not to sound like a stupid, naïve child. He was desperate and he knew it. If Lee and Rebecca learned to communicate in the same way, without him knowing...

'What the fuck are you talking about, Jason?'

Lee was angry with him, but he couldn't stop the words coming from his mouth.

'I don't trust her. I don't want her involved. Why can't you see how dangerous she is?'

Lee stood up, fists clenched.

'Do you have any fucking idea how much trouble we're in, Jason?' he hissed through his teeth. 'We're being hunted. We don't know who the fuck by. We don't know why they're after us or what they'll do if they find us. We've no money, nothing. We could fucking die! And you think she's the problem?'

'Do you love her, Lee?'

Lee stared at him in disbelief and then sat down slowly. When he spoke, his voice was calm again.

'What?'

'Is that why you wanted to come here? Do you love her?'

The boy stared at him, not replying, face expressionless.

'If you do,' said Jason. 'Just tell me.'

Lee managed a crooked smile. He giggled.

'No, of course not. Where the hell did you get that idea?'

Jason tried to think of an answer but none would come. There didn't seem to be any good, rational explanation that he could give. Only that he had been afraid and confused. Overwhelmed by emotions he had no control over.

'I don't want you to leave me, Lee.'

The boy took his hand. His skin felt warm against Jason's.

'I never would.'

And then they were kissing and it was good.

Chapter Twenty-one

The house must have been abandoned for a year at least. Phillip had searched the rubbish-strewn kitchen, relieved to find it free of any infestation, and had managed to uncover a few tins of food. He had opened one and discovered that it contained lumps of some sort of fruit in a syrupy liquid. He was feeding them to the Seeker. The empty-eyed young man sat at his feet, expressionless face upturned. Phillip lowered the spoon into the tin and scooped out another couple of yellow chunks. He held it out to his slave, feeling uncomfortably like a mother feeding her baby. The Seeker's mouth opened and he gently eased the spoon in. The mouth closed around it. Phillip pulled the spoon back out, watching as the food was chewed and swallowed. It wasn't really necessary to feed it. Usually Seekers were kept alive only for as long as they were needed. They were a field tool, of no use in the Fracture itself. Their average life expectancy was three days. But there was no telling how long it would take to find Jason and Lee. It was as well to keep this one healthy. Besides, it helped to have someone to talk to as he gathered his thoughts. While he spoke, he carried on scooping out fruit for his slave.

'We have done very well. We know which direction they are heading in. We know that they must be looking for a commune.'

The Seeker looked at him, eyes attentive, understanding nothing. Phillip had a sudden urge to stroke it. It reminded him of the pet dog he had had as a child. The day that the vet had put it down was one of the few times in his life that he had cried.

'We cannot betray our presence yet,' he continued. 'It might scare them into doing something stupid. It could drive them straight into the enemy's hands. So we wait here. We are within easy reach of all the communes that might take them in. It is just a matter of pinpointing which one they choose. Easy enough for you. We will wait for them to come to us.'

The tin was empty. Phillip dropped the wet spoon inside and

set it down on the bare floorboards. He settled back in the creaking deckchair. It was the only item of furniture in the entire house. Everywhere else there were the televisions. Dozens of them. There were at least eight in this room alone. Some were attached to walls, others sat on the floor. One dangled precariously on a chain from the ceiling. They were all damaged, with cracked screens and chipped casings. A few were hollow shells, completely stripped of their innards. Plugs and aerials littered the floor. Photos of televisions, the programmes they were showing fuzzy and indistinct, were pinned in clusters to the doors. Patches of silver foil were glued, seemingly at random, over the dirty, yellow wallpaper. The only other decorations were pages torn from listing magazines and nailed to the floorboards in a symmetrical pattern.

Phillip had heard of places like this. They were hideaways where affluent, secretive groups had once met. These self-consciously postmodern sects had believed that television would soon perform the final rewrite on mankind's reality. They had foreseen a future in which people walked through ever-changing virtual constructs of their own creation, where, to learn about something, all that was needed was to generate a simulation. In some ways they were right, of course. But mostly they were wrong. Technology alone was not enough to attain freedom. Their lives had been passive, absorbing signals but making nothing new of them. Ironically, for all their supposed radicalism, they came to fear change more than anything else. The rise of the web shows had left them suddenly out of date and obsolete. The very devices they worshiped now tied them to the past. Eventually they had switched their allegiances to other, more fashionable movements.

The Seeker was still staring up at him. Patiently awaiting orders. It would do nothing without Phillip's say-so. Such a total dependence was slightly unnerving. It was what he imagined true love must be like. He decided to try a little experiment.

'Can you speak?' he asked.

Nothing. The blank eyes maintained their steady gaze.

'Would you like to? You can if you wish.'

Still nothing. Would it have made a difference if he had been angry, if he shouted and threatened? Would fear force words to its lips?

'Say something,' he said, his voice harder and louder.

'Something.'

Silence as they observed each other. The word had come easily and calmly, without inflection. Then Phillip began to laugh, the red flesh in the aperture of his mask wobbling rapidly with each chuckle.

'So you can speak! Say "Fracture".'

'Fracture.'

'Phillip.'

No response. Ah, of course! He had forgotten to make his order clear. He should not expect too much of this thing.

'Say "Phillip".'

'Phillip.'

He was intrigued. He could never recall having heard of a Seeker that spoke. They were receptive but silent creatures. Was it that they had simply never been told to speak? If so, what else might they be capable of if asked? A further idea came to him. Cruel, but it would be interesting to see the response.

'Say "Graham Billington".'

'Graham Billington,' it said obediently. There was no change in its tone, nothing to indicate that the words had any special meaning.

'It was your name,' pressed Phillip. 'When you could think for yourself. Before the Block agent wrecked your mind and before I erased what was left. Doesn't that mean anything to you?'

The young man blinked but did not reply. For a while, they remained in silence. Eventually Phillip grew bored with waiting.

'Never mind. It's better that you don't remember. Better for both of us. Go to sleep. Wake up in four hours. Oh, and if you need to empty you bowels, there's a toilet on the second floor.'

Without a second's delay, the Seeker curled up and went straight to sleep. For a while, Phillip watched it, pondering what other surprises it might hold. Then his thoughts returned to home. The pathway that had led them to the outskirts of the city was obscure and little used. It reduced a journey of days to one of hours. The Fracture knew of a million such roads. Even a city like this had its secrets. You might explore the world for a thousand years and still not know its full geography. The thought gave him comfort and he slipped into a dreamless sleep. At his feet, the slumbering Seeker whimpered slightly but did not awaken.

Chapter Twenty-two

In his dream, Johnnie Varney was talking to his grandfather. The old man was wearing the People's Medal he had been awarded for saving a child's life. He was smiling indulgently at his grandson as he poured out his troubles.

'I need to find the little girl,' Varney was saying. 'I need to save her life too. Then I'll be a hero.'

His grandfather held up his right hand. It was smeared with vomit. 'You have only to obey.'

'But—' begun Varney.

The old man leaned forward and puked violently. A thick yellow pool lay at his feet.

'Obey,' he repeated, spitting out lumps of food.

He vomited again and now he was sinking into the pool, chuckling as his legs, chest then head were submerged.

Johnnie woke to find his sheet soaked with sweat. He lay still for a while in the half-light of morning. Savouring a few moments peace. There would be more horrors to come today. More people that had to die. But for these brief minutes he was safe. Why had his grandfather come to him in a dream? Was it to reassure that him everything would turn out well? Or was it because all hope was lost?

A sound disturbed him and he forced himself to sit up. The other Staunchers were lying around the bedroom, sleeping peacefully under sheets torn from the bed. The bus driver's bed, he thought, the one who had... but he couldn't remember that.

Professor Hayden was standing over him. His eyes were open and his cracked lips were moving. Varney struggled to hear what he was saying. Was the Professor giving him secret orders that the others mustn't know about? That didn't make sense. Of all people, why should he be trusted?

'Soon. Close now,' mumbled the Professor. 'The weapon. Kill.'

He wasn't talking to him, realised Varney. He wasn't even aware of him.

'Protect. Homelands. Protect. Birth,' continued the Professor tonelessly. 'No revision. Protection. Essential. Kill. Kill. Glory. Kill.'

I can run now, thought Varney. While he's like this, I can get away from all this. Go somewhere I'll be safe, somewhere I can start again. He won't try and find me; I'm too pathetic to worry about.

All he had to do was to move very slowly and very quietly.

The Professor's gaze shifted. He was looking straight at Johnnie.

'Good morning, Varney,' he said with a sardonic smile. 'Keen to get started I see.'

Jason watched Lee sleep, waiting for the boy to wake up. Their heads lay so close together on the single pillow that their noses almost touched. Jason wanted to kiss him again, to run his hands all over his skinny body again. But he couldn't, not yet. The anticipation was a pleasure in itself. Morning light was beginning to seep its way in through the minuscule window and in the distance he could hear the sounds of cars and construction. From the kitchen came the sizzle of a frying pan and the bubbling of a percolator. At last, Lee's eyes opened. He smiled at Jason.

'Morning, Jason.'

'Morning, Lee.'

'Have you been awake long?'

'No, not really. Anyway, I liked watching you sleep.'

'I could feel you watching me. Even when I was asleep, I could feel it.'

'Good.'

They were becoming accustomed to talking without words. It was a natural part of their intimacy. As they had made love in the night, their thoughts had mingled and caressed as their bodies had. Each could tell the other what he wanted without the clumsiness of speech in the way. Jason had understood that Lee wanted to submit without being hurt. His own desires were all the clearer for being revealed to the boy.

Jason drew Lee to him and kissed him. The kiss went on for a long time, Jason stroking his back gently all the while. They were both hard, their penises touching. Finally their mouths parted. Jason could still taste him.

'I love you.'

Love was such an inadequate word. It contained barely a fraction of what they felt. Jason had heard it used in web shows and films, on the bewildering streets and among the thronging crowds. It was an everyday word, incapable of describing the bond between them. Lee was integral to him, a part of him, fundamental to his sense of self. Tenderly, he eased the feeling into the boy, telling him that he loved him in ways that language never could. The boy sighed softly. Jason kissed his neck. They wouldn't have sex this morning, he knew that. They were both still finding their way, unsure and naïve. It would have to wait for a while, until there was no threat of interruption. But this closeness was enough. For now.

A knocking at the door broke in on them. Rebecca's voice called out.

'Do you guys want breakfast?'

Lee giggled.

'She's not gonna be happy when she finds out.'

'Why?' asked Jason, puzzled.

'She fancies you.'

'You're joking, right?'

'No. I saw the way she first looked at you. I think that's why she started talking to us.'

'Guys!' called Rebecca again.

'Are you awake in there?'

'Yeah,' shouted back Lee. 'We'll be out in a bit.'

'Breakfast's in five minutes,' she said. They heard her footsteps recede down the hallway.

'Better get up, I guess,' said Lee regretfully.

The two boys disentangled themselves and got out of the bed, shivering slightly in the cold morning air. Rebecca's spare room was more like a cupboard and there was barely room for them both to move about. Jason sorted through the clothes that lay where they had thrown them last night but couldn't keep his eyes off his lover's body, watching as he slid baggy boxer shorts up his scrawny legs and over his flat rear. It was strange to think that the sight of someone dressing was almost as arousing as seeing them undressing. Lee slid himself into black jeans and tugged the belt tight round his narrow waist. Jason sat naked on the bed, staring at him. The boy pulled a white top over his head and grinned at him.

'Not that I'm complaining, but shouldn't you be getting dressed, too?'

Rebecca laid out the plates of fried eggs on toast and mugs of coffee on the table and then sat down. She held her coffee in both hands, letting the heat from the cup warm her as she sipped at it. She hadn't slept very well. Her mind had kept on turning over the events of the day, reading significance into everything the boys had said and done. It was as though an energy that had lain dormant within her had been awoken only to find it had nowhere to go. She had waited so long for something unusual to break the monotony of her life that her mind didn't know how to react now that it had. She had already decided to call work and tell them she was ill. She wouldn't have been able to focus on the job today and, anyway, she'd never taken time off sick before.

She heard the spare room door open and shut. I'll have to wash the sheets now, she thought, as Jason and Lee walked into the living room. The boys had the unmistakable look of two people who had made love for the first time. Just for a moment, she found herself longing for her adolescence.

'Morning,' she said. 'Breakfast is ready. Enjoy.'

They sat down and started hungrily wolfing down the food. Occasionally they gave each other covert little glances. Rebecca felt like an outsider. She wished she shared their lack of sophistication. Her well-ordered life suddenly seemed a prison that she had built with her own hands. The artefacts and ornaments that decorated the room were not the statements of individuality she had thought but hollow symbols of a life that she had never led. Forcing her regrets to the back of her mind, she made herself speak.

'Did you sleep well?'

Another look between the two, another secret smile.

'Very,' said Jason.

'Good. I'm going to call in sick at work today. We'll need to have a talk about what we're going to do later. I'm sure we can think of something between us.'

'Cool,' muttered Lee, slurping down coffee.

'I could do with one of you picking up some shopping for me this morning. Just some bread and milk.'

'I'll go,' replied Lee.

Rebecca was surprised by Jason's reaction. He suddenly looked frightened, like a child lost in a shopping centre.

'Be careful,' he said quietly. 'Remember what might be out there.'

Kelly was not having a good day. The café was already full, one of the microwaves had broken down and Rebecca still wasn't in. To make matters worse, Mary had decided to start work early. She had been moaning non-stop for at least half an hour now. Kelly wondered if she even knew she was doing it.

'Everything's just going to the dogs,' she droned. 'We need a whole new kitchen, but you can tell they won't give it to us. Just give them the food and get them out; that's what they think. And we have to deal with it but when I ask for a pay rise, they say I'll have to apply. Well, if they don't treat their staff right, why do they expect us to stay?'

'Mmm,' muttered Kelly as non-committally as she could. As far as she could tell, Mary was appalled and enraged by exactly the same things every day of her life. She had probably come out of her mother's womb complaining that it was all downhill from here.

'And of course we don't have any new aprons. It's a health hazard. It's a wonder we don't have roaches, it really is.'

A middle-aged woman at a nearby table must have overhead. With a shudder she quickly put down her half-eaten croissant and left.

'Well, don't say bye or thank you or anything. Just leave,' whined Mary after her.

Kelly had never been more relieved to feel the pulse of her mobile. She reached into her apron and pulled out the small circular phone. She flipped up the cover and read the message on the screen:

CNT CM INDA. FLU. WILL CALL MORROW. BEX

She took a deep breath before breaking the news to Mary. This would require at least an hour to moan about in full. At the very least.

'Rebecca's not coming in. She's ill.'

'Oh, that's all we need! And of course we've no one to cover for her. So we get all the shit and have to like it...'

Kelly tuned out. Today was going to be a nightmare, but at least she had a couple of auditions later in the week to look forward to. One was for a low-budget feature about aliens in a lift and the other was for a prominent part in a ghost story about a military family. She had only had very minor roles on web shows so far, but her agent was optimistic that success was coming her way. Kelly knew that she was unlikely to be a big star, but that didn't matter. She loved acting. It was a chance to occupy someone else's world for a while.

'Bacon and eggs, please.'

She smiled at the customer. A tall boy with long blond hair. Cute in a fey kind of way.

'Sure,' she said.

A face caught her eye. Just for a second. An old man with large, dead eyes and bushy grey hair, staring in at the window. Then it was gone. Kelly shuddered. There had been something inexplicably horrible about the face. She knew she never wanted to see it again.

'You OK?' asked the fey young man.

'Yeah, I'm fine,' she said briskly.

You're just being silly, she told herself. Letting the day get to you. Save the drama for the auditions. As she went back into the kitchen, she was sure she could smell cigars.

'Are you all right, Lee?'

'Yeah. On my way back now.'

'Good.'

'I didn't think we'd be able to do this long distance.'
'Glad we can though.'
'Yeah. Me too.'
'My god, you're talking to him, aren't you?'

Jason looked at Rebecca in surprise. He had almost forgotten that she existed. They were in the kitchen, cleaning up after breakfast. He was drying plates as she rinsed the mugs. He had become restless waiting for Lee to return so he had decided to try and communicate with him. It was surprisingly easy.

'How do you know?' he asked. He was beginning to get over his mistrust of Rebecca but was still wary of telling her too much.

'Your eyes, they were somewhere else. And there was an expression on your face. You were listening. And it sure as hell wasn't to me.'

Jason set the plate he was drying down on to the draining board.

'We can... we can talk with our minds. We only just found out. Last night. I don't know how we do it... we just do. Anyway, I had to make sure he was all right.'

Rebecca touched his arm gently.

'He's only gone to the shops. He'll be all right. He's a tough kid, he can look after himself.'

'All the same.'
'You really love him, don't you?'

Jason was surprised.

'Yes.'

'It's more than that, though, isn't it? The way you two look at each other... it's beyond being lovers. I think he's the only person that's real to you. I'm not sure if that's sweet or scary.'

He found himself reassessing her. This reserved, slightly haughty woman could understand something of what he felt. She could even put it into words, something that was beyond him. He hadn't expected that. Had he misjudged her? Could he afford to trust her?

'Come into the living room, Jason. I want to talk to you,' she said, drying her hands on a tea towel.

He followed her into the living room and they sat together on the sofa. He wondered what she was going to say.

'Could you talk to me like you talk to Lee?' she asked.

Yesterday the idea would have made him uncomfortable. But he was intimate with Lee now in ways that no one else could ever be. It wouldn't hurt to see if he could use his abilities with someone else. Still…

'Lee?'

'Yeah?'

'Rebecca wants to see if I can talk to her like this too. Do you mind?'

'No. As long as you don't want to sleep with her, too!'

'Euurgh!'

'Don't let her hear that.'

'I'll try not to. Hurry home.'

'OK,' he said to Rebecca. 'I'll try.'

She altered poise slightly, sitting upright with her hands in her lap as though she were a pupil in a classroom. Jason tried not to think about what he was doing. It had to be done unselfconsciously.

'Rebecca. Rebecca, can you hear me?'

There was no response.

'Did you hear me?' he asked.

'No. There was nothing.'

'I'll try again.'

'Rebecca?'

'Still nothing,' she sighed.

'I think it only works with Lee,' he said. He wondered if he sounded as pleased as he felt.

'Looks like it.'

Rebecca was trying not to show it but he could tell that she was disappointed. Jason found that he felt sorry for her. After all, she had given them a lot and yet they weren't able to give her anything in return. An idea occurred to him. He had another ability, one she didn't know about yet.

'I'll try something else. What's your favourite place? Where would you most like to be?'

She thought for a while, twirling her hair in her fingers. Suddenly, her expression brightened.

'When I was a little girl, my father took me to a museum. It was full of dusty old things. Some of them were horrible. They must have been wonderful once, but they were so rotten you couldn't tell what they were any more. But there was a room, a library. I'd never seen one before. You couldn't take any of the books off the shelves, but I loved it. It was full of ideas. I wanted to explore every shelf, read every book. It made me sad afterwards when my father told me there are hardly any libraries left now. I'd like to go somewhere like that again.'

Jason tried to imagine a large room full of books. He remembered Cornish's bookstore but he doubted that the place Rebecca was talking about had been like that.

'Tell me more about it,' he said.

'The shelves were very high and made of dark wood. Real wood; mahogany, I think. There were long windows. You could see dust mites in the sunlight. There was a smell, not bad, but old.'

Jason began to build the image from what Rebecca had told him. He had difficulties with the books. As he couldn't read, he had to leave the spines blank. When it was as close to Rebecca's description as he could get, he placed it into her mind. The experience was less tender, more mechanical than it was with Lee.

Rebecca gasped. 'That's amazing.'

Pride swelled in Jason's chest at her reaction. Nonetheless, it had been unsatisfying. A shadow of what it was with Lee. Still, he was pleased that she was happy. He was beginning to like her.

'The image will stay as long as you want it to. Just let go of it when you don't want it any more.'

She nodded.

'I can even smell the varnish on the wood,' she muttered.

There was a rattle of a key in the front door. Jason stood up as he heard Lee's voice.

'I'm back.'

The boy came into the living room, carrying a shopping bag.

'Shall I put this stuff in the kitchen?' he asked Rebecca.

Jason could see her reluctantly letting go of the image he had created for her. There was sadness in her eyes as it faded away.

'I'll take it,' she said indistinctly.

Lee handed her the bag and she vanished into the kitchen. Jason took his hand.

'It doesn't work with her. I can make images for her but I can't talk to her.'

'Oh well, never mind. I'm kind of glad.'

'Me too.'

They kissed. Jason wrapped his arms round Lee, relishing the feel of the boy's scrawny frame against his stocky body.

'I hate to interrupt…'

They reluctantly broke away from each other at the sound of Rebecca's voice. She was standing in the doorway, smiling at them. There was no hint of embarrassment on her face.

'You need money, right? To buy your way into a commune?'

'That's right,' said Jason.

'I think I've had an idea.'

Chapter Twenty-three

As far as Kelly could tell, her character was a cross between a hippy and a mercenary. She settled back in the comfortable old chair, thumbing back and forth through the freshly printed script, searching for clues. It was important to find an angle, a lynchpin. Once she had that, Kelly knew she would feel confident enough to audition for the part. She could already imagine the sort of costume the character would wear: bright lurid colours, a long battered coat and the inevitable fake dreadlocks. But the motive behind it all eluded her. Was she a hard-bitten cynic? A hurt child? A spiritualist? The writing was loose, allowing plenty of room for interpretation.

Some actors didn't think that rehearsal was even necessary in this day and age. After all, it wasn't as though you would actually appear on the screen. Everything was animated; you just had to supply the voices. Some were happy just to show up and read the script out. But that wasn't enough for Kelly. She had to know that her voice sounded right and to do that she had to understand the character.

Her phone throbbed. She picked it up from the magazine-strewn table beside the chair.

'Hello?'

'Hi, Kelly.'

'Oh, hi, Ash. How ya doin'?'

'Good news – I don't have to sell no more cutlery sets. I got fired!'

'What, again?'

'It's a natural gift. What are you doing tonight?'

'Prep work for an audition.'

'You don't fancy joining us for some medicine, then? We've got some good shit. Cheap, as well.'

'Better not. I've got to get this done. Anyway, I need an early night.'

'Doing your knitting, Grandma?'

'Fuck off, Ash! I've had a bad day. Bex was off and Mary didn't stop moaning all day.'

'I didn't think Bex allowed herself to get ill. Isn't she supposed to be some sort of superwoman?'

'Yeah, it's kinda weird. Yesterday she went off with two boys that came into the café.'

'Maybe she wanted a threesome. She could do with a good seeing to.'

'They didn't look like the kind of guys for it. They looked scary.'

'Well, if she gets killed, I'll come and work with you. I always had a thing for aprons.'

'You're just too compassionate for your own good, y'know that, Ash?'

'Yeah, I know. My heart just never stops bleeding.'

'Anyway, I've got work to do even if you haven't. Talk to you tomorrow.'

'OK, bye. Good luck with the audition.'

'Thanks.'

Kelly ended the call and put the phone back on the table. She started scanning the script again, trying to focus. But it was no good. Ash had reminded her of Rebecca's strange behaviour yesterday and now she couldn't stop thinking about it. She had always got on well with the older woman. True, she could be a bit distant and reserved, but there was no malice in her. If anything, she had always seemed slightly sad, as though waiting for something that she knew would never come. Kelly hoped she wasn't in trouble. You heard of people disappearing all the time. Ash was always talking about secret state tests with captured humans as live subjects.

It was no good. She couldn't concentrate. She needed something to help her relax. Kelly looked round the small, cluttered living room, trying to remember where she had left the pill jar. Her home was one of a dozen converted Mydia Hycron mobile homes on a concrete plaza, each with its own tiny living room, bedroom, kitchen and bathroom joined by an extremely narrow hallway. It wasn't much, but it would do until regular work started to come in and she could afford somewhere better. The only problem was the family of neo-politicos who lived in one of the other cabins. They were always trying to get her to come to their meetings. Kelly always refused. An evening of being shouted at didn't appeal to her. Still, they persisted. One of them, named after a deceased and disgraced president, seemed to have taken a liking to her.

The pills must be in the kitchen. She got to her feet, stretching her stiff and aching back. The curtains were still open. For a moment, she stared out of the window into the night. A thousand lights glittered back at her from the looming corporate tower blocks. All those rooms, all those lives. Perhaps some of them were staring back at her. She shivered. Definitely time for some tablets.

Her kitchen was almost as untidy as the living room. Not unhygienic as such, but a challenge if you wanted to cook something more complicated than soup. After searching through the cupboards, she finally found the pill jar under a saucepan on the draining board. Kelly unscrewed the top and tipped two codeine and paracetamol capsules on to her hand. She had never really taken to the soluble kind. They gave her stomach cramps and made her dizzy. Swallowing them down with a glassful of water, she returned to the living room.

It was a few seconds before she noticed them. Faces. Faces at the window. Expressionless, their cold eyes scrutinised her. She tried to open her mouth to speak, to shout at them to go away, but she couldn't. One of the faces moved closer. A hand rose and pointed at her, the finger pressing against the glass. One by one, the other faces followed suit.

Kelly's nerve broke. She turned and ran from the living room to the kitchen. There might be something there she could use as a weapon; a knife or even – absurdly – a rolling pin. But the faces had followed her. They crowded silently at the kitchen window. In unison, they pointed at her once more. And then they started laughing, a mechanical, joyless cacophony.

'Go away!' she screamed. 'Get the fuck away from here or I'll call the police!'

She snatched a long, serrated knife from the drawer and made for the hallway. If she could get to the front door before them, could make it to the safety of one of the other cabins… She was sure some of the other residents would take her in. They might even have guns to drive the faces away.

Kelly unlocked the door, every desperate, panicked breath hurting. She flung the door open. She half expected to see the faces grouped outside waiting for her. But there was nothing. Sobbing with relief, she crept stealthily from her home. The cold air bit through her clothes. Still there was nothing. No sounds of pursuit. She looked round at the other mobile homes. Most of them were shrouded in darkness, curtains pulled and the occupants locked safely inside. It all seemed normal. Perhaps it had just been a sick game and they had gone away now.

A figure appeared from behind one of the cabins. It started to walk towards her. A man in grey armour, his eyes fixed on her. Kelly turned to run. But they were coming from all around her now, looming out of the darkness. Predators circling their prey. The knife fell with a clatter from her hand. With a cry of despair, she ran back into her home, slamming the door behind her. With trembling hands, she turned the lock and rammed the bolts into place.

Her phone. She could still call the police. The windows were reinforced and the door was strong. It would take the faces a while to break in. Terrified of making the smallest noise she tiptoed into the living room and picked up the phone. Her hands were shaking so much now that she could barely tap in the number for the police. At last it was done. She heard the ringing tone. She could get help now. End the nightmare.

'Your call is important to us. Please stay on the line and an adviser will deal with your call as soon as possible.'

'No!' she whimpered. 'No, no, no, please, no!'

The feeling of breath on the back of her neck. The stench of cigars.

'Behind you.'

She turned. An old man with white hair and the most terrible smile she could ever have imagined. A smile that would enjoy seeing her die.

'Please,' she gasped.

'No time to waste.'

Something smashed into her mind. Massive, unstoppable, certain, absolute. It tore her apart, read every secret, every experience, every fear, every desire. Kelly was torn open before the old man as he searched through her with the brutality of a dog devouring meat. With the last shreds of her mind, she heard the old man's voice.

'Rebecca.'

She felt oblivion come for her. Kelly reached out for it, welcomed it. Life could never mend the damage the old man had done to her. Death was a sweet release. The darkness descended, like a blanket wrapped round a child. Then she was gone.

Johnnie Varney looked at the corpse of the girl. She had been pretty. Even through the horrified rictus of her face he could see that. The sort of girl he had once hoped to marry and later dreamt of protecting with his army. Another victim. The Staunchers trooping into the room did not spare her a glance. He was sure some of them had daughters of their own. If they could even remember such things now.

The Professor was smiling, rubbing his hands together briskly.

'We are getting closer, Varney. Closer all the time. Soon I'll have them.'

Varney nodded.

'Yes, Professor,' he said.

I hate you, he thought. I hate you. I hate you. I hate you.

Chapter Twenty-four

'I sit here?'
'Yes.'
'OK. Do I need to do anything?'
'No. Have you got the money?'
'Sure.'

Jason remembered Rebecca introducing this man to him. His name was Steve. He was small and muscular, with long brown hair. His chin sported a covering of stubble that did not in the least suit him. Like the other people at the party, he was dressed in brightly coloured clothes; a red and black ringed top and blue bell-bottomed trousers. When he spoke, his voice seemed to come from the roof of his mouth. Steve drew out a wallet and produced a plastic card with curved edges.

'Can I pay by card?'
'No, it has to be cash.'
'Oh. How old-fashioned. Well, never mind.'

The room in which they had left him could have comfortably contained Lee's entire house. The walls were patterned with red and blue circles. He was seated behind a table that appeared to have been made from an old noticeboard. His chair was made of heavy mahogany with an ornately carved back. It was extremely uncomfortable. The chair opposite was of a similar design, though less grandiose. In each corner of the room there was a large cone full of swirling lights that cast strange shadows on the wooden surfaces. According to Rebecca, it was meant to be a statement. Of what, he couldn't imagine.

With no more than a flick of his wrist, Steve had produced two three-hundred notes. Jason took them and added them to the already bulging wad in his jacket pocket. Considering how rich they were, it was strange that none of them were prepared to pay him without fuss. There always had to be some minor ritual, some performance to reassert that they were in the dominant position. Jason didn't see the point. It made no difference to the transaction.

'How's it going?'

'OK. It's that Steve guy now.'

'That tosser dressed like a sailor?'

'Yeah.'

'How many more are there to come?'

'Four. Not long now and we can get out of here.'

'Good.'

Jason smiled inwardly. A day ago he could not have sat in a strange room demonstrating his abilities to people he had never met before. The mere idea of it would have scared him. But Lee's presence at the back of his mind gave him a confidence that he would not have thought possible. He could feel the boy's strength within himself. Whatever these over-dressed partygoers did or said to Jason, he would withstand it. They came into this room alone. He was never alone.

'I'm ready,' said Steve petulantly, like a customer at Rebecca's café wanting to know where his croissant had got to.

Jason used one of two images on them. Either a rich, lush forest or a golden field under a perfect blue sky. It was a matter of judging which they would prefer. He was rather proud that so far he hadn't made the wrong choice once. Steve, he decided, would probably like the forest. His long hair pointed to a passing interest in nature – what Lee called 'New Age'. Of course, his expensive clothes probably didn't have a natural fibre in them, but that wasn't the point. Briefly, Jason wondered how it was that he was able to read these people so easily when he still knew so little of the world.

'The image will last as long as you want it to,' he explained. 'Once you want it to stop, just let go of it.'

He created the image in seconds and transmitted it. Steve's mouth opened in a soundless 'Ooooh'. Jason watched him dispassionately. Normally, they hung on to it for about five minutes and then let it disperse. During that time they were almost oblivious to him.

Rebecca's idea had been simple but brilliant. Several of her friends from her student days had done very well for themselves.

Many of them had moved high up in a company called Mydia Hycron, which, from what Jason could make out, was considered the most prestigious and powerful organisation in existence. These people had money to spare and time to waste. Any novelty interested them. It had been a simple matter for Rebecca to call one of her friends – a man called Callum – and tell him to arrange a party at his flat for tonight. She had found a new and exciting experience for them, as long as they were prepared to pay for it. Which, naturally, they were.

Callum's flat took up the second to top storey of a massive corporate tower block. Rebecca had said this meant that he was very successful indeed. Most people had to wait for years before getting an apartment so high up. Her other friends that lived there had had to settle for apartments closer to the middle. The lower floors were taken up by the office complexes where all the residents worked. As they had waited for the lift to take them up, Jason had watched the workers troop past. Their eyes were wide, their limbs twitching from too much caffeine and cocaine. Their voices were deafening as they argued over who had sold, spent and fucked the most. One man in a blue velvet suit had openly stared at Jason, grabbed his own crotch suggestively, and then moved on. Lee had wanted to go after him and confront him, but Rebecca had said they couldn't afford to draw undue attention to themselves. From the look on her face, she understood his anger.

The party itself was just as noisy. Loud music blared out of a monolithic speaker system. Pills of a type he had never seen before were being swilled down with bucket-like glasses of wine. Callum's elaborately costumed friends danced and talked and laughed. None of them looked the same but Jason couldn't tell any of them apart.

In all the maelstrom of conversation and comment that had greeted their arrival, he couldn't remember a single thing the partygoers had said. He doubted they could, either. Each of them played out a perfect role, as though reading from a script. The party felt like a machine that had been operating for so long, no one could remember what it was for. The people were the parts of the machine, worn down but still driven on by a remorseless mechanism. A cybernetic carnival.

He had been pleased to see that Rebecca didn't want to join in. After hurried conversations with various people, she had led them to this room. They would come in one by one for a demonstration of his gift. There were seventeen of them in all, each having already agreed to pay six hundred for the experience. Then she and Lee had left him. They said they were going to the kitchen. A day ago he would have been suspicious and jealous. Now he was glad that they would have each other to talk to.

Steve blinked and sighed. He had let go of the image. His face broke into a broad grin of polished teeth.

'That was amazing. Just amazing. Will you... will you be coming back?'

'Maybe,' lied Jason. 'Send the next one in, please.'

'OK,' he murmured and ambled away. Jason didn't even watch him go. The experience of creating and transmitting the images for so many strangers had left him hollow. He'd be glad when it was all over.

Once they were done here, Rebecca would drive them to one of the communes. They hadn't decided which yet. They would use the money they made tonight to pay their way in. Rebecca's only cut would be repayment for the clothes she had bought them before they came here. Then they would say goodbye. To his surprise, Jason realised that he was going to miss her.

'Er, hello?'

A tall girl with red hair, trousers that looked like an explosion in a paint factory and breasts full of silicon. Jason scrutinised her briefly. This one will want the field, he thought.

'There you go,' said Rebecca, handing Lee a plate. 'Enjoy.'

He looked at the sandwich, fries and side salad in some surprise. He obviously hadn't expected such a large meal.

'Thanks.'

Rebecca studied the kitchen appreciatively. It was massive, full of appliances, some of which she didn't even know the names for. There was even art on the walls – huge, blown-up photos of misshaped clay figures doing disturbing things with cigar butts. They had come here to get away from the revelry in the other rooms. Lee had mentioned being hungry and cooking might take her mind off just how alienated she suddenly felt from friends she had known for years.

She was surprised at how underdressed she felt. She had chosen a cream ankle-length skirt and matching jacket with delicate gold trimmings. It had been a treat for herself a few months ago and had cost her a fortune, yet she was sure she looked dowdy when she compared herself with the flamboyant figures in their bold costumes. Perhaps the time had come to accept that she had fallen behind the in-crowd and would never catch up. After all, it was hardly the worst that could happen. Lee seemed very happy with the clothes she had bought him – black jeans and a baggy, grey hooded top. Fashion obviously didn't interest him much and she couldn't blame him. He had told her she looked nice, which was sweet.

Rebecca watched Lee as he slowly ate. She hoped he'd finish the meal and not just because she'd prepared it. The boy was painfully thin and could do with getting some proper food into him. She wondered if he was suffering from some form of anorexia. Adolescent boys were often afflicted by it these days. As Lee nibbled at the sandwich, his eyes seemed elsewhere. In his way, she thought, he was just as mysterious as Jason. He was capable of violence if need be, that much was clear, and he certainly didn't lack confidence. But she suspected that there were other aspects of him that only Jason ever saw. Occasionally it was hard to be certain which of them was the more vulnerable.

'How's he getting on?' she asked.

Lee looked up at her.

'It's the ginger girl with the horrible trousers.'

'Oh God, Jackie! She always ends the night by throwing up over someone. It's like a ritual for her.'

Rebecca went to the palatial cupboards and produced a small bottle of scotch and two tumblers.

'Would you like to join me in a drink?'

He shook his head.

'No, I don't drink.'

'Sorry, forgot.'

She poured herself a measure and sipped at it. The warmth was reassuring as it hit the back of her throat.

'Hope you're not gonna get wasted like those pricks out there,' said Lee. 'You've gotta drive afterwards, remember?'

She flashed him a look of annoyance.

'I know that, Lee.'

'Good,' he muttered.

He's worried, she thought.

The glass still in her hand, she sat down next to him.

'You don't have to worry. It's all going very well. By early morning you should be in a commune. Once we've decided on one.'

'I hope so.'

Rebecca touched his bony arm gently.

'You really do look after him, don't you?'

'I have to. He needs someone to protect him and I...'

He broke off, cheeks flushing red beneath his acne. She could tell he wasn't used to talking about how he felt.

'Go on.'

'I need him. More than I ever needed anyone. So I can't let anything happen to him. I'll do whatever it takes.'

She nodded. Now the big one, she thought. I have to know.

'Including murder?'

A pause. He scratched nervously at his neck.

'I had to. They would have killed him. There were two of them. They were trying to kill Jason just after he... arrived. I couldn't let it happen.'

'Was that the first time?'

He took a deep, shuddering breath. The memory was a bad one, she thought, long buried.

'No. Once before. I needed money bad so I broke into this old warehouse. It was full of crap no one wanted no more. On the way out, this big, fat bastard jumped me. He hit me and I went down. I though he was finished but he kept hitting me. I think he planned to do me some serious damage before he was finished. Somehow I got my knife in my hand. Got it into him once and then again. And he was dead. Police found him a few days later. Woman I know, Kerri, she took me in for a while and gave me an alibi.'

'You must have been very frightened,' she said quietly. Lee shivered slightly at the recollection.

'Yeah… yeah, I was. It was round about the time they first started showing executions on Web News. They even used to invite the fucking Prince to give a speech first, remember?'

Rebecca nodded. Her friends at university had always stayed in to watch the hangings. The Regent of Rope was a pin-up throughout campus and the Royalist cause had never been so popular.

'I didn't want to die like that,' continued Lee. 'With people watching. Didn't want people to be glad I was dead. But the police never even questioned me. It was like I had, I dunno, a guardian angel or something.'

He looked her in the face, daring her to judge him.

'I didn't enjoy it. I didn't kill him 'cos I get off on it. I did it 'cos I had no choice. I still… see his face sometimes, y'know? But I didn't enjoy it.'

'I believe you,' she said.

She meant it. Rebecca couldn't begin to imagine the life he must have led. But she knew he was telling the truth. No wonder he needed Jason so much.

'What ya doin' in here, Bex? You'll miss all the fun.'

In the kitchen doorway stood an unconvincingly elegant young man with spiked hair. He was wearing a black and white patterned jumpsuit. His eyes were glazed and his speech slurred. Rebecca sighed with relief. It was only Callum. Even if he had overheard them, he'd have forgotten it by morning.

'I'm not staying long,' she explained. 'Once Jason's through entertaining your guests, we're off.'

'Shame,' replied Callum. Just watching him sway made her feel nauseous. He turned his wine-sodden attention to Lee.

'Your boyfriend's amazing. Just incredible. Even made old Jackie unwind a bit. She's normally coiled like a… a…'

'Spring?' supplied Rebecca.

'Yeah. One of them. Anyhoo, what are you gonna do with the money? Go into business or something?'

Inspiration flashed through her mind. Callum might be an idiot, but he seemed to know everyone.

'Callum, do you know anything about the communes? That's where they're heading for. A good one. Not some stupid religious sect or hideaway for people who think their cheese is spying on them.'

He tried to tap his lips, missed a few times and settled for tugging at his cheek.

'There's one I heard of. Very liberal. Not all, like you say, religious and cheese. It's called, er, Dancing Devil. That's it. The Dancing Devil Retreat. Not religious though. No cheese.'

'Where is it?' she asked.

'Just off the R45. Take the new B8 off it and you're there.'

She looked at Lee. He was studying Callum with a mixture of amusement and contempt.

'It sounds OK,' she said. 'Want to try there?'

'Yeah,' he agreed. 'As long as they don't ask too many questions it should be OK.'

Callum grinned at them.

'Pleased to be of service to you both.'

He waved extravagantly, nearly overbalanced and staggered away. A few seconds later they heard him talking to someone in another room about cheese. The silence left in his wake was broken by Lee's high-pitched giggle.

'What's so funny?' asked Rebecca.

'I never thought of Jason as my boyfriend before.'

'Why, what did you think of him as?'

'Just… Jason, I guess.'

'I wouldn't tell him that, if I were you!' she said with a chuckle. He returned her smile.

A few moments later, Jason appeared. He looked tired but pleased. He held up a wad of notes triumphantly.

'We've got enough' he said. 'Almost as much as we had' – a look at Rebecca – 'before.'

Lee stood up.

'Nice work, Jason. We've found somewhere to go. It's called the Dancing Devil Retreat. It sounds like the kind of place we're looking for.'

'When do we go?' asked Jason eagerly. Rebecca could tell that he didn't like the partygoers any more than Lee did.

The two boys turned to look at Rebecca. She had been about to take a mouthful of scotch. With a rueful grin, she put down the glass.

'All right, all right. We'll go now. But before we do, I've got something for you. Call it a present.'

She reached into her pocket and produced a small flick knife. Carefully she handed it to Lee.

'For eventualities.'

Their eyes met for an instant.

'Thanks.'

Before they went, she took one last look round the kitchen. It truly was a thing of wonder. The very best that money could buy. Heaven for an amateur chef like herself. Much better than a grotty café where all she could make was tea and toast. But it belonged to a world she had been slowly leaving for months, a world with no future that was worth having. She turned her back on it and walked away.

Chapter Twenty-five

Jason watched the city as it rushed past the car window. It was less inexplicable than it had been on the night that he had arrived. The massive, impassive buildings with their exoskeletons of scaffolding and patchwork surfaces of transplanted brick, the small, ever-changing establishments that lurked beneath them and the crowds swarming ceaselessly from place to place – it was all beginning to feel familiar. One day he might even understand the city, might perceive the structures and rituals that bound it together and guided its movements. At night, it was reduced to its most basic nature: glittering lights, deep shadows, anonymous figures flitting across empty spaces. The truth of the city would be found in darkness, he decided, when it was most fully revealed.

And now he was leaving. Heading for another mystery, another place that he would have to search for the words to describe. But Jason wasn't afraid. He could sense Lee at the back of his mind. The connection was always there now. A signal that never stopped transmitting back and forth between them.

Jason turned to look at Lee. He was curled up on the seat next to him, sleeping like a child. He reached out and ran a hand through the boy's blond hair, fingertips brushing the dark roots. Lee stirred slightly. Jason closed his eyes for a moment. He could feel Lee's dreams. For once, they were happy ones that did not frighten him.

'You OK, Jason?'

He looked to the front of the car where Rebecca was at the wheel. It had been a long time since either of them had spoken. The monotony of the roads was hypnotic and dulled conversation.

'Yeah. A bit tired, though. How about you?'

'The same. Once I've dropped you guys off at this Dancing Devil place, I'll check into a motel and grab a few hours' sleep.'

'What will you do after that? Go straight home?' asked Jason.

He had only spent two days with Rebecca, yet it seemed a lifetime. It was difficult to believe he might never see her again. Strange to remember how much he had distrusted this woman at first.

Rebecca hesitated before replying.

'No. No, I'm not going home just yet. I'm going to travel for a while. I've some money that's been sitting in an account growing interest for years and it's time I used it. Maybe I'll spend some time in another city. Or maybe overseas. Just for a few months while I decide what I want to do with my life.'

Jason looked back out of the window. He had difficulty with the idea that there were other cities, let alone other lands. But then, he wasn't even from this one. His eyes were drawn upwards, to the eternal, ruthless light of the stars. The memory of the battlefield returned unwanted. Snowflakes and the screams of the dying. A war so vast as to be beyond comprehension. Himself a nameless weapon with only one thought: to defeat the enemy. Fighting alongside billions of others exactly like him and yet always alone. Wherever he ended up, whatever this commune held, it would be better than that.

Lee's eyes opened.

'Are you all right, Jason?'

'Yeah. I was scaring myself a bit. Thinking of the place I came from.'

'Don't worry. They won't take you back. We'll not let them.'

Johnnie Varney looked at the young man sprawled awkwardly in the bed before them. He was called Callum. Soon he would be dead. Varney was resigned to that. He would force himself to watch and try to remember it afterwards. He owed it to the others. To that poor girl. To the memory of his grandfather. Perhaps, even to himself or, at least, the man he had wanted to be.

'So close now,' breathed the Professor. 'We find the Dancing Devil commune this degenerate told them of and then we attack.'

'What about their friend, Rebecca?' asked Varney. I don't want to see any more women die, he thought.

'She is of no importance.'

Johnnie was relieved. They had found the woman's flat empty

but an address book had told them about this place. A name – Callum – and an address circled in red with a time written next to it. They had arrived too late for the party – he shuddered to imagine what Hayden would have done to the partygoers if they hadn't – but they had found Callum, alone in his expensive flat. He had greeted them with drunken roars. They soon turned to screams. The Professor had ransacked his mind and found what he was looking for. The hunt was finally drawing to a close.

Professor Hayden rubbed his hands together enthusiastically. His aged face creased into a smile.

'When I have them, I shall draw the Fracture agent out into the open. And then I shall put an end to their vile scheme.'

'Scheme?'

'To undermine us. To pervert the order of things. You couldn't understand, Varney.'

The old man wandered away from the bed to the large window of the opulent room. It occurred to Varney that the Professor had seemed unusually at peace ever since they had entered the tower block. There had been an uncharacteristic glint of admiration in his eyes as he watched the bustling, rowdy workers as they hurried to and from offices that never closed. Now he was gazing down from the window, hands resting on the sill, like a king looking down at his people.

'This building is a wonderful, wonderful place, Varney. A testament to all that humanity can and will achieve. All that we must protect.'

He turned to face him and smiled once more. It was only in that moment that Johnnie understood how much he wanted to kill him. He wanted to throttle the old man, to burn him, to smash the smile from his repulsive face. But how could he? How could Johnnie Varney, who had always failed, who had never been good enough and who had always been powerless, kill this thing?

A Stauncher entered the bedroom. He must once have had a name, but Varney didn't bother to try and recall it. What was the point? The Professor walked away from the window, still smiling.

'Strangle him,' he said to the Stauncher, indicating the bed with a nod of his head. 'Come, Varney.'

Johnnie wanted to stay and watch the man die. It was his duty. His penance. But the Professor had given an order and he must be obeyed. So, obediently, he followed his master from the room. The rest of the Staunchers were lined in the wide hallway, waiting. Hayden grunted with approval and then addressed his troops.

'Gentlemen. The time is upon us. History will look back on you and envy you your part in this moment.'

From the bedroom, there came a gurgling cry and then silence.

'The enemy think they can evade us, but we have found them. We shall strike at them without mercy. We shall do our duty without fear or doubt.'

The remaining Stauncher emerged from the bedroom and joined his compatriots.

'We shall protect that which must be preserved. The Block will prevail as we always knew it would and its past shall not be taken from it. We march forward with determination, to glory.'

In unison, the Staunchers beat their chests in perfect rhythm. As one they cheered. It was the sound of a pack scenting blood. As Johnnie added his voice to theirs, only one thought was in his mind.

He has to die. And so do they. And so must I.

Rebecca's car came to a halt in front of a high wire fence. The road they had been following for the last ten minutes stopped here. The gate was shut and the squat wooden hut beside it was empty. Behind the fence and all around them was empty scrubland. In the distance, the lights of the city sparkled. It was odd to be so far from any buildings. A glance at the digital clock on the dashboard told her that it was half-past three in the morning. Would there be anyone to let them in at this time?

'I suppose we better get out,' she said. 'There might be an intercom or something like that.'

All three of them got out of the car. After a few hours on the road, the ground was unnaturally steady beneath their feet. The air outside was mercilessly cold. Still wearing her white party dress, Rebecca wrapped her arms protectively around herself. She hoped they wouldn't be waiting all night before they found a way in.

Lee limped towards the gate, Jason close behind him. They examined it, searching for an intercom of any sort. There didn't seem to be any. Rebecca watched the white clouds of her breath as the wind carried them away. Maybe they would have to come back later, she thought. She hoped not. She wanted to get this done.

Lee had tried the door of the hut and found it unlocked. He pushed it open and disappeared inside. Jason followed. Seconds later he called out.

'I've found something!'

Rebecca hurried forward. For a few moments, she had absurd visions of a secret entrance in the floor of the hut. When she entered, she found the two boys crouched over a tatty desk. Lee was pressing a button and speaking into a grill.

'Is there anyone there? We want to join your commune. Hello?'

Nothing. Then someone broke the silence.

'How many of you?'

The genderless voice from the grille was barely discernable.

'Two of us,' said Lee.

'On car or on foot?'

'Car. A friend's dropping us off.'

Rebecca was pleased to hear herself described as a 'friend'. Even if it was by someone who she was about to say goodbye to, probably for ever.

'OK, you can come through. The gate'll open for you now. Keep on driving until you come to the end of the road.'

There was a click from the intercom and the voice was gone. Rebecca looked at Jason and Lee.

'Are you guys ready, then?'

They nodded. Silently, the three of them returned to the car. As the voice had promised, the gate opened automatically for them, swinging shut after they had passed through. The road on this side of the fence was badly rutted and uneven. Rebecca had to swerve several times to avoid the bigger holes. All around there seemed to be only wasteland. In places, hollow metal tubes jutted out of the ground, the tops jagged and torn. The occasional bench lay splintered across the roadside. On the horizon, a dark object loomed. At first glance it looked like a hill, but it was too regular to be entirely natural.

'There's something kind of familiar about this place,' said Lee suddenly.

'You've been here before?' she asked.

'Maybe. But I can't remember when or why.'

Suddenly, Rebecca realised that they had almost run out of road. She screeched the car to a halt. In front of them was a small, brick building, not much bigger than a shed. There were no windows and only one door – a large, circular metal hatch like a manhole cover. As they watched, the hatch opened. Framed in the circle of light was a short, heavy-set man. A ginger beard covered the lower half of his face. The man was wearing baggy blue overalls and carried a walking stick. He remained where he was, waiting for them.

Rebecca sighed. The time had come.

'Well, I guess this is it.'

'Guess so,' agreed Lee.

The two boys got out of the car. Jason was carrying a holdall containing their clothes and money, plus some drugs she had given them. She wound down the window.

'I hope… I hope it works out OK for you both.'

Lee smiled at her.

'Thanks, Rebecca. We couldn't have got this far without you.'

'Yeah, thanks, Rebecca,' said Jason. 'Take care. I hope you find what you're looking for. I hope you find your library.'

She studied them both for a few moments. Such strange boys. But they had given her the adventure she had wanted. A glimpse into things that her friends could not have imagined. Rebecca would never forget these last two days. They had pushed her life in a new direction. All she had to do now was find out where it led.

'Goodbye,' she said. 'Look after each other.'

She watched as they approached the building. It looked like the entrance to some kind of shaft. The commune must be underground after all, she thought. Lee spoke to the man with the beard, though she could not hear what he said. Jason showed him the money they had earned at Callum's party. The man took it, examining the notes carefully. Then he nodded and led the boys into the building. The hatch closed behind them.

Rebecca sat motionless behind the wheel for a while. The freezing night air was pouring in through the open window but she ignored it. Tears trickled down her face. Whether they were of joy or sorrow she could not have said. Eventually, she took a deep breath and dried her eyes. She pressed the button to close the car window, started the engine and drove away.

Chapter Twenty-six

At first, Jason had thought that their guide was leading them into the sewers. The curved tunnel of dirty brown brick sloped gently but noticeably downwards. Even with the glaring illumination from the long neon lights that were set into the ceiling, it still felt as though they were entering a dark, buried place. The bearded man in the overalls hadn't explained where he was taking them. He had accepted their payment with grateful thanks and then told them to follow him. Since then, he hadn't said a word. Perhaps it was all a trick. Once he had fooled someone into giving him money, they were lured down here and then...

They had been walking in silence for about five minutes when Jason spotted the first rat. Its hairy body was bloated and the tail was thick and long. But for the cracked plastic round the jaws, it was very realistic. Just as he realised it was fake, he heard Lee trip and swear.

'Mind your step, there,' advised the bearded man. His voice had an accent that Jason hadn't heard before. Lilting but with a hard edge.

At Lee's feet lay another model rat. Its fur was tattered and worn with age and both its eyes were missing.

'Old friend, that is,' said the man. 'Always gets the new people. Like saying hello, isn't it?'

He smiled at them both with crooked buck teeth. All of a sudden, Jason realised that they were completely safe with this odd little man. He wasn't the sort to hurt anyone, even two boys who had woken him up in the middle of the night.

'What is this place?' asked Lee.

'Old theme park, isn't it?' explained the man. 'Used to be a big underground roller coaster, this did. Came here myself before they shut it down. This ride was called the Dancing Devil—'

'And that's where you got the name,' completed Jason.

The man nodded enthusiastically.

'That's right. Seemed a good name, it did, so I thought we might as well keep it! Me and the others got together enough money to buy the place off the owners and have it converted. Lots of room down here.'

Lee looked as though he were trying to recall a distant event. Jason could sense him searching his memory.

'I think I came here when I was a kid,' he said suddenly.

The man grinned at Lee. Jason wondered how he managed to remain so constantly enthusiastic. Perhaps he was on very good drugs.

'You must have been very young... Lee, you said? It closed down a good nine years ago.'

'Yeah,' said Lee slowly. 'I was about seven I think. I could only go on the little rides but I remember thinking how the big ones looked really exciting. My mum told me we'd come back when I was older.'

Jason could feel the sadness attached to the memory. A bright summer's day full of things to do and see. The smell of grass and the splash of water. Places to dream of going when you were bigger. Mysteries that were never solved. He moved closer to Lee.

'That must have been the last summer,' said the man. 'Well, you've come back now, isn't it?'

It was peculiar the way he finished so many sentences with a question. As far as Jason could tell, he wasn't expecting an answer.

'What's your name?' Lee asked. Jason could feel him roughly shake aside the memories that had momentarily gripped him.

'Oh, didn't introduce myself, did I? Harvey. Harvey Butler. Other Dancers call me Harv.'

'Dancers?' asked Jason, puzzled. Were they joining some strange, underground circus troupe?

'Yes,' said Harvey. 'Dancers. As in Dancing Devil. Seemed appropriate. Some of them wanted to call us Sharks, after one of the other rides, the, ah... Shark's Reef, it was called. But I thought it'd put new people off. I wouldn't trust people calling themselves Sharks, would you?'

Lee giggled.

'No, I guess I wouldn't.'

'Anyway, let's not stand about here. We'll find you somewhere to sleep. Not so far to go now.'

He led them further on. There were more artificial rodents on the wall, along with fake spiders and the dismal wreckage of plastic bats. Eventually the tunnel branched to the left. They found themselves in a narrow room decorated with bold pictures of massively horned, grinning demons dancing round bubbling cauldrons. Set into the floor was a shallow pit which led to an arched opening.

'Just through here,' said their guide.

There were metal steps which took them down into the pit. Jason noticed a rusted rail running down the centre of it. It was a little like the tracks outside Lee's house.

'Where the ride used to start, this is,' said Harvey. There was a touch of regret in his voice, as though he would have liked to have kept it all running if he could.

They followed him through the opening. Jason heard a sharp intake of breath from Lee. They were on a narrow balcony high above a huge room. Beneath them were rows off heavy wooden tables, almost twenty in all. Bulky machinery was lined against the walls. A domed ceiling, laced with the remains of gantries, reached over them. There was a smell of oil in the air and the occasional clattering of an automatic mechanism left running through the night.

'Factory floor. Where we make all the things we sell to support ourselves. Jewellery, ornaments, that sort of thing. Lot of demand for the home-made.'

Jason was barely listening. Lee's face was pale and he was trembling. Sweat had broken out on his forehead. Jason quickly took his clammy hand.

'You'll be OK, Lee.'

Harvey had noticed them holding hands and smiled gently.

'Scared of heights, is it? Well, don't worry. Hold on to your friend there and keep to the wall when we go down.'

Lee straightened slightly. Jason could sense his embarrassment at having a stranger see him so afraid. All the same, he didn't let go of his hand.

'I'll be all right.'

'Good, good. I'm sure you will. Well, let's go. This way.'

As they trailed along the balcony behind him, Jason fed Lee

reassuring images. He surrounded him with guardian angels that wouldn't let him fall and warriors that would defend him to the death. As they approached a staircase leading downwards, he felt Lee relax. Still he held on to him. In Jason's other hand was the holdall, the weight beginning to make his arm ache.

The metal stairs rattled and clanged beneath their feet. The structure looked sturdy enough, but sounded as though it might collapse at any moment. As Harvey had suggested, Lee kept to the wall. Jason studied the walls of the chamber, noticing how rough they were with none of the lurid decoration they had seen elsewhere. If this was where the roller coaster itself had been, maybe the people had ridden in pitch darkness. It must have been very exciting.

At last they reached the ground. With a grateful smile, Lee let go of his hand. The two boys stood looking around. The work tables were covered with tools and half-completed projects. Chairs and stools were scattered chaotically around. The machines ranked against the walls were old and some appeared to have been converted from their original purpose. Most had a stool to one side, suggesting they were designed for a single operator.

Harvey beamed at them.

'If you want, this is where you'll work. Don't have to though. You've paid for your first six months here already. How you get the money for the rest is up to you. No need to worry about food. We've got good stocks, plain but healthy, and medical stores.'

'We'll check out those tomorrow, Jason.'

Jason barely contained a smile.

'I hope they've got enough pills to last us!'

'There are forty-three of us here,' continued Harvey, like a tour guide running through a well-rehearsed list of facts. 'Most work down here, though a few have their own lines of business. We've got an artist, a comedian, a couple of musicians. Good variety – it's what we like.'

Bet they've never had anyone like us before, thought Jason.

'So, are you in charge?' asked Lee. He didn't seem able to meet Harvey's eye. Jason knew that he was still ashamed of having been seen to be scared by a stranger.

The older man looked surprised and then laughed.

'No, I'm not in charge. No one is! If we have a decision to make, we all sit down and talk about it. Round table, like. There are timetables and a few rotas for cleaning the kitchen, but they're agreed between us. We want to get away from having to have people in charge, don't we? Making bad decisions that affect other people. Ah! Here's Freddie!'

A tall man in his early thirties was approaching them. He wore baggy red trousers and a tight black top which accentuated his muscle-heavy torso. Like Harvey, he had a thick beard, though the effect was faintly ridiculous. As he came closer, Jason could see a thick gold chain around his neck. The newcomer studied them through narrowed eyes.

'Hatchetman,' he growled.

'What?' asked Lee.

'My name's Hatchetman,' he replied, as though astounded that anyone should be unaware of such an important fact.

Jason wanted to laugh.

'Freddie, sorry, Hatchetman is a singer,' said Harvey brightly. 'Always trying to teach himself to play some instrument or other, he is. Anyway, Hatchetman, show them to the rooms, will you?'

Freddie sighed theatrically. Clearly he had more important things to do than look after newcomers.

'Come on, then, if you're coming,' he muttered.

'See you in the morning, boys,' said Harvey. 'We really are very glad you've decided to join us at the Dancing Devil.'

Jason watched as Harvey walked away, disappearing though a door in the far wall. For all his jollity and friendliness, there was something curiously sad about him. It was as though he had found that the world was all too eager to hurt him and had retreated beneath the ground to escape disillusionment.

'Come on,' repeated Freddie angrily.

He led them to a small green door beside one of the bigger machines and shoved it open. Beyond it lay a long, brown-carpeted corridor. The white walls were covered in multicoloured swirls. There was a row of doors on both sides, each one different from its neighbour in design. The smell of incense hung in the air. From one of the rooms came the sound of laughter.

'There are a couple of free rooms at the end,' said Freddie.

'We'll just need one,' replied Lee.

The man frowned at them, nose wrinkling in disgust.

'You two fags?' he asked.

There was a threat in his voice, as though he expected them to instantly deny it. Jason felt rather than saw Lee's knife in his hand, the blade glinting.

'So what if we are?' asked Jason, pleased at how calm he sounded. Combined, they were more than a match for this idiot.

Freddie swallowed, eyes suddenly wide with fear as he saw the knife. When he spoke, his voice was much higher.

'Nothing... nothing. Just wondered, that's all. Number thirty-eight's free. Toilets are at the end. Gotta go.'

He turned and hurried down the corridor. He opened one of the doors and scuttled inside, slamming it behind him.

Lee snorted as he slid the knife back into his pocket.

'What a prick!'

'Think he'll give us any trouble?'

'Doubt it. Let's find our room.'

The door to number thirty-eight was painted in a patchwork of different shades of blue. The room itself was cramped but clean. There was a single bed with just enough room for two. A wardrobe stood in one corner. Next to it was a ceramic washbasin with a mirror above. One of the walls was entirely covered by a dramatic mural in orange and brown of an octopus-like creature with a single bulging eye; its many tentacles were wrapped round a metal tower. Lee studied it appreciatively.

'That's cool.'

Jason nodded in agreement. The image appealed to him. Its eye seemed to look deep within him, though with curiosity, not malice.

'You wanna get some sleep?' asked Lee.

At the mention of sleep, Jason realised just how tired he felt. The party, the car journey and the descent down into this place had all taken their toll.

'OK,' he said, throwing the holdall on to the floor.

They kicked off their shoes and began to undress. Jason found that he still couldn't stop looking at Lee as his scrawny, pale body was revealed. When he was down to just his boxer shorts, Lee crouched down beside the bag, rummaged through it and produced a toothbrush and a tube of toothpaste. He must have taken it from Rebecca's bathroom.

'I guess I should start brushing,' he said, smiling at Jason. 'Now I've got a... boyfriend.'

He stood up and went over to the mirror. Critically he examined his grey teeth. 'Don't think they'll ever be white again, though,' he sighed.

Now naked, Jason stood behind Lee and wrapped his arms round the boy's emaciated torso.

'I don't mind, Lee,' he said softly. 'It's not important.'

Lee hesitated before he spoke again.

'What do you see when you look in the mirror?'

Jason thought, remembering when he had first seen his own reflection. The sense of disappointment at something so fleshy and fragile.

'Myself, I guess,' he replied. 'Jason. Nothing great but... me.'

'When I look in the mirror,' said Lee. 'I see a little boy. Like I've never grown up. I see a stupid, ugly little boy.'

Jason tightened his grip on his lover's body.

'Close your eyes,' he whispered.

'What?'

'Close your eyes.'

Lee's eyes closed. Jason reached out to him. He built a new image, the most intricate he had ever created. He showed Lee how he saw him. The beauty in his skinny body, the poetic fragility and strength of his bony face. He kissed his neck and shared how good it felt to touch him. Jason felt his cock harden and eased the sensation into the boy's mind, letting him see himself as an object of unceasing desire. In his arms, Lee groaned with pleasure. His eyes opened and he smiled. They kissed.

'Let's go to bed,' said Jason.

He took Lee's hand and led him to the small bed. They slipped beneath the covers, holding each other in a tight, passionate embrace, exploring each other with fingers and minds. In the basin, the toothbrush lay forgotten.

Chapter Twenty-seven

'You have found them?'

The Seeker nodded, no shadow of satisfaction in its eyes. Phillip reached into his slave's mind. Where once there had been thoughts, memories and dreams, there was now a map. Every part of the city was detailed, down to the smallest cracks in the road. The map was continually changing as buildings were built or demolished, redecorated or damaged, painted or burnt. Tiny grey shapes drifted across the map, the ebb and flow of the inhabitants. As he contemplated the chart, Phillip was amazed that he had ever lived in such a confined place. Surely the claustrophobia should have driven him insane? The Fracture had tool sheds more complex than this city.

There. On the outskirts. Two tiny flames, burning at the corner of the map. Jason and Lee.

'Closer,' he commanded. 'Find me a signpost. I want to know the name of the commune.'

The contours of the Seeker's mind altered. The corner of the map expanded, rolling forward until the rest of the chart was covered. Phillip could see a fence, a brick hut with a door, an artificial hill on the horizon. They must be underground, he mused. At least that showed some sense on the part of whoever had built the place.

'Pull back a little.'

The fence receded. Roads were revealed, tarmac streams branching and criss-crossing. Austere grey signs giving directions and route numbers. One stood out. It was a different colour to the rest – a sickly off-green. Orange lettering gave the name: The Dancing Devil Retreat.

'Good. That's enough.'

Phillip retracted himself from the Seeker's mind. Now he knew where the boys were, he had to act. But when would be the best time? If he waited until nightfall, there were less likely to be other people about. He wouldn't have to take into account anyone but the two boys. But he was impatient. He wanted to bring the project to a close. Furthermore, to wait would give the Block agent more time to attack. No. He would not give the enemy the opportunity. He would not let them win. He remembered the wreckage of Graham Billington before he had saved him.

'Not this time,' he muttered.

The Seeker put its head slightly to one side. It seemed puzzled by its master's words. Phillip studied the creature. They weren't designed for combat situations like this. Its loyalty might conceivably be a liability. Perhaps it should be left behind.

'Would you like to come?' he muttered, more to himself than the slave. 'Would you like to help me defeat the man who destroyed you?'

Slowly, almost imperceptibly, it nodded. Astounded, Phillip wondered if he had imagined it. Was this another effect of being away from the Fracture for too long? Was he just seeing what he wanted to see? Maybe. Maybe not.

'Come then,' he said briskly. 'We've waited long enough.'

Johnnie Varney had watched the sun rise, certain that it marked the dawning of the last day of his life. The orange ball had been colder than the night, as though it were a personal messenger of his doom. The others, even Professor Hayden, had been sleeping soundly inside the garage. Varney had roamed the forecourt all through the night, tormented by memories and self-hatred. He had examined the shells of the petrol pumps, in case they still contained a little fuel. All it would have taken was one match to burn the nightmare away. But the garage had been abandoned for years and the pumps were all empty.

So he had passed the long hours reading the ancient notices and adverts, examining the bullet holes left in the walls by robbers and inspecting the skeletons of the cars that had migrated here to die. The garage shop where the others slept was still intact, but the stone was crumbling and generations of squatters had taken their toll. Eventually it would be forced to give up the struggle and expire. It seemed to Varney that this was an appropriate place for the beginning of the end. Behind him was the city he had wanted to protect. Before him there was an empty road surrounded by barren scrubland. He felt as though he were standing on the edge of the world, waiting to fall.

The metal panel that covered the gaping hole where the garage's glass door had once been was heaved to one side. The Staunchers trooped out in unison. They didn't even look at him. They formed into two rows – four behind, three in front. Each one had a gun holstered on his left hip. Johnnie took his place in the front row. The morning air was sharp, but it didn't touch him. The only sensation left to him was the heaving emptiness of his stomach.

Professor Hayden strode out of the building. He smiled. A terrible smile that knew that every man before it would soon be dead.

'Gentleman. It is time to meet with destiny. To deliver the final punishment. To ensure that that which is most important is protected.'

The Staunchers pounded their chests in perfect unison. The old man smiled once more. His eyes were suddenly distant, almost wistful.

'There is a glorious place, a place that you can for the moment only dream of. The roads are straight and clean and lead ever upwards. There is but one journey that can be taken there. The journey to the summit. To glory. Those too weak to walk the path are left behind. But those of us that are strong enough never slacken their pace.'

Once more they pounded their chests. Varney felt his own trembling hand slap against his breastbone. He hadn't even realised he was joining in.

'It is from this place that I came,' said Hayden. 'It is to there that I will lead those of you that survive. It is the absolute certainty on which all things depend. It is a towering and remorseless future. It is the Block.'

Fists against chests once more. Varney joining in once more.

'It is endangered. Weakness and uncertainty and dissent threaten it at its very roots. But we shall protect it. Your bodies shall be its shield against degeneracy and corruption. Your true journey begins here.'

The Staunchers began to stamp their booted feet in time with the pounding of their chests. Their faces were joyous, without any flicker of doubt. Flesh against flesh. Boot against stone. In the midst of it all, Johnnie Varney wondered if any of them even knew what the old man had said.

Lee broke two tablets into a plastic beaker full of water and then handed the strip to Jason. Gratefully he took them and dropped two into his own beaker. The water bubbled, the usual haze forming above. He contemplated the fizzing fluid, anticipating its soothing caress.

'We've enough for the next couple of weeks,' whispered Lee. 'After that, unless we get some money, we might have to pay their medicine cabinet a visit.'

Jason nodded. He knew that he was addicted to the numbing sensation of the drugs. It didn't concern him. It was another bond, another connection between them. Besides, there were more important things to worry about.

'They all seem friendly,' he said quietly.

The kitchen was full of the sound of conversation. It was a long blue room with four lines of crowded tables running down the middle. At the far end of the room stood a much bigger table covered with plates of toast, bacon, salads and omelettes. An open doorway led to a kitchen from which the clattering of dishes could be heard. People moved from table to table, swapping greetings. A few had introduced themselves to the two newcomers, asking polite questions and telling brief stories about the place. All of them appeared to be suffused with an almost manic energy, but their faces were drawn and there were heavy bags under their eyes.

The food was all free. It seemed serving in the kitchen was part of the rota Harvey had told them about. Jason hoped they would have moved on before his turn came round. They had deliberately chosen to sit at the end of one of the tables, as far away from anyone else as possible. Jason had chosen a full breakfast of bacon and eggs. Lee had settled for a couple of pieces of toast. An elderly woman in charge of drinks had given them two cups of coffee and the beakers of water. If she knew they were going to use them to take drugs, she didn't comment on it.

'Seems kind of unnatural to be this cheerful in the morning,' said Lee with a grin. He gulped down the contents of his beaker. 'Maybe they're on better stuff than we are.'

Jason laughed. He wanted to kiss him again, but not in front of all these strangers. Last night had been good. The sex itself was frantic and soon over. They were both too desperate for each other to make it last. But even after it was done, their minds had remained entwined, each deep inside the other. They no longer even needed words to talk. When they chose, they could communicate through impulse and image.

'Enjoying your first morning at the Dancing Devil?'

The man who had sat down next to them was small and lean. It was difficult to make out much of his face behind the thick black beard and curly hair that reached down past his shoulders. Behind thick glasses, his blue eyes were bright. His tone was that of an old and trusted friend.

'Er, yeah,' replied Lee.

'Good, good. Always pleased to see some new blood. Need all the help we can get!'

He chuckled heartily. Jason forced a smile.

'My name's Bill,' said the man. 'Bill Bradley. Been here a long time now. Great place this. Hard work, but worth it. Listen, I hope you don't mind me asking this when you've just arrived, but have you done much in the way of manual work?'

Lee shrugged.

'Not much.'

Bill seemed unperturbed.

'You see, I have a plan I want to try out. We still have to buy our food from wholesalers. Not a problem; we make good money from the stuff we sell. But I think we need to be more self-sufficient. What's the point of leaving it all behind if we're still dependent on other people? Some of the others agree with me. A few months ago, one of the machines caught fire and I was left with burns on my leg. I was laid up for a while and it gave me time to think. Why don't we start our own farm? There's a lot of land round here that we could try to cultivate. All it would need would be for enough people to lend a hand. Ploughing, planting seeds, that sort of thing. Would you be interested?'

'I don't know how long we'll be staying,' said Lee.

'Fair enough, fair enough. But think about it. I think working with the soil could be a very rewarding experience. Well, I'm going to get some breakfast. I'm ravenous!'

He got up and headed for the food table. Lee watched him go.

'I don't fancy life as a farm hand, do you, Jason?'

'No,' said Jason. 'I was hoping they'd just leave us alone.'

'I think they're expecting us to work for them one way or the other.'

'We're not going to, though, are we?'

'No.'

'Ooooh, sitting all by ourselves are we?'

A colossus of a girl loomed over them. Her hair was dyed a bright red and a floral dress struggled to contain the rolls of her blubber. One hand clutched at a long, delicate chain round her neck from which dangled a drop of amethyst. Jason guessed she wasn't much older than twenty; she looked almost forty.

Her jowls wobbled as she spoke.

'Well, don't worry, you'll soon fit in. Friendliest place on Earth this. Before I came here I had a job with Mydia and, well, it could be days before anyone even spoke to you. Everyone far too self-conscious to talk to someone new. My mother and father were just the same. But here, well, it's totally different. Everyone's welcome.'

Jason could not think what to say to this bizarre woman. She hadn't blinked once yet.

'I'm Suzanne,' she announced. 'Though I prefer Sue or Suzie. Whichever you like. If you have anything you need to talk about, I'm a very good listener. Everyone says so. I think I might be a bit psychic sometimes. I pick up on things, y'know? Like when Gill's dog died, I just knew before she even told us.'

'Right,' said Lee, taking a fortifying mouthful of coffee.

'Of course, you can't keep a secret in this place! Everyone knows everyone else's business! But we've no prejudices, so you don't need to worry about that.'

She still hadn't blinked.

'We have lots of activities. Work hard together and play hard together; that way, everyone gets to know each other. No holding back. I want to arrange a disco night. A touch of Mardi Gras!'

She struck a dramatic pose and clicked her fingers. A large portion of dress vanished into her armpits. Lee sniggered.

'It'll be a great night,' she enthused. 'Gets rid of everyone's inhibitions. Lots of wine, too. I know a lot of people prefer all these pills nowadays, but give me a bottle of red any day. So much more civilised, don't you think?'

Lee downed the remainder of his coffee in one and stood up.

'Well, we're off for a walk now. See you later.'

Jason regretfully pushed his half-finished breakfast away, drained his beaker and followed Lee from the kitchen. Behind them, Suzanne was already talking to someone else.

The corridor from the kitchen led to the workroom. Already people in blue overalls were at the benches. Some of them nodded in greeting, others were too engrossed in what they were doing to notice them. The machines were all chattering away busily as though happy to be awake and in use. Plastic containers at the end of each bench were rapidly being filled with jewellery. Jason noticed that many of the workers had minor injuries, with arms wrapped in bandages or fingers covered with plasters. A few of them bore the traces of deeper cuts and scars that were unlikely to ever fully fade.

'That was… odd,' said Jason.

Lee giggled.

'She's a bit keen, isn't she?'

A door between two of the machines opened and Harvey emerged, walking stick in hand. Another, younger man with curly hair followed behind him. He was wearing a tattered overall and his hands were covered with oil and dirt. Like the other men, he had a thick beard.

'Good news, everyone,' announced Harvey. 'Austin's got it fixed. The generator's back up to full power again. No more blackouts in the middle of the night.'

There was a ragged cheer. Austin took an exaggerated bow.

'Oh, hello lads,' said Harvey. 'Just had breakfast, is it?'

'Yeah,' replied Lee. 'We thought we'd go for a walk.'

'Oh, right-o. It's a nice day for it. Bit chilly, but not too bad. Some of the Dancers are out already, rehearsing a play.'

'A play?' echoed Jason.

'Oh yes. Justin, one of our oldest residents, he's a bit of a scribbler on the side. He's preparing a show for us all. Drama, a few sketches, that sort of thing. Probably be parts for you both if you're interested.'

Jason felt Lee's laughter in his mind. 'Not really our kinda thing,' said the boy.

'Oh well,' continued Harvey, completely undeterred in his cheerfulness. 'Never mind. Not involved in it myself, but looking forward to seeing it. Before you go, let me show you our generator. Quite an achievement.'

Reluctantly they followed him through the door he had just emerged from. The generator room was cramped and very dirty. The air was heady with a bittersweet odour of gas. The floor was slippery with oil and strewn with tools. In one corner of the room sat an extraordinary machine: a collection of steel drums, turbines, tubes and belts. It throbbed loudly to itself, like the heart of a metal giant.

'Built it ourselves we did,' announced Harvey, proudly indicating the machine as though it were a famous landmark. 'Took a month to get it right. Keeps us all warm now, though. Odd breakdown, of course, but that's only to be expected, isn't it?'

'Is it safe?' asked Jason nervously. He could feel his concerns in Lee's mind too. They had had to escape from one fire already.

'Oh yes,' replied Harvey breezily. 'Safe as houses, as long as people are careful. Anyway, I shouldn't keep you. Enjoy your walk. Take a stroll round the lake; it's quite nice on a morning.'

When they reached the lake, Jason thought Harvey's description was a bit generous. It was more like a very large pond. The water looked shallow – only three or four foot deep at most. Heavy green algae clogged the surface. White birds skimmed its surface, hunting for insects. The water had an unpleasant, diseased stench.

On the far side was the hill they had caught a glimpse of the night before. In the light of day, its regular sides looked even more artificial. At its peak was a huge shark's head, its jaws open to reveal a dark tunnel beyond. From the mouth, tracks led down the side of the hill and carried on a few metres into the lake. At the edge of the water there rested the wreck of a metal carriage. It too was shaped like a shark, with a tail arching up behind and a triangular snout at the front.

Lee looked at the scene sadly.

'It all looked really exciting when I was a kid. It reminded me of this old film about a shark I once saw.'

Jason looked up at the shark's head at the top of the hill. He found the ruin curiously intriguing. He wanted to see where the dark tunnel led. What would it be like in the shark's belly?

'I wonder if we could get up there?'

Lee shrugged, obviously still unhappy at the state the place had fallen into.

'Maybe. There must have been steps or something and it doesn't look too steep. Guess we could look for a side entrance. As long as I don't have to go near the drop.'

'There are people coming.'

A small group was approaching them from further round the lake. Jason recognised one of them as Freddie. He was dressed in an ill-fitting tweed suit and broad-brimmed hat. His companions were all similarly dressed, except for a tall man with silver hair who was wearing a black overcoat and narrow trousers. A cape fluttered from his shoulders. He was talking loudly to the others.

'Well, I'm quite pleased with how our first dress rehearsal went, but we need to make it snappier. Especially when… ah, newcomers!'

He stopped and smiled broadly at Jason and Lee. 'You two arrived last night, I believe?'

'Yeah,' replied Lee.

'I'm sure you'll fit in well. Most people do. Harv has very much an open-door policy.'

Jason noticed Freddie was staring at the ground and looking very uncomfortable.

'I'm Justin,' continued the silver-haired man. 'We're working on a little production at the moment. It's going rather well. You must be sure to see the finished work when it's ready.'

Lee was deliberately looking at Freddie as he answered.

'We will.'

Justin smiled at them.

'And what brings two boys like you here?' he asked. 'A spiritual revelation?'

'We...' started Jason, then faltered.

'We needed to get away from things for a while,' said Lee quickly.

'Ah... I see. Well, I'm sure you'll find it a good place for that. Where are you headed for this morning?'

Lee pointed up at the huge shark head on the hill. 'Is it safe to go up there?'

Justin gazed up at the hilltop.

'The Shark Reef ride? Yes, it's safe. Keep going round the lake and you'll come to some steps. They'll take you up to the old entrance. It's all quite sturdy.'

'Thanks,' said Lee.

Justin nodded and led his group beck in the direction of the commune.

'This place gets stranger,' said Jason when they were out of earshot. 'They all seem happy but... weird.'

'I know,' said Lee slowly. 'We'll have to be careful.'

Jason nodded and then turned his attention upwards, to the shark's mouth and the dark space beyond its jaws.

Chapter Twenty-eight

There were still traces of the countless tourists that had once walked up the wide, stone steps that led to the ride. Ancient litter was scattered everywhere, as brown and desiccated as the piles of leaves that had fallen from the deformed, stumpy trees. Shreds of lost clothing laced the dense bushes that closed in from either side. The corpse of a pushchair was spread across five steps, with no indication as to whether or not the occupant had survived its destruction. There were patches of graffiti in places. Lee read some of them to Jason. Matt had once loved Susan and Alexander had been a fuckwit.

The higher they got, the colder the air. The stench of the slime-clogged lake was smothered beneath the dank smell of the heavy greenery that clustered around them. There was no sound. Even the voracious, scavenging birds had forgotten that this place existed. Jason felt as though they were leaving the old world behind, climbing a stairway to an empty and mysterious realm.

Something emitting an angry buzz crashed into his face and he jumped back with a cry. The ugly, fat dot rushed forward again, collided with his cheek and retreated. A black insect with furiously pounding gossamer wings. It circled his head a few times, chattering in agitation, and then darted away. Jason watched as it flew away, the motion clumsy and lopsided. He shuddered.

Lee was laughing.

'It's just a bug, Jason.'

'You're not the one it tried to attack!' he replied, with mock indignation.

'Guess it knew you were a soft target!'

They both laughed as they carried on up the steps. A few minutes later, Lee stopped. They had come to an oranging noticeboard which displayed the faded remnants of a map. Lee squinted at the almost-illegible printed words and symbols.

Something caught his eye and he pointed to a green squiggle in one corner.

'Hey... the Dragon! I remember that! It was a ride for the little kids. Just a few carriages and a green engine. Lots of tunnels.'

He looked at Jason.

'I went on it loads of times. It was great.'

Once again, Jason could sense his sadness for this shattered theme park and what it had once represented. It was stronger now.

'I'm sorry you had to see the place like this.'

Pause. A thought half formed, half hidden.

'Yeah. It's a shame. But I guess things have to change.'

'Not us though,' said Jason aloud. 'I don't want that to change.'

'It won't.'

'Have you ever...' began Jason and then broke off. The question had only just occurred to him and he wasn't sure if he wanted the answer.

'Go on,' prompted Lee and he could tell the boy already knew what he was going to ask.

'Have you ever been with anyone else? Like we are, I mean.'

Lee scratched at his neck before he replied.

'No, not like we are. But... there was this one guy. It wasn't much; we didn't, y'know, sleep together or anything. But something sort of happened.'

'What was his name?'

'Joseph.'

Lee was staring into space as he spoke.

'He was about thirty. A real hard bastard people said, but he was kind of smart, too. Read a lot and used to go to museums. He used long words all the time; I didn't know what half of them meant. He had this weird thing about undelivered letters. God knows why. I think maybe it was something to do with knowing people's secrets. But I'm not sure. Anyway, he'd heard about me, knew I was good at getting stuff people wanted. So he paid me to break into this little depot were they kept all the letters they didn't know where to send. I thought it'd be easy. I got in, no trouble. But there was this big fucking dog I didn't know about. I was lucky to get out in one piece. But I couldn't get the letters he wanted.

'So I had to go back and tell him. No point in trying to run; he'd have found me straight away. No one ever got away from him. And so I just stood there in front of this guy, crying my eyes out and telling him over and over how sorry I was. He came towards me and I thought, this is it, he's gonna break my neck, right here, right now. But he put his arms round me and he said, "Don't be afraid. I'm not gonna hurt you." And then he kissed me. And it was... good.' Lee broke off. Jason could feel the memories turning in his mind.

'Did you see him again?' he asked.

'Yeah. He told me to come back the next day. He took me to this place full of stuff from the movies.' He smiled at the memory. 'It was awesome. They had old monsters and spaceships. Not drawings; real models. I guess he knew I'd like it. When the guy that owned it had gone, he kissed me again. Said he'd see me soon. Promised to take me to some more places. And that was the last I saw of him.'

Lee sighed sadly.

'I reckon he had to do a runner. Pissed off the wrong people or something. I don't think he was that serious about me, not really. But it was the first time I'd ever thought about being with another guy. Before that I used to think I must be... I think they call it non-sexual or something. I'd met gay guys, but the way they acted... I just thought they were fags, didn't see how I could be like them. And all the ones on the web shows were more like pretend women. But after Joseph, I started thinking about it more.'

Jason remembered his own dawning sexuality. The bewilderment and confusion. His body crying out for nameless things.

'And then I found you,' Lee said softly. 'And right from the start, I knew I had to be with you.'

Jason moved forward and kissed Lee's emaciated neck and then his lips. The kiss carried on, neither wanting to relinquish the moment. As he sensed his lover's hurts and regrets dissipating, Jason held him tight, easing images and dreams into him. Lee was responding with pictures and sensations of his own. His impulses were raw and made Jason shiver with pleasure. All the adolescent's fragility and strength were laid bare before him. He was open and accessible and wrapped all round him, protecting Jason and submitting to him at the same time. He could taste Lee's life, felt the breathlessness of violence and the ache of loneliness. He knew what it was to be a thief and to dream of adventures and miracles. He had a knife in his hand, was light-headed with the thrill of the blade.

Their lips were still joined, but he was barely aware of the physical touch. He was travelling deeper into Lee than he had ever been before. He saw the world through his eyes. Sometimes the details were unbearably clear. At others they were numb with drugs. And then he saw himself. A strange and wondrous creature born of blue fire. A fallen weapon come to save Lee from desperation and despair.

Lee was inside him, too. Jason could sense him exploring the memory of the battlefield, gazing at the falling snowflakes and hearing the cries of the dying. The boy seemed to understand what he was looking at. There was horror at the carnage and a final comprehension of his lover's birthplace. But he had turned from those memories and was running long, tender fingers over Jason's fear and self-disgust. The touch drew Jason further into Lee.

And now he wasn't sure who was who. Their minds were flowing into each other, becoming one relentless, unstoppable movement. They were each other. All that each ever had been or ever would be. He saw all their experiences simultaneously through his own eyes and Lee's. Jason relived the story of his life and he finally understood himself. Before they had met, he had not existed. He had remembered nothing because he had been nothing. A weapon. A device. A thing capable of destroying billions but ultimately less than the insect that had crashed into his face. Lee had created him. He was Jason's lover and parent and child and home.

You... I... Us... Us...

Perhaps they could stay like this for ever. One moment stretched across all their lifetime. Perhaps they could. One day. But not today. The world was dangerous and their bodies could still be broken. Wrapped round each other and within each other, they were vulnerable to attack. Slowly, gently, they disengaged. Each was careful not to tear the other's mind in the separation. They slipped out of each other. Almost. Some parts of them were sealed together and screamed when they tried to part them. So they let them be.

The steps and the overgrown bushes swam back into Jason's sight. He felt the cold breeze and the rusty smell of leaves. Their lips were still pressed together. Reluctantly, their mouths separated.

'Don't move.'

The voice was expressionless, without accent or inflexion. It was the coldest, hardest sound Jason had ever heard. He let go of Lee, aware that the boy's hand was already reaching for his knife and certain that it wouldn't do any good.

'You are coming with us.'

Seven men stood in a circle about them. They were wearing grey body armour and each held a long-barrelled gun. Jason tried to focus on their faces, but for some reason couldn't. His eyes seemed to slip over them as though they were made of smooth putty. He couldn't even tell which one had spoken.

'Who the fuck are they, Jason?'

'I don't know!'

Lee was holding out his knife. The blade looked tiny and useless against the unwavering certainty of the grey figures.

'That won't help you, sonny.'

Again, he couldn't tell who was talking. Did they even have mouths to talk with?

'You're coming with us. To Professor Hayden. You are going to answer for your crimes. You are going to be made to take responsibility. You are going to be punished.'

The voice began to speed up. There was still no expression, but the words spilled out faster and faster.

'We are honourable men and you have sinned against honour. You are worthless vermin and must be dealt with. You are a danger to our families. Our children must grow up in a safe world. You are the reason we pull the trigger. You must be punished. You must be punished.'

The circle began to close in. The guns were raised, aimed directly at the boys' heads. Jason reached inside himself, searching for the power he had used once before. The ability to attack and kill that made him a weapon. For so long he had tried to forget it and now it was the one thing that might save them.

It was gone.

'You will be punished. You will be held to account.'

Jason searched frantically within himself, desperate to find some trace of his offensive capability, but it was hopelessly lost, irretrievably entangled in his connection with Lee. A weapon had always, ultimately, to be alone and Jason would never be alone again.

'I can't stop them!'

The circle was close now. Their faces were still indistinguishable. Jason was sure that they must be there, somewhere beneath the grey, but they had been filed down to make for more effective warriors.

The voice again.

'It is time for justice. It is...'

A scream. Unbearably loud, unnaturally high-pitched. The circle was breaking, the figures collapsing. One rolled down the steps, another slumped into the bushes. Jason and Lee held on to each other, too terrified to move. There was nowhere to run to, the agonised creatures were writhing all around them. One of the figures hauled itself up from the ground. The face was still grey, but now it was decorated with a crimson cobweb. It lurched up the steps towards them, shrieking in agony.

'I dropped the knife, Jason!'

The figure was close to them now, so close they could feel its ragged breath, could see the blood coursing down the surface of its body. It raised a fist. The cobweb expanded, until the whole face was red. With a gurgle, the thing crumpled at their feet. The others were struggling upright now. And running. Still screaming, they fled down the path and into the bushes.

The silence they left behind roared in Jason's ears. He didn't let go of Lee. He held the boy close, looking into his frightened eyes. He had to reassure himself that they were both still alive. Reluctantly, they both stared down at the corpse of their attacker.

It was little more than a lump of red meat now. In unison, they stepped away from it, letting go of each other as they did so.

'What... what happened?' asked Lee. 'One minute they were... what's going on?'

'Jason. Lee.'

This voice was different. Soft and silky. It seemed to caress them, to reassure them that they were safe now. A figure emerged from the bushes to their right. They both gasped at the bizarre creature standing calmly before them.

'My name is Phillip.'

He was tall and slender, clad in brown leather trousers and matching jerkin. His head was covered by a blank metal mask. There was only one opening; a small circular orifice where the mouth should have been, in which red flesh moved as he spoke.

'Don't be scared. I am not as frightening as I appear to be. You must come with me.'

'Who... who...' stuttered Jason. 'Who were those... things? What did you do to them?'

Beside him Lee was staring speechlessly at Phillip, his mouth hanging open.

'They were tools of the Block. And I am a specialist in dealing with such... tools. Among other things. I need to talk to you. To both of you. You have to understand what is happening.'

Lee suddenly found his voice.

'You come from the same place as Jason, don't you? From the war?'

The blank mask swung round to look at him.

'That's right, Lee. We hadn't planned for you be so involved.'

Jason suddenly found he was angry. Very, very angry.

'Why can't you just leave me alone? I made my choice. I left the war. There are thousands like me still there; what does it matter if I don't go back? What fucking difference does it make? Why can't you just let me stay here with Lee?'

Phillip raised a gloved hand.

'You don't know the full story. As you say, there are thousands like you. Billions in fact. But I must explain to you. There is a building at the top of this hill. I believe that's where you were going anyway. We'll be able to talk in peace.'

Jason looked at Lee. The adolescent gave him a small smile, revealing his grey teeth.

'I think we have to know, Jason.'

Lee turned to Phillip.

'You're not going to hurt Jason, are you?'

'No.'

'Then we'll go with you.'

Lee took Jason's hand and gave it a tight squeeze.

'It'll be OK,' he said quietly.

Phillip nodded. 'Come forward.'

Jason and Lee both started as a second figure emerged from the bushes. A long-haired man in black trousers and a white shirt. His unblinking eyes stared vacantly into the distance.

'What... who is he?' asked Jason. 'What's wrong with him?'

'I will explain,' promised Phillip.

Jason and Lee followed their peculiar saviour up the stone steps. Behind them, the young man gathered up the abandoned guns of their attackers before trailing after them. The silence returned. There was still litter and graffiti and the heavy smell of greenery. But to Jason it seemed as though the entire world had suddenly changed. He heard Lee's voice within him and felt the tangled connections to the boy in his mind. They gave him comfort as he walked towards answers he didn't want to hear.

Whatever happens... Whatever happens...

Chapter Twenty-nine

Although the mask locked Phillip in unending blackness, it showed him the weapon in every detail. Things were not as had been anticipated. He had expected to find Jason terrified and bewildered, overwhelmed by the world in which he had found himself. After all, the plan had been to introduce him to the experience of uncertainty. But though the boy – it was difficult to think of him as anything else now – was clearly frightened, he seemed to have found an unexpected source of strength in Lee. The mere presence of the adolescent appeared to empower him.

It was obvious that the two were lovers. This in itself was not a problem. The plan had allowed for the possibility of sexual experimentation between them. But the way that Jason and Lee interacted was unlike anything he had seen before. They moved like two halves of the same person, the body language of each seeming to speak for both. And then there were their eyes. Always slightly distant, as though they were communicating via secret means known only to them. The Committee had intended that the weapon should be left isolated and helpless, useless to his Block creators. But though he was separated from the battlefield, it was clear that Jason was far from alone.

Instinctively, Phillip scanned the room. The building was a shoddy, tumbledown affair set into the top of the hill. The outside had been designed to resemble the prow of a sailing ship, but time had left it a waterlogged wreck. The entrance was long and low, surrounded by cracked motifs of exotic birds and treasure chests. Inside, they had found a hexagonal chamber. The walls were decorated with paintings of sharks attacking absurdly muscular men armed with harpoon guns. Rusted railings ran down the centre, forming a zigzagging pathway that led to a locked and barred door plastered with red DANGER signs.

Holidaymakers had once queued here, impatiently waiting for their turn on the ride. Now it was a dismal place with puddles floating with litter in every corner. A crude mural of a nude man stained one of the walls and a wheelbarrow without wheels lay stranded amidst a pile of bricks. Jason had suggested trying the door, but Phillip had decided against it. The structure within the hill was unlikely to be safe. Besides, it made no sense to stumble around in the dark when the Block agent's troops might strike again at any time. He had set the Seeker on watch at the entrance, a gun in each hand. It appeared to understand its new role as a guard dog.

'You said you were gonna explain,' said Lee.

As ever, the youth sounded confident. Yet the sight of a Fracture representative should at the very least have caused him some confusion. People from non-combat realms usually went into immediate denial and only gradually came to accept what they were seeing. Jason's influence was obviously shielding Lee from the traumatic effects of Phillip's foreign nature and disturbing appearance. Or was there more to it than that? The adolescent seemed to know about the war. Did he have some glimmer of understanding as to what the Fracture was?

Phillip turned to Lee.

'Yes. I will explain. And it may be hard for you to understand. But you must try.'

His mask swung towards Jason.

'You know what you are?'

The slightest of nods.

'A weapon,' he replied quietly.

'Yes. A weapon. You were created by our enemies. By the Block.'

'The Block,' repeated Jason. There was no sign of recognition. No flicker of loyalty to his former masters. A good sign.

'Then who are you?' asked Lee. Phillip had the strange feeling that he was reacting for Jason as well as for himself.

'We are the Fracture. We have been at war with the Block for millennia.'

'The war,' said Jason. 'I saw it. Just briefly. Millions were dying.'

'Millions? More have died in the war than there are numbers to count things.'

'What started it?' they asked in unison. The sound of their voices joined as one was curiously unsettling.

This would be difficult, thought Phillip. Like trying to describe the sound of thunder to a man born deaf.

'The war is about stories,' he said slowly. 'One story and many stories.'

'Stories?' repeated Jason wonderingly.

'There have always been stories,' continued Phillip. 'Humanity was made from them. Stories are the sound of culture talking to itself about itself. There is one particular story. It is about a man. He starts off poor and becomes rich. He starts of weak and becomes powerful. He starts off a peasant and becomes a king. He destroys all his enemies and is never conquered. All the land becomes his. This story has always existed. And for some, it was the only one worth telling. The only one they ever wanted to hear. They did not want tales to frighten them or to teach them or to change them. They wanted this one story and no other. They came to hate the others and sought to stop them from ever being told again.

'And eventually, it became so. One culture. One story. All lessons were learnt from this one story that was told to them from birth. It guided and controlled their entire culture. It became their entire culture. In the end, it became them. The Block. Unmovable. Unchanging. Absolute.

'The Block enclosed their world. A physical prison as well as a cultural one, and they welcomed it. Except there was resistance. Always one in every hundred wanted to hear a different tale. Always those that wanted to remember the stories that had been buried and forgotten.

'Before the Block was fully formed, a few managed to escape. Via secret pathways that had taken centuries to build. They left the Block behind and they created the Fracture. A culture inconceivably different from the one they had left behind.'

'And that's where you are from?' asked Jason.

'Not originally. I was born in this city. But the Fracture and the Block are both capable of journeying across different realms. I was recruited when circumstances made me... receptive to Fracture culture. A creature like myself is much better equipped to slip from realm to realm than someone less... physically altered.'

'Your mask,' began Jason. 'Did they—'

'No. But who better to slip through shadows than a man with no face?'

There was a moment's silence before he continued.

'The Fracture grew. In a million different directions. Until eventually, locked away in the cell they had built for themselves, the Block learnt of it. Learnt that other stories still existed and that new ones were being born all the time. And so they declared war on us. And that is how it began. They fight for their one story. We fight for our many.'

'And Jason was one of the weapons,' said Lee.

'Yes. The war is fought with ideas. What better weapon for such a conflict than one of flesh and blood? You were grown, Jason. On a breeding farm. One of countless others. You were impregnated with absolute belief in the Block and its one story. Those ideas gave you the ability to kill.'

'But ideas can't...' began Jason, and then broke off.

'You saw the battlefield. You saw how many were dying. You know that ideas can kill.'

'And was I... what did I look like? I felt different when I went back. Like I had extra limbs and senses.'

'You looked much the same as you do now. But you had enhanced modes of expression. Organic communications systems. Channels through which to focus and use the beliefs you were given. You still have a shred of them left.'

'How did Jason end up here?' asked Lee suddenly. 'Why can't he remember any of this?'

Now, thought Phillip. Now comes the difficult part.

'The Fracture cannot allow the war to go on. We need to progress. To learn new stories. But while we are locked in this ceaseless carnage with the Block, we are as trapped as those we left behind. So the Committee – our war council – devised a plan. A virus to cripple Block weapons. To erase their genetic programming and destroy the loyalty to their masters. You might say that we plan to tell them a different story. One about the fragility of flesh and blood and the value of uncertainty. And so we decided to test the virus on a single, unimportant weapon. One whom they would never even notice was gone. We tested it on you.'

Jason nodded. His face was unreadable. Perhaps he was in shock. Perhaps he had known all along. Lee's eyes suddenly became even more distant. He frowned slightly and shook his head. Jason appeared to relax. Just a little.

'Go on,' he said. 'Tell me the rest.'

'We could not conduct such a test on the battlefield or take the risk of bringing one of the enemy into the Fracture to apply the virus. So we decided that once infected you would be brought here. In this realm, you were to learn and I was to watch. We thought this was a city where the Block would never come.'

'Why?' they both asked.

'Because it is a place they have tended to avoid. For reasons that I can't tell you.'

Again, they spoke as one.

'Why not?'

'It... it is not knowledge that can be shared outside of the Fracture. All you need know is that we meant you no harm. When the time came and we were sure there was no danger, I was to take you back to be studied by the Committee. If the experiment was a success, the virus would be deployed on a wider scale. Eventually, we might wreck the entire Block army. And so I have watched you.'

'I saw you once,' broke in Lee. 'Remember Jason? Near Cornish's?'

Phillip could not repress a slight chuckle.

'Ah, yes. Cornish. One of our better contacts in this realm. He sent you to the library that night. Didn't he, Lee?'

The adolescent nodded. He was trembling slightly. Phillip felt a sudden pang of guilt. Poor kid.

'We arranged that. We arranged for you to find Jason. The weapon needed a protector. We chose you. Who better than a damaged outsider to teach Jason about humanity?'

Lee turned away to face the graffiti-covered wall.

'You manipulated me,' he said quietly. 'All the time, you were controlling me...'

'Not all the time. We did not know the Block would have an agent here. We didn't know that you and Jason would end up being hunted or that you would run away. We didn't plan on you spending so much time together. I'm... sorry the plan went wrong. You were only supposed to be involved at the beginning. We knew that there would come a time when Jason would be forced to use his offensive ability to protect you. The use of that ability activated his homing instinct and returned him to the battlefield. It was the choice he made there, the choice between fighting for the Block or protecting a friend that would determine whether or not the plan was a success.'

'What now?' asked Jason. He was staring at Lee's back.

'You will come back to the Fracture with me. You'll be safe there. There will be some tests but they will be painless, I promise.'

'And what happens to Lee?'

Phillip turned to look at the adolescent. He was still facing the wall. Silent. Motionless.

'I will make arrangements with our agents in this time. He will be cared for. He has served us well. Without him, you would be dead and the whole experiment worthless. A job, money, whatever he wants will be provided.'

'I see,' said Jason quietly. 'So when does all this happen?'

'Now. I will take you to the Fracture. Lee?' The boy didn't turn round. His voice was toneless.

'What?'

'Go back to the commune. My agents will make contact soon. They will make arrangements for you. You will be provided for.'

Lee stared down at the floor and shrugged. 'Whatever.'

Phillip turned to Jason. The difficult act was done. The plan could be concluded. At last. He had succeeded after all.

'Are you ready now, Jason?'

The weapon took a step towards him, staring into the blank mask. For just a fraction of a second, Phillip was afraid of him. Jason might have lost his original offensive abilities but he was still a product of the enemy.

'I'm not going with you. I'm not leaving Lee.'

Damn. He still didn't fully understand.

'Jason,' he said gently. 'It's because of us that you met him. You—'

The weapon interrupted him, his voice quiet but without any fear.

'I know all that. I don't care. So you manipulated us, so you put us in the right place at the right time, so what? You said you lost control of the experiment? That you didn't know what happened when we ran away? Well, that's when I realised. That's when I knew that I loved him. So it's got nothing to do with you! You can't separate us no matter how fucking powerful you are!'

Lee suddenly turned to face Jason. He was trembling now, close to tears, both arms wrapped round his emaciated torso. Jason held out a hand and touched his acne-ravaged cheek.

'I won't leave you.'

'Even though...' Lee began, barely able to control his voice.

'Yes. I promise.'

Jason turned defiantly back to Phillip.

'I don't care about your war. I've left it behind. I chose Lee.'

Phillip tried to control his growing exasperation as he answered.

'Yes, but the virus was programmed to show you the battlefield at the right time. To give you that choice. The experiment—'

'Yes, I know! The experiment said I probably would. But you didn't know for sure, or why else was there an experiment in the first place? If you'd been certain, you'd have just used the virus. So there was still a doubt. So it was still my choice in the end.'

With a shock, Phillip realised that he had lost control of the situation. Breaking up a friendship would have been difficult but ultimately posed no serious obstacle. Even a normal sexual relationship would have succumbed when faced with the truth of the situation. But the connection between the two boys was so intense, so unconditional, that even the knowledge that they had been manipulated could not damage it. Perhaps it had even strengthened it.

Of course, he could forcibly take Jason into the Fracture. But then he would try to resist the necessary examinations and experiments. Worse, if he regarded them as his enemy once more, he might try to fight them. A rogue weapon in the Fracture did not bear thinking about.

'I know it is hard that you must part,' said Phillip. 'But some things have to be, no matter how cruel or unpleasant. This plan is too important to fail. The Committee will not abandon this chance to end the war.'

'The Committee,' said Lee. He had stopped shaking and his voice was suddenly strong again. 'They came up with all this, right? So why aren't they here instead of you?'

'They never leave the Fracture.'

Jason and Lee looked at each other. They nodded in silent agreement.

'Take us both to them,' said Jason.

'And let us talk to them,' completed Lee.

For a moment, Phillip was too astonished to reply. They were demanding to speak to the Committee! The arrogance! But then... if they went willingly, he could try other methods to convince. With them both in the Fracture, he might be able to persuade these absurdly uncooperative boys of the full reality they faced. And even if he could not, surely the Committee could convince them? Yes, the idea had merit...

'Very well,' he said.

He reached into his jerkin and produced a small bronze pendant on a chain. It was engraved with tiny symbols. He removed it from the chain and placed it on the ground at his feet.

'What now?' asked Lee.

'Wait.'

The lid of the pendant opened. Music began to play. A polka, gentle but building in volume. The air around the pendant began to shimmer and flicker.

'What is it?' whispered Lee.

'A key,' replied Phillip.

The rhythm was faster now and deafeningly loud. The tremendous noise was shaking the rickety building. Steam began to rise from the puddles as the dank water boiled. The wooden door splintered and the DANGER sign was ripped in two. One of the metal railings began to twist and melt, molten rivulets dripping to the floor.

Jason and Lee were standing close together, looking round them in trepidation. A wall behind them cracked and they started backing away.

'Do not be afraid,' commanded Phillip.

At least not for the moment, he silently added.

For a second, the world turned upside down. Philip felt himself plummeting down into the sky. Incomprehensible visions burst into the unending blindness of his world and then faded. He had made this journey before, but he had never got use to it. No one ever did. He could hear Jason and Lee's voices joined once more, this time in a cry of joyous exhilaration.

Mad, he thought. They are both quite mad.

As suddenly as it had begun, it was over. They had arrived. A warm sensation swept over Phillip, wrapping itself round him like a familiar blanket. He was home. Jason and Lee stood clinging to each other, both still twitching from the excitement of their brief journey. Well, he thought, the journey would be the least of it.

'Welcome to the Fracture,' he said.

Chapter Thirty

'Where are they?' asked Jason. 'Where are the Committee?'

Phillip hesitated before replying, savouring the feel of the warm wind against his body.

'We have some way to go before we reach the War Room,' he finally said. 'That is where you will meet the Committee.'

Lee was studying their surroundings.

'Is this a desert?' he asked.

Phillip laughed softly.

'It may appear that way. But there is more to it than that.'

Orange sand stretched in all directions, disturbed into swirling patterns of ridges and grooves by the wind. The sky was shot through with the blood red of approaching twilight. The sun sat full and bloated above them. On the horizon were formations that could have been mountains or buildings but which Phillip knew were neither.

'It reminds me of one of the images you made for me,' Lee said to Jason. The weapon nodded.

So, he had been transmitting images to Lee, thought Phillip. That was something else unexpected. Of course, Jason would have retained that skill – it was a by-product of his offensive capability – but the Committee had not predicted that he would use it to create pictures for his friend. That could prove important. Still, for the moment it would be better if he concealed his surprise at this latest revelation.

'You will still have some knowledge of us,' Phillip told him. 'Buried in your subconscious. But the Committee will be interested to hear about the images you created.'

'We have other things to talk to them about,' muttered Jason.

'Indeed. Come, then.'

He led them across the desert, each step reviving his flagging strength. He knew that all the two boys would see would be sand. But he knew that, here, every grain had significance. Each one was a story that the Block had tried to destroy.

Lee pointed to one of the structures on those horizons. It was an uneven dome.

'What is that? Do people live there?'

'No, it is a terminus.'

'Like for... buses?'

'Not really,' the agent replied kindly. 'They are the focal points and co-ordinators for the journeys to other realms. They elected for a stationary existence so that others might travel. They are much... admired.'

'They're alive?' breathed Jason.

'Yes. Technology born of flesh. Like you. Only not created for war.'

They carried on in silence for a while. The wind was much cooler now and there were no more patterns in the sands. There were fewer and fewer shapes on the horizon until eventually there was only one. A ring of massive stone monoliths. At its centre, something flickered.

'Is that it?' they asked simultaneously.

I wish they'd stop doing that, Phillip thought.

'Yes. That's the War Room.'

He was surprised to find himself feeling nervous. How would the Committee react to this turn of events? Would they be offended that an enemy weapon and his lover were demanding to speak to them? Worst of all, would they decide that Phillip had failed them?

They were very close now. The sand beneath their feet had gone, replaced by enormous flagstones. As they approached the stone circle, the true size of the pillars could be seen. They reached up endlessly into a sky that was suddenly dark and starless. Each column was inscribed with words from every language ever written. Phillip led Jason and Lee between two of the columns and then stopped. In the centre of the circle, a blue fire blazed without warmth. Round it stood the Committee.

There were ten of them. Ten tall figures in silver armour. Some were missing arms or legs. One was missing its head. The suits moved continually, joints creaking and scraping. Green and brown fluids were smeared on their chest plates. From deep within them came gurgling, hissing sounds. The light from the cold flames danced ceaselessly across the metal figures. As long as the war went on, this fire would blaze and the Committee would study it. Each flame represented a different part of the battlefield. Ground taken or lost was reported in each flicker. A spark held the death of billions. Only when the war was done would the fire go out. Only then could the Committee cease to be.

Phillip stepped forward, leaving the two boys behind him. One of the Committee raised an arm with no hand. In the open hole at the end of the sleeve, things moved.

The voice was deep and harsh.

'So, Phillip, you bring us visitors?'

'Yes.'

'And one of them is the infected weapon of our enemy?' continued another.

Jason and Lee came forward. The Committee gurgled and chattered among themselves. Outrage? Amusement? There was no way of telling.

'We want to talk to you,' said Jason.

A pause.

'Very well. Speak.'

'I'll tell you whatever you want to know,' said Jason. 'But I won't stay here. I won't leave Lee.'

'And what interest does a Block weapon have in a crippled, impoverished adolescent criminal?'

'I love him.'

Laughter. Loud, but not without sympathy.

'Oh, but the virus has taught you well. But now it is time for us to learn from you. Time for us to study you.'

Lee limped towards the Committee until he stood before one of the armoured figures. In the cold light of the fire, his pale face looked even more sickly.

'I won't let you hurt him.'

It was such an absurd sight that Phillip almost laughed out loud. This scrawny, spotty boy standing up to the unimaginable might of the creature before him. Another of the Committee moved closer to Lee with an ear-shredding scrape of metal on metal. One of its legs appeared to be on back to front. Its voice was gentle as it spoke to the boy.

'We are not without compassion. But these things must be done. And we do not need to hurt him to learn from him.'

It raised an arm and a stiff glove pointed at Jason. The weapon took an automatic step backwards, as though sensing its intention.

'Now,' it said. 'Let us begin the examination.'

Music started, the slightest sound. A waltz for surgical instruments, played on strings of stainless steel. The rest of the Committee were all turning in the same direction. The music grew louder and sharper. Jason looked confused. His head was cocked to one side, as though listening for a harmony that wasn't there. Lee hurried back to him. He took him by the shoulders.

'What are they doing to you?'

Jason blinked, his face still puzzled.

'Nothing. They're trying to do something, I'm sure. But it's not working.'

'I think... I think I can feel it too, Jason. You're right. They're not strong enough.'

Lee turned to the Committee with a grin.

'You hear that? You're not strong enough!'

The suit of armour lowered its hand. The helmet shifted to one side in a gesture of curiosity.

'Odd,' it muttered. 'Very odd indeed. Most puzzling.'

Unnoticed, the music had stopped. The Committee swung as one towards Phillip. And now, for the first time in decades, he was truly terrified. He felt their anger boring into him.

'You have failed,' said the one without a head, the voice rasping from a slit in its belly. 'You let them be together for too long. The virus has rewritten them both.'

'They are not as we expected,' said another. 'Not two creatures but one now.'

'They are unique. And becoming more so every minute.'

'They are beyond the reach of our techniques. They are so enmeshed; we cannot tell one from the other.'

'We cannot read the weapon.'

'We don't even know what it is any more.'

'We cannot learn from him.'

'The plan has failed. The experiment is worthless.'

'You have failed us, Phillip.'

Phillip heard Jason and Lee laughing with relief, saw them hug each other. The Committee were no longer paying attention to them. All ten had turned to Phillip now.

'There were unexpected problems,' he said quickly, wondering if he was talking for his life. 'There is a Block agent in the city. We did not foresee that. And these two ran away. I had to create a Seeker to find them. Even then it was not—'

A voice of tempered fury silenced him.

'The responsibility for this plan was given to you and to you alone, Phillip. We trusted you as a man of guile and cunning. So the responsibility for salvaging it is yours also. Take these two back to the realm from which you came. Return only when you have a solution. When this can all be turned to some good.'

'But—'

'Enough!'

The blue fire suddenly roared and billowed. Even as he shrank from its freezing grasp, the ground was falling away...

...and once more they stood among the litter and graffiti of the tumbledown old ride building. It was oppressively hot after the chill of the war room. Jason and Lee were kissing each other, laughing and talking at the same time.

Phillip leant against one of the railings. All he could think of was that he had failed. Events had overtaken him. His great mission had come to nothing. Whatever the nature of the mental connection that had formed between the two boys, it was strong enough to shield them from the Committee's powers. The virus had changed Jason and he had transmitted it to Lee, perhaps when he was feeding the boy images. The more images were sent, the more Lee had been affected. And, without knowing it, he had been transmitting the virus back to Jason. Each time the virus and the boys had been changed. An unending circle, all leading... where?

Phillip would have to find a way to resolve the situation. Something had to be produced from all this. At least then he might be allowed to retire to the archives with a few scraps of his dignity left. But he seemed to be surrounded by chaos and bad luck. What chance did he have?

A voice he had not heard before broke in on his dismal thoughts.

'What the hell is going on here?'

Chapter Thirty-one

Rebecca was sure that she had been dreaming but she couldn't remember much about it. There had been a shape, an object. No, not an object; something alive. It had been talking to her. It had seemed friendly enough but she couldn't remember what it had said. It must have been important, though, because she had been straining to hear its voice.

She turned on to her left side, trying without success to get more comfortable on the bed. The mattress seemed to be made of awkward lumps and bumps. She definitely wasn't staying here for another night.

With a sigh, she gave up the struggle and sat up. The room looked even worse in the morning light than it had when she had arrived a few hours ago. The yellow walls were covered in pink hieroglyphs. A plastic pharaoh mask was nailed to the door. Even the wardrobe was shaped like a mummy's casket. Each room in this hotel was designed to look as though it came from a different time. She had opted for the Egyptian room, which had sounded quite romantic until she had actually seen it.

Still, after two hours on the road, she had had to stop somewhere and this place had been the closest. It seemed there was a small archaeological site nearby and the proprietors of the hotel had been quick to cash in on the tourist trade. After she checked out this morning, she might take a look at the ruins. They were Norman, apparently, though strangely the hotel didn't have a Norman room.

Her mind went back to the dream. She usually remembered her dreams, but the memory of this one was very vague. It had seemed important, but then didn't they all? After the events of the previous day, it was no wonder that her subconscious was a bit mixed up.

What would Jason and Lee be doing now? Waking up in their new home, presumably. Saying goodbye to them last night felt very distant now, as though that too had been a dream. She tried to picture the lives that they would live in the Dancing Devil commune. Probably they would be safe. Certainly they could look after themselves. All the same…

Breakfast. She should order breakfast. She didn't expect it would be very nice but a meal would give her some energy to start the day with. The first day of her new life. She had been clear about that yesterday. She was going to travel, visit new places and meet new people. But in the cold light of morning, she was no longer so sure. How could she start her travels when she didn't even know what kind of place she had left Jason and Lee in? And then there had been her dream. She was certain it had something to do with them.

I have to be certain, she thought. I have to know that they're OK. She had known Jason and Lee for barely two days, but they were the most important friends she had ever had. All her life she had wanted something unique. She had found it in them.

Rebecca reached for the Sphinx-shaped phone by the bed. She would order breakfast. Once she had eaten, she would drive back to the commune.

Just to make sure.

Johnnie Varney was glad of the silence. If he didn't have to speak, he didn't have to think. If he didn't have to think, he didn't have to feel. If he stayed motionless and silent for long enough, the hollowness in his stomach might consume him. He would be free then. Free from the shame. Free from the memories of the pretty girl lying dead at Hayden's feet. Free from having to be Johnnie Varney.

They had been waiting for more than two hours now. Each second lasted an eternity. Nothing moved in the empty landscape before them. There was not even the sound of distant cars. Standing beside him on the garage forecourt, the old man seemed unable to keep still. He clicked his tongue against the roof of his mouth, fiddled with the cuffs of his dusty jacket, drummed the fingers of one hand against his chest. His eyes constantly scanned the horizon, waiting for his troops to return with the two boys. Varney hoped they would soon. While he was alone with the

Professor, he had the perfect opportunity to kill him. To be a hero and avenge the innocents that had died. But he was far too afraid of his master. At least when the Staunchers were here, he had an excuse not to act. Alone with the old man, he had only fear and shame.

It came as a shock when Professor Hayden suddenly turned to him and smiled. Varney was sure that the stench of cigars was even stronger now.

'Soon, Varney, we will both get what we want.'

'Yes, Professor,' he responded dully.

'I shall have the two boys. The bait to draw our enemies out into the open. And then they shall all die. And you too will die. That's what you dream of, isn't it, Varney?'

The bastard knew. Knew everything. He had not even allowed Johnnie secrets. He must have read every thought. And what was worse, he simply didn't care.

'I shall give you that gift, Varney. I shall let death wrap you in its grey arms and free you from the misery of yourself. You might suffer a little first. Just for my entertainment, you understand. But then you shall have your freedom.'

'Thank you, Professor Hayden.'

'The Block is generous, Varney. We know the true shape of your desires. You have craved death from the moment your wretched existence began.'

'Yes, Professor.'

What else was there to say?

Hayden turned back to the horizon. He gave a sharp exclamation and Johnnie felt a flood of relief as he followed his gaze. Figures were racing towards them. It was over.

And yet... seven had set out. With the two boys captive there should have been nine of them. But as they drew closer, he could see only six, each in the grey Stauncher armour.

'Something has gone wrong,' spat Hayden, fists clenched tight. 'They have failed me.'

The Staunchers reached the garage and clattered to a halt on the forecourt. They were hunched over, panting with exhaustion. Their uniforms were drenched with sweat and they had lost their guns. Even though he was unable to focus on their faces, Varney could tell that something terrible had happened to them.

'Where are they?' roared Hayden.

One of the figures straightened. When it spoke, there was barely contained terror in its voice. Varney couldn't remember the last time he had heard one of his former soldiers sound afraid.

'I am so sorry, Professor. We were attacked. A man in a mask. He got into our minds—'

'The Fracture agent!' hissed the Professor.

'He confused us... made us think we were the enemy we were attacking... it... hurt.'

The voice was a whimper now.

'We dropped our guns... ran away. Couldn't help it... so tired now... Professor.'

The old man moved closer to him.

'Not good enough.'

The Stauncher emitted a choking gasp and toppled over. Hayden's face twitched into a bitter smile as he scrutinised the five that still stood.

'Perhaps the rest of you don't fully understand my point. Let me explain further.'

Another Stauncher gurgled and fell. The four survivors drew themselves stiffly to attention. They paid no heed to the corpses sprawled across the tarmac.

'That's better! I will not tolerate failure. We attack again. The agent and the two boys are in the commune. So we go there and we kill them. You have no weapons now, but your bodies will serve as my shield. You will all die, but that is unimportant. Your lives will be sacrificed to a greater cause. You understand now?'

'Yes, Professor,' they chanted in unison. Varney found his own lips moving in time to theirs, though no sound emerged.

Hayden turned to him.

'You go, too. Time for you to earn your freedom.'

Johnnie Varney nodded. He found himself looking at one of the corpses. He was sure he remembered the name. Was it Levine? Or perhaps Brooks? A man who liked onions and luxury holidays in the summer and who... No, it was gone. It didn't matter anyway. There was nothing that he could have done that would have saved him, even if he could have recalled the man's name. Instead he thought of his own death and the comfort it would bring.

Chapter Thirty-two

Harvey might not have been in charge of the Dancing Devil commune, but he was certainly the one who ran it. His room was more like an office than a place to live. A desk sagging under the weight of mounds of paper faced the door. On the wall behind it were shelves stuffed with binders and box files. The small bed in one corner seemed like an afterthought, a token acknowledgement that he occasionally needed to rest.

When they had entered, Harvey had been studying a sheaf of yellow documents covered with neatly written figures. Both of his hands and one eyebrow were stained with blue ink. He had not looked up, but he had recognised the knock.

'Hello, Freddie,' he had said. 'A good month we've had. Three per cent increase on the jewellery sales. That's great, isn't it?'

Still sounding stunned, Freddie had replied, 'I've brought some people to see you.'

And then Harvey had looked up at them. At Freddie, dazed and trembling. At Jason and Lee, standing close together. At the expressionless, unblinking Seeker. And finally at Phillip. He had gasped and pulled back in his chair, as though thinking he could hide away from his visitors in a corner of the room.

Phillip had walked towards him, his voice smooth and calm. 'We don't have much time. You must listen.'

Since then, Phillip and Harvey had been talking. The Fracture agent had only explained so much about what was happening. Enough to make it obvious that the Dancing Devil commune was no longer a safe place for anyone. Jason stood with Lee by one of the shelves. Sometimes he listened to them talk. Other times he tuned it out, focusing only on Lee.

'Think Harvey will listen?'

'Don't see he's got much choice. If they don't go they'll probably all die. Phillip's sure that Block agent will come here.'

'Harvey looks like he's scared of Phillip. I think you're right. Are you?'

'Not any more.'

Jason touched the adolescent inside and heard the pleasure in his mind. They were together. That was the important thing. They had defied the Committee and won. He remembered Lee confronting them, his frail figure dwarfed by the massive, armoured creatures. He had been so proud of him. When they had returned, Jason had felt happier than he would have thought possible.

And then Freddie had appeared, the Seeker at his back with a gun. After he had seen them at the lake, he had decided to follow Jason and Lee at a distance, wanting to know more about the two new arrivals. As the Staunchers had fled back down the hill, he had been forced to hide in the bushes. When they had gone, he had cautiously emerged and continued up the steps. He had just found the corpse of the Stauncher when the Seeker appeared behind him. It had no orders to kill him, so it had taken him to Phillip.

The Fracture agent had told him that the two boys were in danger and needed a way out of the commune other than the main gate. That was where their enemies were waiting. Still stunned by the sight of the strange man, Freddie managed to stammer that, if there was another exit, only one man would know where it was.

'So let me get this right,' said Harvey, his tone expressionless. 'Jason and Lee, who only joined us yesterday, are being hunted by an organisation called the Block. And, though you cannot tell me who exactly these people are, you are asking me to accept that they will kill everyone here just to get at them?'

'They may kill you all anyway,' interrupted Phillip. 'You would be an automatic enemy.'

'I see. So, not very nice people, then?'

It was hard to tell if he was being sarcastic.

'I saw them,' interjected Freddie. 'There was something... wrong with their faces.'

'Not just theirs,' said Harvey evenly, looking at Phillip.

'I was... injured in a skirmish. I assure you I'm not a monster.'

Jason saw Harvey nod, apparently accepting the answer. It had been the same with Freddie. It was as though they found Phillip's appearance so unsettling that they were happy for a simple explanation to explain it away.

Harvey turned his attention to the Seeker. It did not respond to him. It was waiting to be told what to do. Jason and Lee had yet to exchange a single word with it. Its blankness made them both uncomfortable. A mind so silent.

'He is a deaf mute,' said Phillip, anticipating Harvey's question. 'A loyal friend. But you will not be able to communicate directly with him. His name is… Graham.'

'I see,' said Harvey.

'Do you think that's true?' Lee asked Jason silently.

'What?'

'His… its name?'

'Could be.'

'What do you think Phillip's planning?'

'Not sure. This is taking too long, though.'

'You've got to listen to Phillip,' said Lee loudly. 'We've got to get away from here before they come back.'

Harvey turned to him.

'And why exactly are these people trying to kill you? What have you done?'

'Does it fucking matter?'

'Yes, Lee. It does matter. And there's no need to swear at me.'

'We—' started Lee.

'I killed one of them,' said Jason. 'He was going to hurt Lee and so I killed him.'

A silence descended on the room. Jason remembered that night. The power surging through him, burning the man from existence. A power that was gone now, replaced by something far better. Could he make Harvey understand that he had had to do it? That it had not been a matter of heroism or cruelty, but an instinctive response?

Harvey ran a hand through his beard, frowning slightly. He picked up a pen and drummed it absently on the desk before him. Eventually, he seemed to come to a decision.

'Well, at least you're honest. Hmm, I suppose we'd better do as you say. I'd rather not take the chance of putting everyone here in danger.'

He looked directly at Jason.

'You have to look after the people you care for, don't you?'

Jason nodded.

'Yes. You do.'

Harvey stood up, rubbing his hands briskly.

'We'll tell everyone we need to temporarily evacuate. Bare essentials only; we can come back for the important stuff. Half an hour and we should be ready. Some people will complain, of course, but then some people always do, don't they?'

He smiled at them, as though he were arranging a day trip, but Jason could see a gleam of sadness in the man's eyes. He came round to their side of the desk, picking an apparently random folder from a shelf on the way.

'We can't use the main entrance,' said Phillip.

'No, well, I suppose that's obvious enough. But don't you worry, there's a rear exit. Not what you'd call an official one, just a gap in the old fence. Very overgrown, it is. Should be all right, though. Well, I'd best be going, hadn't I? Get things started.'

Harvey left the room, the door swinging shut behind him. Seconds later, they could hear him giving the orders for evacuation. Protesting replies were quickly silenced. Soon there were the sounds of doors opening and shutting as people rushed from one room to another and back again.

Phillip turned to Freddie.

'Do you think they'll be able to do it in time?'

Freddie managed a smile.

'The amount of cocaine pouring into this place, speed is never a problem.'

He headed for the door, some of his old swagger returning.

'Still I'd better go kick their arses or they'll want a sing-song before they go. I'll see you later.'

After he had gone, Phillip turned to the two boys.

'Leaving with these people will have its advantages,' he observed.

'Cover for us, you mean?' said Lee.

'Exactly.'

'And then?' asked Jason.

There is a lost pathway nearby and—'

'A what?' interrupted Lee.

The mask turned in his direction.

'An old route, overgrown by time and all but forgotten. It will take us straight into the heart of the city. And then—'

'Yes?' they chorused together. Jason liked the sound of their voices in harmony.

'And then we shall think. The Committee want me to find an answer. I cannot do that while the Block agent knows where we are. We need a respite to consider our situation.'

'Our situation?' echoed Jason. There was a tone of bitterness in Phillip's reply.

'Yes. It seems our fates are joined together.'

'What you did to that other guy, can't you do that to the Block agent?' asked Lee hesitantly.

'No. With his troops, I could confuse them, transmit conflicting information to them and make them see themselves as their own enemy. The conflict devastates them. But he is far more powerful. I can kill him, of course. But he is as strong as I am. And while we are here he has far too many advantages.'

The Seeker suddenly spoke, its voice as flat as ever. 'The enemy is moving.'

'How close?' asked Phillip sharply. Jason was sure there was a note of trepidation in his voice.

'An hour and they will be here.'

The masked man swung towards Jason and Lee.

'Remember, we may have to stand and fight. If so, the Block agent will show no pity. And neither shall I.'

Chapter Thirty-three

Rebecca had never seen a dead body before. She had heard that they didn't look as real as the ones in the web shows and, certainly, the two lifeless figures at her feet seemed artificial. Their expressionless faces were too alike, as though they had been cast from the same mould. There was no lingering expression to indicate whether they had died slowly in agony or quickly and painlessly. Both corpses were clad in grey body armour that made her think of a paramilitary organisation. A sickening stench of tobacco that caught at the back of her throat hung over the bodies.

With a shudder, she forced herself to turn away. She ought to call the police and report this. It would most likely be a long time before anyone else found the bodies on such a desolate stretch of road. She had been driving at speed and had given the abandoned old garage only a second's glance as she passed. At the sight of two unmoving figures sprawled across the tarmac, Rebecca had brought the car screeching to a halt. For one terrible moment, she had thought it must be Jason and Lee. When she had found that they were strangers, her first reaction had been relief. She wondered if she ought to feel guilty about that.

She couldn't delay, she decided, not even to make a phone call. She was certain that whoever these people had been, their deaths were linked to her two friends. The hunters must be drawing closer.

Rebecca got back into her car and started the engine. She made herself take a deep breath. Guilt would have to wait for the moment. She was heading into danger, of that she was certain. A danger that could quite easily take her life. But there was no turning back now. It had been Rebecca's choice to involve herself in this. Right from the start, as she had surreptitiously listened to Jason and Lee talking in the café, she had understood that she was taking a massive risk entering their world. Now she had to face the consequences of that risk. Head on and without flinching.

Gripping the wheel with steady hands, she drove at full speed for the commune.

The fat girl was annoying Phillip. She kept trying to rouse the others into song. One or two joined in half-heartedly but most of them pointedly ignored her. The warbling of her voice seemed to echo through the dense, overgrown woodland around them. A few birds replied with angry screeches from the tops of the trees.

There was a sudden rustling as a rodent scurried out from one of the bushes, zigzagging round the strangers tramping through its home. The girl gave a scream of delight and started squealing at a tall man with a particularly absurd beard. Was the stupid bitch trying to draw attention to them?

'That's Suzanne,' explained Lee, with a sour smile. 'She organises discos.'

'I can imagine.'

Phillip and Lee had been walking side by side for some time. Just ahead of them was Freddie, who was talking to Jason.

Freddie the Hatchetman, thought Phillip wryly. How absurd. The would-be singer was telling the weapon about his recent musical projects. He was still in denial, of course. All the people around them, the 'Dancers' as they called themselves, were participating in these events as though in a trance. Occasionally one of them looked at Phillip's blank mask or at the Seeker, trailing behind him with a gun slung over its shoulder, but they would invariably turn away. In a day's time, their memories would be hazy and unclear. They would recall only that there had been strangers in their midst.

It was a peculiar experience to be surrounded by people once more. Phillip was more used to being alone. Still, they were making swift progress. The rutted path was narrow and they could only walk in lines of twos and threes, but he was certain that they would reach the exit before the Block agent found them.

'Those guys that attacked us,' said Lee quietly. 'I couldn't see their faces. I tried, but it was like there was nothing there.'

Even in his bleak mood, Phillip couldn't help liking the adolescent. He had stood up to the Committee as if he faced such awesome beings every day. His recklessness verged on madness but there was no doubt he had been well chosen to protect Jason. He had embraced his mental connection to the weapon with a fervour known only to the young and the desperate.

'The Block agent has altered them,' he explained. 'Now they only have one purpose. Everything else has been removed. They have no need of expression, so their faces appear blank.'

'So, they're becoming weapons? Like Jason was?'

The boy was quick. He might not fully understand what was happening, but he grasped what was important.

'A crude form, yes. Weapons like Jason are manufactured with precision. These are handmade. Designed to be used once and thrown away.'

'I still don't get what you did to them.'

'The agent's methods were clumsy. He left them susceptible to attack. I introduced chaos and confusion into them. They were unable to cope with it.'

'You put ideas in them? Like Jason does?'

'In a way. I used the Seeker's mind to project and enhance my attack.'

Lee nodded. Looking at him, Phillip thought the boy was even paler than usual. Beneath his acne, his skin seemed almost translucent. The way he moved was different, too, as though his centre of gravity had shifted slightly. It must be another effect of his relationship with the weapon. Where would it end? he wondered.

Jason stopped and turned to face them. 'We've reached the exit,' he said.

Ahead of them was a chain-link fence, sagging in places but still upright. An uneven gap had been torn through one section, the edges on either side twisted and jagged. The Dancers were moving slowly through the opening. Some of them looked frightened now as though they were walking into a new land.

'I'd better go and talk to Harv,' said Freddie.

He determinedly made his way to the front of the line. Jason watched him go and then turned to Lee.

'He told me he was gonna write a song about all this. About us,' Lee giggled.

'Proximity to war agents often affects people from different realms in strange ways,' observed Phillip.

He would be glad to be away from this odd little commune. From what little he had seen, the people here were just as trapped as those in the city. In the end, they would most likely end up recreating the life they thought they had left behind.

As they passed through the gap in the fence, he saw that the trees on the other side were less dense. The path was broader and split to the left and right.

He became aware of a concerned babble from the crowd.

'Where is he?'

'I'm sure he was behind us – near Jeanie,' said a long-haired man. 'When I was talking to her about the likely pH content of the soil here. I was hoping he might overhear and—'

'No, that wasn't him,' interrupted someone else impatiently. 'That was me and I just wanted you to shut up!'

'Who do you think—'

'Don't start, you two!'

'Well, he must be here somewhere!'

Freddie came up to them, his forehead furrowed with worry.

'Harv isn't here. He must have stayed behind.'

'Maybe he didn't want to come with us,' said Jason. 'He looked kind of sad when we were getting ready to leave.'

'Stupid old fool,' muttered Freddie. 'He's stayed underground for too long.'

The last few stragglers had come through the gap in the fence. None of them knew what had happened to Harvey. Without him they looked lost. Suzanne began screeching in dismay until someone sharply told her to shut up.

Phillip inwardly cursed. He didn't have time for this. Jason and Lee were his sole responsibility and concern. He could not tolerate delay. He turned to Freddie.

'You'll have to lead them away from here. It's too dangerous to go back.'

Freddie pointed at the Seeker. It did not respond to the attention. 'What about him? Couldn't he go back and find him?'

'No. There isn't time. You must lead the others away from here.'

Phillip knew that the Seeker could have found the missing man. But the longer they waited, the greater the danger. If it was necessary to sacrifice Harvey, that was the way it must be.

'I doubt the Block agent would pay much attention to Harvey anyway,' he said. 'He is of no importance to him.'

'So you think he might be all right?'

'There is every possibility,' lied Phillip.

Freddie sighed. Then he turned to address the anxious throng.

'OK, everyone, Harv has decided to go it alone. He always likes to do things his own way. We'll have to go on without him.'

There were unhappy noises from the crowd. Freddie carried on regardless.

'There's a place about two hours' walk from here. Another commune. Smaller than ours, but there should be room for us all. I know some of the people, so there won't be any problems with us staying as long as we want. All right?'

Gradually the rumbles of disquiet turned to murmurs of agreement. Their relief was palpable. They had found someone new to make decisions for them. Phillip wondered if Freddie realised he had just appointed himself as their leader. He wasn't going to have much time for singing from now on.

Freddie held out his hand. 'Goodbye, then.'

Phillip shook his hand, noting the other man's barely perceptible shudder at the contact.

'Thank you for you help, Freddie.'

'No problem.'

Freddie turned to Jason and Lee.

'I don't know who you're really running from and I don't think you'd tell me. But good luck, anyway.'

'Thanks,' muttered Jason.

Freddie looked at the Seeker for a moment. It stared back at him without moving. He shrugged.

'We'd better be going.'

He raised his arm as an indication to the others that it was time to resume their journey. Like obedient children, the group followed behind him. They took the path to the left, away from the city. The woodland swallowed them up. For a while their voices could still be heard. Phillip was certain he could make out the fat girl singing. Then there was silence.

'What do you think happened to Harvey?' asked Jason.

'I don't know,' replied Phillip. 'Come, we must hurry.'

They took the path that led back to the city. It would take them round the perimeter of the old theme park and to the beginning of the Fracture pathway. They might yet escape their pursuers. If not, they would have to stand and fight. All of them: a former weapon, an adolescent criminal and a mindless Seeker. If it did come to a fight, reflected Phillip, he would have a very unusual army.

'It's strange,' said Lee quietly. 'We were here a day and everything changed. They've had to leave their home, get a new leader. Just 'cos we arrived.'

'You are causing new stories to happen,' replied Phillip. 'It is what the Fracture has always wanted.'

'New stories?' repeated Jason.

'Yes.'

'And how do you think our story will end?' chorused the two boys.

Phillip stopped. Both of them were staring at him, their faces unreadable. He had the sense that they knew something that he didn't, that they were waiting. But for what?

'I don't know,' he said. 'We'll just have to wait and see, won't we?'

Chapter Thirty-four

Varney could see Hayden's lips moving soundlessly. Was he talking to himself or to the rest of his people? He was sure that the old man never stopped scheming. For decades there had been stories of computers that planned wars down to the finest detail, dispassionately sacrificing hundreds of troops to gain an advantage. Considering how ineptly most wars were fought, the idea was hardly a credible one. All the same, the rumours persisted. For a while he had suspected Professor Hayden was the legend made flesh, a computer with skin. Now he was certain that he was something even worse.

Johnnie hadn't thought about what they would find waiting for them at the commune. He was going to his death and that was all that mattered. It was an easy matter to get into the enemy stronghold. The Staunchers had disabled the electric lock on the fence during their first attack. No one had repaired it since.

Silently, they had made their approach in a tight formation with the Professor and himself at the rear. There were no guards. No one about at all in fact. The wasteland around them was as empty as it was desolate.

Then they had seen him. A short, heavy-set bearded man with a walking stick. Even at a distance, it was obvious that he was unarmed. He was standing in front of a small brick building. Behind him was a metal hatch; some sort of entrance. As they drew nearer, Varney could see that the hatch was open to reveal a tunnel leading downwards.

The bearded man studied them for a while before speaking.

'Here already, are you? Should have guessed, really. Should have gone with the others. But I couldn't do it. Couldn't bring myself to leave. Stupid, I know. But, you see, it was the only place I've ever been happy. Suppose that's all over now though, isn't it?'

'Where—' began Hayden, but the man hadn't finished.

'Wanted somewhere I could be free from it all. Where everyone could live in freedom. But I think I might have got it wrong. They all had to work so hard. Day in, day out. Never time to enjoy being free. The machines weren't right, people were always getting hurt. Never wanted that.'

'Where are they?' demanded Professor Hayden. 'Tell us and it will be quick.'

The man shook his head.

'Couldn't tell you that now, could I? Met them, you see, the boys you're chasing. Whatever they've done, they deserve their chance at freedom.'

One of the Staunchers stepped forward and punched him in the face. There was the crunch of bone and his beard was suddenly full of blood. He collapsed, whimpering with agony. His stick clattered to the ground beside him. A boot smashed hard into his ribs. A cry of pain. Another kick, harder. The other three stepped forward. They kicked in perfect time with the first.

Varney closed his eyes, trying to shut out the sound of toe cap against flesh, the low chuckle of the stinking old man beside him. These were people he had once known. His loyal troops. His friends. And this is what they had become: a circle of faceless monsters beating a sad, harmless old eccentric. He heard a despairing gurgle and forced himself to look. This was his fault. He must see the results of his actions. The Staunchers stepped away from the bloody ruin at their feet. Hayden studied their work with a satisfied smile.

'Varney, you and the others search down there. See what you can find. I shall see what I can learn from our friend here before he dies.'

He heard himself say 'yes' and walked towards the hatch. The things that had once been people fell into step behind him. Their boots were bright red now. Johnnie Varney entered the tunnel without looking back and began the walk downwards. He was certain that they would find no one here, but it was of no importance. He knew what he was going to do.

Chapter Thirty-five

'It doesn't look very safe,' said Jason.

He stared down into the blackness. A faint light glittered in the depths, but he couldn't make out the source. Whatever he had been expecting of the pathway, it wasn't this. He and Lee had almost walked past it when Phillip had called them to a halt. The city was now visible through the trees, though still some way away. They could just make out the faint sounds of construction work. At their feet was a rusted square hatch set at an angle in the earth and shrouded by leaves. The Seeker had heaved it open, the hinges muttering in annoyance. Beneath was a narrow, vertical shaft. There was a ladder set into one side but only the first few rungs were visible.

'It's only a short climb,' said Phillip. 'There are lights at the bottom.'

Jason looked around. The trees weren't as numerous here. They were very exposed now. He told himself they would be safer beneath the ground.

'OK,' muttered Lee. 'Let's go then.'

'Go down first if you want, Lee.'

'No. Phillip said it was only a short climb. I'll be all right. I'm getting a bit better with heights.'

Phillip went down first. Then Lee. Jason waited only a few seconds before he followed. The metal rungs were dry and brittle under his hands. An unpleasant smell, like rotten fruit, drifted up from the darkness. Only a little daylight seeped down from the open hatch, illuminating his way. Glancing up cautiously, he saw the shape of the Seeker above him. The ladder creaked beneath their combined weight. He found himself holding his breath, terrified that the whole structure would give way and send them plummeting into the depths.

With a sudden echoing clang, the last trace of light was gone. The Seeker had closed the hatch.

Jason forced himself to start breathing again, tried to think only of the action of climbing, hand over hand, downwards. The hard, unyielding rock of the invisible walls pressed close, threatening to swallow him up. Then Lee's voice was inside him, reassuring and strong.

'It'll be okay, Jason.'

'My hands are slippery.'

'Yeah, mine too. But don't worry, I won't let you fall.'

'I never thought I'd be scared of the dark, Lee.'

'I reckon everyone is.'

Jason forced himself to look down. He could just make out Lee on the rungs below him. The light beneath them was a little brighter now.

'Nearly there now, Jason.'

'Lee, I feel...'

'So do I.'

Phillip had reached the foot of the ladder. The illumination was now coming from his hand. Jason heard Lee jump to the ground. He quickened his movements and at last there was the welcome feel of a solid surface beneath his feet. Gratefully, he let go of the ladder. Seconds later, the Seeker jumped down beside him. Its face showed no sign of exertion or relief.

Phillip was holding an ornate brass oil lamp, the flame dancing in a long glass tube. It must have been left here by whoever built the tunnel, thought Jason, burning in solitude until it was needed. Phillip fiddled with the base and the flame blazed higher. They were in a wide tunnel. Brown brick walls sloped away from them on either side. Heavy flagstones paved the floor, thick clumps of moss forcing their way up through the cracks.

'This way,' said Phillip, his voice calm, almost contented. Jason had the impression that he liked it down here.

The masked figure led them forwards. Jason and Lee followed side by side, the Seeker bringing up the rear. The walls were not regular, but were broken up by strange protuberances. Long, spindly shapes emerged from the brickwork, reminding Jason of limbs. Some were shaped like arms and legs, others more resembled the claws and antennae of lobsters. There were occasional low archways leading further downwards. Jason didn't like to imagine what lay beyond them. The heavy, rotten odour was overpowering.

Lee broke the silence.

'This reminds me of a story my mum used to tell me.'

'Go on,' said Jason. He knew the boy was trying to take his mind off their strange surroundings.

'It was about a man called – I can't remember his name – but he was a prince. And he lived on this island where they had to send people to be sacrificed on another island, 'cos the people there were more powerful than they were. The prince decided he wanted to put a stop to it. So he went to the island on the ship with the people that were gonna be sacrificed. And he found out that they were all sent into a big labyrinth. And there was a monster that lived there, half man, half bull, and it ate all the sacrifices. So he went into the labyrinth and he took a ball of string so he could find his way back. And he found the monster and he killed it before it could eat the sacrifices. And then he took them home.'

'The Minotaur,' said Phillip.

'What?' they asked in unison.

'The monster was called the Minotaur. It is a very old story. It's been retold many times. The original is in the Fracture archives.'

'Right,' said Lee. 'Well, I always liked it. It's like... however frightening things are, you can find a way out.'

Phillip's sheathed head nodded.

'It is a story with many possible interpretations.'

They carried on in silence. The tunnel began to widen, the walls reaching higher and higher above them. The smell was much less pungent and the shadows less dense. Looking up, Jason saw an irregular crack in the roof, through which daylight was leaking. The further they went, the broader it became. Soon, they could see the sky. There were sounds, too: the throb of motors, the rumble of production lines. From somewhere there came the crackling voice of a tannoy system.

'We're under the city,' said Lee quietly.

'That's right,' said Phillip. 'We'll soon be near the centre. This route cuts a journey of hours into minutes.'

He set down the now unnecessary lamp and strode on. As calm, confident and determined as when they had first met him.

The surface of the walls were broken up here by geometric, metal shapes of all sizes that thrust outwards, like half-born machines. Industrial pipes wormed their way across the brickwork and cables trailed down from circular orifices into bulky terminals that were set in the flagstones.

The crack in the roof was huge now and they could see enormous warehouses glowering down at them from the world above. 'Won't someone see us?' asked Jason.

'Why should they?' asked Phillip rhetorically. 'This is where they generate the power for manufacturing. Who would think to come here? No one even stops to think that such places must exist. If they did, they would be afraid.'

Lee was staring upwards.

'Must be one of Mydia Hycron's compounds,' he said.

'Possibly. The lost pathways run through the guts of the city.'

'How did they start?' asked Lee.

'I don't know. Perhaps they started themselves.' The deliberately evasive answer annoyed Jason for some reason.

'Stop trying to be so mysterious,' he said.

'You're not very good at it,' Lee laughed. Phillip didn't reply.

The air about them was thick with a new smell: the odour of oil. Jason began to feel giddy and light-headed. From some of the openings in the walls, he could hear what sounded like the hiss of gas and the churning of dense fluids.

Beside him, Lee was searching his pockets anxiously. 'What's the matter?'

'I just remembered. I dropped my knife when we were attacked. I thought maybe I'd picked it up again and forgotten, but it's gone.'

Jason knew that Lee felt vulnerable without a blade. He indicated the Seeker, and the gun slung over its shoulder.

'We've still got a weapon.'

'Yeah,' said Lee. 'I just hope that's enough.'

'If not... we'll find a way,' said Jason.

Lee was looking at his hand again. He held it out to Jason. The palm was wet with a silver fluid.

'Do you know what this means?'

Jason looked at his own hands and saw the same fluid seeping through the skin.

'Yes. Do you?'

'Yes.'

'Are you scared, Lee?'

'A bit.'

'Me too but…'

'Yeah, I know.'

'Soon, then.'

Lee smiled.

'Soon.'

Johnnie Varney was dying. Blood gushed from his slit wrists, forming a pool at his feet. He lay slumped back in the chair, eyes roving absently over the workbench before him. He could still hear the Staunchers banging on the door. They would be dead soon, too. Perhaps they would be pleased. Perhaps they too had been suffering in silence all this time, some small shred of humanity left to them that was horrified by the atrocities they were committing. He hoped so.

It had been easy in the end. They had made their way down here to the commune workroom. It was a cluttered place, long benches full of tools, chairs scattered about, machines against the walls. There was evidence of half-completed, abandoned tasks everywhere.

They had soon found a door leading to the dormitory. Varney had sent the four surviving Staunchers in to search for clues. Then he had shifted the heaviest machine he could find in front of the door. He was surprised and vaguely pleased by his own strength. It had seemed to take them a long time to realise he had tricked them. Maybe the possibility just hadn't occurred to them until it was too late.

Varney had found the generator room close by. There was plenty of fuel for a fire. Once it was begun and he was sure it could not be put out, he returned to the workroom. Finding a blade sharp enough had been tricky, but he had finally chanced upon a small knife used for carving pendants. The blade had neatly sliced open the veins.

After that, he had sat down to wait. The pain had been unbearable at first, but it was starting to fade. It was getting difficult to breathe with the heavy smoke filling his lungs. He could hear screams, but he was sure they weren't his own. Somewhere he could see his grandfather's face. He seemed disappointed in his grandson, but that was only to be expected.

This wasn't the death he had hoped for. He had dreamed of dying a hero, mourned by the whole city. But it was not to be. His life had always been leading him to this place, to this lonely ending. Perhaps if he had realised that sooner, he might have been spared all the sorrow and regret. But he knew now and that was all that mattered.

Up above, Professor Hayden had finished with the shattered lump of meat. The last dregs of information had been taken. This meat had run the commune. The meat had spoken to the weapon, to its adolescent friend and to the Fracture agent. There had also been someone else. A fourth figure the meat had not been able to properly focus on. But what did that matter? The meat had been full of useless information. It had been stupid and had returned to this hole in the ground for no good reason.

He let it die. There was so little left of the meat's mind that it barely noticed. Professor Hayden could smell the structure beneath the ground burning. Soon the inferno would consume it. Varney had betrayed him. The gutless, spineless piece of excrement had destroyed both himself and the remaining troops.

No matter.

Professor Hayden knew where the enemy were headed. He knew the name of the Fracture agent that he must face. And he knew that he could defeat him. When the fight was done, he would return home to where roads of gleaming metal stretched as far as the eye could see.

Chapter Thirty-six

Phillip could feel his vitality returning. The shadows and mystery of this place comforted him. The pathway was an old one, possibly one of the first. He found himself looking up through the gap in the roof at the buildings that loomed over them. Built by people addicted to certainty, they were ugly in both design and intent. It was good to think that the Fracture had left such structures behind.

Phillip was beginning to think that success might still be possible. He had suffered massive setbacks, interminable waiting and, worst of all, humiliation before the Committee. But this hidden pathway reassured him. There were always possibilities. It was just a case of looking for them.

'There is something approaching us. Very fast.'

Phillip swung round in alarm at the toneless sound of the Seeker's voice. It stared back at him dispassionately.

'Oh, fuck!' whispered Lee.

An object was racing up the tunnel behind them, clouds of dust billowing in its wake. At the centre of the maelstrom, there was a shape. An old man with white hair, wearing an ancient suit. He was running on all fours. It was difficult to believe that anything could move so fast. As he came nearer, they could hear that he was emitting a hooting roar.

'What do we do?' asked Jason.

'Stand still,' ordered Phillip. 'Don't run, you understand? Don't run.'

He was prepared. He was a Fracture agent. A representative of his culture, confronting the enemy that had waged merciless war on them. He would not yield. He would protect his charges or die. It was that simple.

The two boys had moved closer together and were staring at the approaching shape. It was hard to tell if they were frightened. Their faces were shining and just for a moment he thought he glimpsed a clear fluid trickling down their hands.

Realising that the refugees were not running, the Block agent was slowing down. Phillip could make out his face now and he recognised the enemy. Not the individual but the type. This one must be millennia old, born during the early days of the Block's formation. A veteran of countless campaigns, with all the knowledge of his people to draw upon. His biology would have been altered; only a little but enough to make him a highly efficient killer with the ability to wield authority in any realm.

Phillip knew he could not have been faced with a more dangerous opponent. And even now the thought came: why was the agent here? Why was such a specialised creature chasing just one errant weapon?

The old man ground to a halt only a few metres away from them, the dust settling all around him. He rose to his feet, his face glowing a healthy pink, as though he had taken a brisk afternoon walk. Beside him, Philip could hear Jason and Lee coughing. His mask told him that the agent stank of ancient tobacco and other, more rotten, things.

The old man smiled a victorious smile.

'I am Professor Hayden of the Block. You cannot escape. You will surrender.'

Typical Block arrogance.

'My name is Phillip,' he replied evenly. 'I won't let you harm them.'

'And how could you stop me, little castrato boy?'

'You have no army to hide behind now.'

'True. But I no longer needed them. You will be just as easy to dispose of, I assure you.'

A rattle of gunfire. Bullets ripped into Hayden's chest. The Seeker, the gun in its suddenly shaking hands, had discharged both barrels into the old man's body. Phillip was so focused on his enemy that it was a few seconds before he realised that he had given no order to start firing.

Professor Hayden looked down at the holes in his suit. He grinned at the Seeker.

'Billington. As incompetent as ever. Do you really think that I would be so stupid as to give my troops weapons that would harm me?'

The Seeker dropped the empty gun. Its face betrayed nothing and its hands were steady once more.

Hayden turned his attention back to Phillip.

'We have known your plan right from the start,' he crowed.

But that was impossible!

'How?' demanded Phillip. 'How could you possibly have known?'

'You have a contact here, a man called… Cornish.'

'Cornish?' Phillip was unable to keep the surprise from his voice. Had that fat bastard betrayed them after all?

'A clever man, in many ways. Well read, to be sure. But not clever enough to realise that the woman he took his occasional pleasures with is in our employ. From what she learnt, we were able to piece together your plan. It became obvious! You know what this city is. You know why we have never allowed our agents to come here.'

'Yes, this city is one of the places where the Block will begin. But…'

'Not one of the places, castrato boy. The first place. The cornerstone of the Block. The root from which it will grow. And you would stop that growth! You brought one of our weapons here. You experimented on him and on one of the city's inhabitants, this repellent boy. You are trying to unlock the secrets of our past. Of how we came to be. You are trying to prevent the Block from being created. You plan to change history!'

Silence followed as Professor Hayden awaited a response to his speech, a self-satisfied smirk on his face.

Phillip began to laugh. Jason and Lee were looking at him in surprise but he couldn't stop himself. The Block had got it wrong!

'You fool!' he finally managed to say to the dumbfounded Hayden. 'You stupid fools! Of what interest is the past to the Fracture? We want the future! We are the Future!'

'You lie!' raged the old man.

'Why should I lie? Why bother to lie to you when you can invent paranoid fantasies for yourself? It's the only way you can understand anything outside of the Block, isn't it, Professor Hayden? To come up with convoluted, ridiculous conspiracy theories.'

'Don't try to deceive me!' shouted Hayden. 'We know! We know the depths to which your kind would sink to undermine us and—'

'We don't even care about you!' interrupted Phillip. 'Have your Block! We aren't interested in it! We never were! We were happy for you to stay where you were. It was you who attacked us. But we will end this war. We will progress while you stay locked away in your precious prison.'

'You're lying! You're fucking lying!'

Phillip could hear the doubt in the agent's voice. Perhaps it was the first time he had ever been unsure of anything.

'How many people have you killed, Hayden? How many died because you got it wrong? Change history? Have you any idea how stupid that is? Why we would we want to change a history in which we exist? Do you really think we value ourselves so little? Do you think that we would destroy ourselves just to defeat you?'

'You hate us! The Fracture has always hated the Block. That's why you left us.'

'Are fear and hate all the Block understands now?'

'Then why are you here? Tell me that! Why?'

'Don't be absurd. I'll tell you nothing.'

The old man turned to Jason. The weapon returned his gaze. Two creatures once the same, now so different.

'Tell me, traitor, why did they bring you here? What did they do to you?'

Jason shook his head. The Professor's tone changed. It was almost pleading. Almost desperate.

'Don't you remember what you once were? Have you forgotten the power and the certainty? I can give you those things back. I can make you what you were before. All you have to do is tell me. Tell me what the Fracture are doing here and your treachery will be redeemed.'

'You don't have anything I want,' said Jason.

'You were a wonderful creature once. A glorious weapon.'

'And now I'm something better.'

The old man's voice was insinuating now.

'Is it companionship you crave? Is that how they corrupted you? We can give you that, I promise you. We understand desire.

You don't have to be dependent on this ugly, pimple-ridden boy. There are companions for you in the Block. Strong, healthy men. They can be yours, if you come back to us.'

'Go away.'

The Professor seemed to sag as though he had accepted defeat.

'The weapon no longer belongs to you,' said Phillip. 'Go now, Hayden. Go back to the Block. You have nothing to gain here.'

'No!'

Hayden's livid eyes begun to bulge. Phillip felt the enemy's mind in his. Pushing into him with a renewed aggression.

'Time to die, Phillip.'

'We shall see.'

Phillip pushed back into the old man's mind. He filled its desiccated confines with chaos, stories and pictures that wound round each another and through each other without end. He heard the enemy whimper in terror. He tangled them further, spinning them into limitless possibilities.

But now there was a second wave of assault. Block faces. All the same. Determined and confident, obedient to their one story. They stared into him, a terrifying indomitable army. The certainty of their gaze was enough to turn a man to stone if he looked too deep into their eyes. Phillip found he was retreating into himself, terrified of the merciless scrutiny of so many. The Block in all its entirety was looking at him through this one old man.

Somehow he forced himself to meet their gaze. And then he showed them the face of the Fracture – fragile and strong, wounded and powerful. He showed them visions of beauty and ugliness melded into a perfect unity. The faces turned away, confused and afraid of riddles they could never solve.

Phillip pressed home his attack. He used the sound of the Fracture like a scythe. The bewildering multitude of harmonies sliced through the enemy's defences. He could hear the sound of the Block as the Professor attempted to retaliate. A repetitive, ceaseless beat. But it was muted, drowned by the whirling, soaring fusion of music that crashed against it. He increased the volume and then began combining the sound with images. The music and the pictures spiralled around each other, forming a quadruple helix. Then they merged, complementing and contradicting each another. The Professor was caught at the heart of a fathomless puzzle. A web that spun its own spiders.

Still the Professor managed to resist. Phillip could feel him searching for something in the midst of the chaos. The old man still had a finger hold in his mind and was hunting for something – a place, a feeling, a memory.

And then he found it.

Phillip remembered. He was in a hospital bed, blind, his body wrecked by a car crash. He was alone and there was only darkness. Just for a second, he recalled how that had felt. He tried to banish the memory, but the enemy wouldn't let him.

He heard voices: Hayden's voice and those of everyone he had known as a child, his friends, teachers, parents.

You are alone. No one is coming. No one will save you. You are alone. You are alone.

Philip's defences weakened. Just for a second. But it was enough. Hayden's assault smashed through him without mercy. He staggered, trying to gather himself, to recover. But it was far too late. A final devastating thrust through his mind and Philip was flung, defeated, to the ground.

His mask could only give him an indistinct vision as Professor Hayden stood over him. His whole body was racked with agony. Even breathing hurt.

'Memory,' said the old man softly. 'Always a weakness. I told you I would win. But before you die…'

The old man turned to Jason and Lee. They were holding on to each other. Their faces resolute. Philip wished he didn't have to see what was to follow.

'Traitor!' Hayden spat at Jason.

The boy did not flinch. He regarded the Professor with contempt. Almost disinterest.

'You betrayed the Block,' went on the old man. 'You betrayed everything it stands for. You could have had the glory and the honour of a true warrior. Instead you will die here with your lover.'

Jason's voice was steady when he spoke.

'Get on with it, then.'

'You still think you can defy me? You and this stupid boy?'

'Come on, then,' said Lee. 'What are you waiting for?'

Phillip wondered what good they thought this could possibly do them. Perhaps if they didn't anger the agent, he would allow their suffering to be brief.

'You will be pleading with me to stop before this ends,' said Hayden.

'Well then...'

'Come on...'

'What are... you scared of?'

Philip couldn't separate the sound of their voices. Hayden's ancient face creaked into a leer. Philip watched in despair as he focused his terrible power on the two boys, power that had already overcome a Fracture agent. He waited for them to start screaming, to fall dead in each other's arms. At least they would perish together. There was some small comfort in that.

Nothing happened. The veins on Hayden's head pulsed, spittle dribbled from his hanging mouth and pools of sweat became visible on his suit.

Still Jason and Lee stood unmoving, their eyes fixed on the Block agent. Phillip remembered how they had withstood the Committee's attempts to study them. Could it be that Hayden, too, was incapable of overcoming the unearthly connection that shielded them? He could sense Hayden fighting harder but the more determined his efforts became, the more of his vitality they sapped.

'What... are... you... what are...' whispered the Professor, tears streaming from his eyes.

He can't win this time, thought Phillip. They're like nothing he's seen before. Nothing he could even have imagined. Part Block weapon, part adolescent boy, part Fracture virus, part something else altogether.

'You... will... be... submit...' gasped the old man.

They replied with one voice that made the air quiver around them.

'Come on, Hayden, is that the best you can do?'

And now it wasn't just their voices that were joined. Their bodies were locking seamlessly together. Arms and legs joined together in impossible combinations and new limbs began to grow.

They rose above Hayden, hovering over him like a bird of prey. They were glowing now and Phillip struggled to make out their new form. It was narrow and almost triangular, with lines of long, constantly moving tendrils running down both sides. A complex lattice of bone ran down its middle. The surface of the body glistened with a silver fluid. There was only one head but two faces.

A voice echoed back and forth along the tunnel.

'You've been...'

'...following us for...'

'...too long...'

'...now...'

'...you will...'

'...DIE!'

At the last word, Professor Hayden staggered away from them, sobbing with terror. His body was suddenly wasted, drained of the ferocious energy that had animated it for so long. His white hair was tumbling out in huge tufts. The pupils of his eyes were lost beneath swelling lines of blood. Bile pumped from his gaping mouth.

Jason and Lee had won, thought Phillip. In the end, they were stronger than all of us.

Hayden was lurching towards him now. Withered arms outstretched, his twisted hands were reaching for Phillip's mask. Determined to claim the only victory left to him. Nothing I can do now, thought Phillip. He prepared himself for oblivion.

A blur of movement. Someone was standing over him. The Seeker. In its outstretched hand was a blade. Lee's knife.

'Billington... out of... out of my way!' gurgled Hayden. It was half an order, half a plea.

The Seeker struck with perfect precision. The knife opened a wide gash from corner to corner of the Professor's throat. It slashed again, deeper. Rich, dark blood erupted in a fountain over the musty suit, painting the green material a vivid red.

Hayden tried to scream but found he had no voice. He collapsed to his knees, mouth opening and closing piteously. The

Seeker stood over him. Its eyes were without expression, its face motionless. Then it spoke, calmly and without inflexion.

'Not this time.'

The light glinted on the blood-splattered blade as it was thrust into the Block agent's heart. Professor Hayden looked down at the handle jutting out from between his ribs. Slowly, his wondering gaze drifted up to the Seeker. He managed a final cough. Then he slumped, dead in the spreading pool of his own blood.

Phillip tried to get to his feet, but he couldn't.

Jason and Lee were hovering over him. The form had only one face now but when it spoke he could somehow hear both their voices.

'You tried to protect us,' said the voice. 'So we will help you.'

There was a void rushing towards him and soon, he thought, it would be over. Still, there were worse ways to die.

The voice carried on gently.

'You won't die, Phillip. Tell the Committee they will never find us now. We have our own stories to find.'

Phillip tried to focus, but the shape above him was becoming indistinct.

'Thank you for your help, Phillip. We will not meet again.'

Then he felt the darkness closing round him and then there was nothing. For a while.

Chapter Thirty-seven

When she had been a little girl, Rebecca had sometimes played nurses with her friends. It had seemed like an exciting profession. You must meet all sorts of interesting people with unusual stories to tell. Some of the other girls liked to pretend they were in love with handsome surgeons. Rebecca had preferred to imagine herself in the middle of a crisis, calmly dispensing help, finding miracle solutions at the last minute. Once she had entered adolescence, her childhood fantasies quickly faded, lost beneath the weight of academia.

And now here she was, playing nurse once more. There was little she could actually do. Philip didn't eat or drink and she dared not administer any medicines. All that Rebecca could do was sit by his bedside and make sure that he was no worse. The Seeker was always there. He refused to be separated from his master. Sitting on a chair in the corner, he kept a constant vigil. Rebecca had quickly realised that he had to be fed or he would allow himself to starve. Every four hours, she gave the empty-eyed young man a plate of sausage sandwiches. He seemed to like them. After a while she became used to his presence. She was growing accustomed to having strange beings in her spare room.

The important thing was that Jason and Lee were safe. She had arrived at the small building above the Dancing Devil commune to find flames belching up from beneath the ground. The bloodied corpse that lay close by was already half roasted. She had run on, heading for the lake and the woods beyond, hoping against hope that Jason and Lee had escaped the inferno.

Then she had seen them. Two figures, one supporting the other. She had not recognised either of them and the sight of the man in the mask had scared her at first.

And then she had heard them. Jason and Lee telling her to help these two strange people. She had felt their presence for only a few moments, but she had known what had to be done.

The darkening sky had been seared orange with flame as they drove away. Rebecca had called the fire service on her mobile and the scream of sirens was approaching from the city. She had broken every speed rule in the book to escape the inevitable and impossible questions that the authorities would want answered.

When she was sure they were safe, Rebecca had pulled over at the roadside. She had thought about taking Phillip to a hospital but it quickly became obvious that that would be impossible. How could she explain this man who had no face? So instead she took them both home. The Seeker had driven. She told it where she wanted to go, mumbled a few instructions on how to drive and then fell asleep beside him. She had woken as the sun was rising to find that the car had just come to a stop outside her block of flats.

That had been over a week ago. Since then, she had not stepped outside the flat. Philip's condition gradually improved. He was confused at first, to find himself in a strange room with an unknown woman. Slowly, he began to talk, just a few words every now and then to begin with. Gradually she began to piece together the incredible story. She doubted whether he would have her told her so much if he hadn't been so weak. She got the impression that talking about Jason and Lee made him feel better.

The only other person she saw aside from Phillip and the Seeker was the locksmith. She knew now who had broken into her home and how lucky she had been. Her mobile was full of voice messages from her friends. Kelly and Callum were missing. She wished she could have seen Professor Hayden. Wished she had been there when he died. Maybe she would feel less guilty then. Phillip told her that she shouldn't blame herself and that Hayden had killed thousands in his lifetime. It didn't help.

The Seeker never spoke. But Philip's mask was often turned in its direction, contemplating his enigmatic slave. Rebecca was sure that its presence was a comfort to him.

Today he was sitting up in bed. He seemed stronger. Perhaps he was getting back to normal, though what that would mean in his case she couldn't imagine. Rebecca was sitting at his bedside, sipping at a cup of coffee.

'Do you ever eat?' she asked.

'It's not necessary,' he explained simply.

'Right.'

Silence.

'Why did you want to help them, Rebecca?' he asked suddenly.

She had the unpleasant sensation that he was mentally dissecting her. The blank metal seemed to gaze deep into her. She hesitated before replying.

'I liked them. I wanted to make sure that they didn't come to any harm.'

'But that's not all?'

There was little point in lying.

'They were... unique. And I've always wanted to be involved in something unique. To see things no one else has.'

Philip nodded.

'Understandable,' he said with a note of approval.

'What do you think will happen to them?'

Philip leaned forward.

'I don't know. We chose Lee to protect Jason because he was strong but damaged. An outsider. We never expected they would affect each other the way they did. They became so open to each other that in the end it was natural for them to become one. As you say, they were unique. They are unique still, whatever and wherever they are.'

Rebecca sighed. If only she could have seen them, just once, before they were gone.

'What will you do now?' she asked.

'Even with the Block agent dead, the Committee will want a solution. They will want to know where the plan goes from here.'

She nodded, turning over what he had said. 'What will they do if you can't think of something?'

'It depends how angry they are. We are at war, remember. This plan was meant to bring it to an end.'

A frightening thought occurred to her. One that made her skin suddenly cold. 'Will the Block send another agent after you? Will they send someone here?'

The red flesh in the aperture of the mask trembled slightly as Philip chuckled.

'No. They thought we were trying to change the past. They will see their present has stayed the same and assume that their agent died victorious.'

'That's ridiculous!'

'Fear makes them ridiculous.'

'I see.'

'And they have a very limited imagination.' Philip turned his attention to the Seeker. 'Has it eaten today?'

'No, not yet.'

It made her uncomfortable the way he referred to the Seeker as an object, not even acknowledging it as a living person.

'I'll feed it today.'

'Very well. Philip?'

'Yes?'

She wondered if he already knew what she was going to ask.

'Is there anything that can be done for him?'

'For the Seeker? I have done all I can. Most of them don't live for more than a few days. But I shall see to it that this one survives. I am… indebted to it.'

'There are others?'

'Our battle-wounded. We found a use for them. It was that or kill them.'

'And they only do what they are told?' she asked.

'Yes. They are slaves. I understand that such a concept must make you uncomfortable. But as I said, we are at war.'

'But it… he killed the Block agent. Without orders from you.'

'Yes. That is… unusual, to say the least.'

'So, there might be hope for it? It might become something else? Like Jason and Lee did?'

She was probably clutching at straws but she couldn't stand by and let this tragic young man be condemned to a life of mindless slavery. Surely it deserved some reward for its loyalty?

Philip seemed to pause for thought before he answered.

'Perhaps.'

He fell silent. Rebecca waited for him to continue but his mask was turned away from her and he seemed to have forgotten she existed.

She stood up.

'Anyway,' she said. 'I'm glad Jason and Lee are together. I think that's what they wanted all along. To be as close to each other as they could. Not to be alone.'

Phillip nodded but did not speak. Rebecca waited a few moments but he still didn't say anything. She turned and left him to his thoughts.

He watched her go, pondering what she had said. She was a clever woman, he thought. Certainly she had unusual insight.

He had to find a solution.

The Seeker was watching him. Waiting for orders. It was still dependent on him. Like all the converted battle-wounded, it needed someone to guide it.

Rebecca's words came back to him.

Not to be alone.

A sharp intake of breath came from beneath the mask.

Of course!

Chapter Thirty-eight

In many ways the Committee were a contradiction. The Fracture had been created by refugees from the authority of the Block. It had never been intended that it should have a ruling class. And yet the Committee had been given power. They had the instant use of any resource that they required and could punish those that disobeyed them.

The Committee owed their existence to the war. Without it, they would not have been created. To retaliate against the onslaught of the Block, the Fracture had been left with no choice but to unify. A council had been needed. No one could remember where the ten armoured figures had come from or whether or nor they had had a life before. But that wasn't important. As long as the war went on, they were needed. When it was over, the Committee would die at the hands of those they had presided over.

They understood this, naturally.

Philip wondered if the news he brought them would bring that death closer. His plan might help extinguish the blue flame that had burned for so long in the centre of the war room. Would they be pleased? As the Committee plotted and schemed, were they working towards victory for the Fracture or towards their own release?

The harsh voices did not betray their feelings on the matter.

'So. You think you have found a solution?'

Philip tried to steady both his voice and his nerves. He must not think of failure.

'Yes. And I have brought the solution with me.'

'This is the second time you have bought us visitors.'

'We trust this time will prove more productive,' added a second voice from a limbless torso.

'For your sake,' completed a third, its one arm grating agitatedly in its socket.

Philip turned to the figure beside him. The Seeker seemed no more impressed by the Committee than it had been by the journey here.

'You know what this is, of course?' he asked rhetorically.

'Obviously,' came the impatient response.

'Do not waste time, Philip,' rattled another from its battered helmet.

'Very well. The Seekers are supposed to respond only to the orders they are given. Everything else, every trace of personality, is removed. As they normally die within a few days anyway, it has never seemed important. But this one has lived far longer than most.'

'Because of you. Are you trying to move us with your compassion?'

'No, of course not. But this Seeker hasn't just lived. It has learned to act without orders. It acted to protect me without instructions. It showed concern for me. It had a concealed knife I knew nothing about. It watched over me while I was recovering. We have what you might call a connection.'

A heavy pause. Grinding noises emanated from the Committee, as though they were literally turning the idea over within themselves. Finally, one spoke.

'And this connection, you feel, echoes that between the weapon and the adolescent, the one that put them beyond our reach and rendered the plan worthless?'

'Yes. Jason and Lee became something we had not planned for. They are beyond our ability to control, but also beyond the Block's. They resisted the agent's power and fought back against him. They have chosen a life independent of the war.'

'And so?'

'And so I suggest that we deploy the virus on the battlefield as we had intended. Leave the Block weapons stripped of their purpose and connection to their masters. And then we send our own wounded, converted into Seekers like this one, to bond with them. There are billions of weapons and billions of wounded. Their joining will change the whole nature of the war. In a day, the battlefield would be reshaped by a third faction. Symbiotic pairings with no interest in fighting for either side.'

Again there was silence as the Committee considered.

'Once they were bonded, we would have no control over them,' observed one without arms, its torso thick with oil.

'True,' agreed the headless one.

'But neither would the Block,' said Philip. 'And besides, they would be repellent to the Block. They would represent a new story. One beyond their understanding.'

'With the war over, the linked weapons and seekers would become another part of the Fracture. Another alternative.'

'And this is your plan? The solution you offer us?'

'Yes.'

Phillip waited for the Committee to reply. He had said all that he could and now his fate was out of his hands. He was surprised at how glad he was to have the Seeker by his side. Whatever happened, he could at least be sure that it would not abandon him. After so long alone, it was good to have company once more.

The scream of metal on metal was deafening as the ten figures moved forward. Their harsh voices roared as one.

'Then let it begin!'

Rebecca had never imagined there were so many books in the world. The wooden shelves stretched endlessly beneath her as she descended the shaft. Warmly glowing bronze lamps were placed at irregular intervals between the books, bathing her in a warm light. At first, the slow falling motion had been hypnotic in itself. She had felt like Alice tumbling down the rabbit hole and half expected to find bottles labelled 'Drink Me'. Lewis Carroll was one of the first authors Rebecca had read. She was fairly certain that was why she was experiencing the Fracture's archive in this way. To fans of horror, it would have probably assumed the form of a gothic mansion. To others there would not even have been books, just ranks of shiny discs and humming terminals.

You didn't read these books. It took her a while to understand that. At first she had thought the words filling her mind were a hallucinogenic result of the strange atmosphere. Gradually, she had realised that the books were speaking to her. She was being told stories in a language more direct than the written word and yet just as intimate.

Focus would take a while to learn. It was not easy to choose the stories she wanted to hear. Phillip had told her that the skill would come in time. Apparently, agents like him sometimes retired here. After a lifetime in the field, they were able to enjoy an easier existence as they maintained and updated the library. She found it hard to imagine Phillip coming here. What on Earth would it look like to him?

Sometimes she caught glimpses of the other minds here. It was only the faintest of impressions, yet she knew she was being watched. Not with any intensity, just a casual observation. They didn't seem surprised that a stranger had joined them. There was no trace of fear. Perhaps they were used to newcomers. She hoped that, in time, she would be able to learn from them.

This had been the reward the Fracture had given her for helping Jason and Lee. She would spend the rest of her life here, uncovering the mysteries of this place. At first she had worried that she would die without food and drink. Phillip had assured her that this would not be a problem. She would adapt to the archive just as it would adapt to her. It was ironic that, after spending so long wanting to find something unique, she was becoming something unique.

The words were changing now. There were stories beneath the stories. No, not beneath: within. Hidden narratives as alien to their hosts as could be imagined. A tale of a hero was also a love story for a monster. A song of triumph was underscored by a lament for the lost. A comedy carried the agony of despair. A single sentence was a thousand alternatives. She could not read them all. Not yet. But one day...

Phillip felt sorry for the city. Beneath the sunset it was almost beautiful. The buildings were painted with an orange light that gave the brickwork surfaces the texture of skin. The latticework of scaffolding that wound around them was like the beginnings of a skeleton for a new and wondrous form. So many futures there could have been.

But it would all come to nothing. This city – the place where he had been born and where he had seen his childhood dreams rise, fall and finally metamorphose – already belonged to the enemy. It would become the Block and all its possibilities would be lost. It wasn't much of a future for it to look forward to.

He would not come back here again. He had decided to carry on in the Committee's service as long as they needed him. With luck, they might let him oversee the operation on the battlefield. The virus had already been mass produced in readiness. Very soon, it would be used. Perhaps then, the war would finally end. If so, what would he do then? He did not want to join the Committee in death. He might retire to the archive after all. He and Rebecca might have much to teach each other. She was already a beautiful woman and life in the Fracture would make her more so.

The Seeker stood by his side, studying the city without interest. Soon Phillip would release it from his service. He would send it to the battlefield, to join with one of the infected weapons. He hoped it would be happy.

Where were Jason and Lee now? As they had predicted, the Committee had not been able to find them. Perhaps they were building a city of their own somewhere, patiently waiting for the rest of their kind to follow them.

The thought cheered him. There were still possibilities.

He would walk these streets one final time. He would take in every detail. As ever, the people would turn away from him as though he were not there. But he would allow himself to enjoy the city and forget the fate that awaited it.

For the moment, thought Phillip, the present was all that mattered. The future could wait for one day at least.

Printed in the United States
86557LV00001B/41/A